POLITICS OF LOVE
Book Two in the San Diego Trilogy

ANNETTE MORI

ALSO BY ANNETTE MORI

SINGLE STORIES

Co-authored with Ali Spooner
Heart Strings Attached- TWC3
Free to Love
Trouble in Paradise -TWC4

SERIES

San Diego Series

Politics of Love
Undercover Love

Politics of Love

Book Two in the San Diego Trilogy

Annette Mori

2023

Politics of Love
© 2023 by Annette Mori

Affinity E-Book Press NZ LTD.
Canterbury, New Zealand

Edition First (1st)

ISBN: 978-1-99-104020-6 (paperback)

Editor: Angela Koenig
Proof Editor: S.M. Lee
Cover Design: Irish Dragon Designs
Production Design: Affinity Publication Services

ACKNOWLEDGMENTS

A huge thank you to Ali Spooner, who was the only beta reader I sent this book (hopefully that will not end up being a mistake). I would also like to express my gratitude to Affinity Rainbow Publications—JM Dragon and Nancy Kaufman—who continue to provide feedback to tighten up manuscripts that need help and publish my unconventional work. I am eternally grateful for the opportunities they give me to let my stories see the light of day. Thanks to Angie for her magic as the final editor to further tighten the story. She is a delight to work with. Inevitably, those pesky errors slip through, and I am thankful that the final proof editor, S.M. Lee caught those before the book went to print. Thanks to Nancy Kaufman for the final cover. A huge thanks to all the other readers and fellow writers who have sent personal emails, written reviews, and posted nice things on Facebook (you know who you are). The Affinity authors are an incredibly supportive group and often share posts or send words of encouragement. Finally, my wife, Jody, continues her support even when it interferes with our time.

DEDICATION

Once again, to all the powerful men and women who work to keep our country from becoming a hotbed of extremist views and may we all prevail during these scary times. And to my beautiful wife as always.

TABLE OF CONTENTS

CHAPTER ONE

She supposed today was as good as any other day to die. Her only regret was that she hadn't experienced that one great love. Keeping too focused on her political career and listening to her mother's advice over the years had made it impossible for her to maintain any relationship for more than a year or two, much less gain a lifetime commitment.

Regret would soon be over, or the shelter she'd insisted on at her mother's house would keep them safe. Nothing much Sandra could do now.

The spunky Hispanic woman, Jimena, had left the safety of the panic room. No matter how impressed Governor Sandra Murphy was with the young woman, she was under no illusion that either of the formidable women guarding her would save the day. She had seen the regret and concern in the taller woman's commanding eyes. Nevertheless, she had begun barking orders the second she walked into her mother's house. Although the war heroine wasn't giving up, it looked dire. There was a connection beyond work association between Jimena and the war heroine. Sandra had caught the flicker of emotion. Then Jimena left the shelter to join the other woman, taking away any chance of her survival.

The explosion was a lot quieter than she'd anticipated. She supposed the twelve inches of solid steel that formed a barrier between everyone in the shelter and whatever had occurred in the rest of the house had done its job. Sandra opened her eyes and immediately found her mother's panicked face.

Finally, the man the FBI had sent to protect them spoke.

"Wait here while I check things out," the large man ordered.

Sandra wasn't in any hurry to leave the safety of the reinforced steel room, considering it had done a bang-up job of keeping them safe. She simply nodded her acknowledgment of the directive.

After the man opened the door to the panic room, dust seeped into the small space. Her mother coughed first. He pushed against the heavy steel door, and more dust encroached on the small area, finally causing Sandra to cough. With her trembling hands, she pulled her shirt over her nose and mouth to keep from inhaling the noxious material floating in the air.

Curiosity got the best of Sandra, and she decided to follow the man assigned to her security detail. Her mother accompanied them. As the three gingerly made their way inside the once opulent home, Sandra gasped at the destruction. The only thing remaining was the panic room Sandra had, thankfully, built at least a year ago when she'd started receiving threats to herself and her family.

Sandra stepped over the debris, continuing to put a barrier between the dust and her nose and mouth. She had the ridiculous thought that she was wearing the wrong shoes for this jaunt across the demolished house. Then, hearing faint sirens, she looked to the east and found a flurry of activity surrounding the two women who she had assumed had died in the explosion.

Sandra began to make her way to the women, but the man assigned to her security detail held her back. He quickly shuffled her mother and herself into a waiting SUV. Sandra sighed in frustration. She wanted to at least thank the two women but wasn't afforded that opportunity.

†

"Governor Murphy, Governor Murphy," the cacophony of press voices called out. The press was going to have a field day with today's events.

Sandra kept her hand securely plastered to her side, not wanting to use it to pinch the bridge of her nose. That would not play well on live TV. She looked up as one voice rose above the din—a pleasant alto voice she quickly recognized in any room full of eager reporters. This woman had been at previous press conferences, and although she worked for a network that Sandra despised, the woman knew how to dig out a story. Sandra didn't always enjoy answering her questions. Still, she respected the woman for doing a thorough job, even if the way she worded each question was slightly aggressive and sometimes accusatory.

"Governor Murphy, when did you learn about the plot to kill you and your mother?" The woman continued with her second and third questions without taking a breath. "How are Jimena Aguilar and Emma Schmidt involved? Did you authorize the lies told to the press about Jimena Aguilar's death?

Sandra forced a smile on her face and attempted to answer each question. "I'd need to be a rich woman to react to every threat against my family and me. As it turns out, this one was credible. Jimena Aguilar and Emma Schmidt are both heroines. The FBI is a vast organization that does not need nor is required to seek permission from me on their choice of tactics and strategies to make our nation safe, Ms.—"

"Wynter. Wynter Holmes," the reporter offered before barreling into her most pointed question. "So does that philosophy also apply to what you choose to do when ignoring Ordinance Number 10014 Section 91.1.105 requiring a permit for any improvements made to a home, such as the panic room in your mother's house?"

Well shit. Sandra had hoped this would not come up, but it wasn't like she wasn't prepared for the question. She'd talked with her mother and other advisors in great detail about how to answer the probe.

"No, Ms. Holmes. If you are asking, do I believe anyone is exempt from the law? Of course, I do not. This is not an excuse for failing to obtain the correct permit before completing the project, merely an explanation. When the threats extended to my family and not only myself, I chose the most expedient route to ensure my mother's safety should one of these terrorists make good on their threats. While I don't believe I should face zero consequences for my choice, I do not regret making it. Had I waited for the permit, neither myself, my mother, nor the agent assigned to protective detail would be alive today. I will readily accept the consequences of that choice and admit that I set a deplorable example. I am not a perfect human being, and this was a valuable lesson."

"Because you got caught?" Wynter asked.

"No, because I ignored an established ordinance that is on the books for a good reason. And I believe this is an opportunity to look at the long process for obtaining permits, including how we can expedite those permits in emergency situations or ones that risk the safety of California residents. Most people have a mother or loved ones they wish to protect, Ms. Holmes, not just me."

Wynter nodded, and the corners of her mouth lifted in what Sandra could only surmise was a grudging demonstration of respect for the answer. Then, with great effort, Sandra wrenched her focus away from those amazing crystal blue eyes that were nearly opaque. The blue was so vibrant. It reminded Sandra of those pictures of the glaciers in Alaska, sometimes with just a hint of blue within the massive ice structures, yet often that brilliant color that awed tourists around the world.

Sandra thanked the universe that Wynter had not pursued a different line of questions. Namely, why she had decided not to use the security detail typically assigned to the governor's office. She didn't want to tarnish their good name simply because she'd had that one bad experience.

She pointed to a reporter from Wynter's rival network which offered a kinder and less antagonistic platform for her policies and liberal political leanings. "Mr. Stone."

"Thank you for taking my question, Governor Murphy," the man responded.

When Sandra heard a muffled *ass kisser*, she momentarily lost her concentration, glancing briefly at Wynter Holmes, who smirked when their eyes met. Thankfully, she tuned back in time to hear David Stone's question.

"The FBI has released the name and photo of the suspect who happens to be Emma Schmidt's brother. Are you sure she is a heroine and not part of the plot?" David Stone asked.

"While I am not at liberty to discuss the specifics of the case, one thing that is clear is that Emma Schmidt is not involved in the terror cell."

"Was she working undercover?" he pressed.

Irritation threatened to bubble from deep inside, but Sandra knew she had to keep her emotions in check. Control was what had made her so effective against her right-wing opponents. Sending her trademark smile in David Stone's direction, she calmly answered, "I'm sorry, Mr. Stone, all other details on the case are not available to share at this time. You'll be the first to know when I have more information to provide to the press. Thank you for your time, ladies and gentlemen. I'm afraid I have another engagement I'm late for."

As she turned to leave, she heard the cacophony of calls for her to answer just one more question, however, Sandra was a practiced politician. Blocking out those calls was child's play. She knew when to end what essentially amounted to a live press release. One that would not hurt her rising star in the Democratic Party. Although many said there was no such thing as bad press, Sandra Murphy disagreed with that advice as she always chose her words carefully. Unfortunately, twisting her words was what the right-wing media did best, something she worked very hard at not allowing, including from the attractive viper, Wynter Holmes.

†

Ever since the people of the great state of California had elected Sandra as their governor, she had avoided going to her favorite bar, which happened to be owned by one of her closest friends. It had been a point of contention between them. Geri insisted that the crowd in her upscale lesbian bar,

Lavender Lips, would never make a scene or even acknowledge the governor's presence. Tonight Sandra wanted a good drink, a relaxing time, and a chat with her good friend. She decided nothing was keeping her from stopping by after work for a drink.

Although it was early evening before the sun had finally set, the dimly lit interior of the lounge differed vastly from the outside. Sandra adjusted to the darkened bar that tried to create a relaxed, intimate atmosphere for the patrons who preferred a low-key visibility for a gathering place instead of the blinding strobe lights and loud thumping music geared toward a younger crowd. Geri barked orders at one of the bartenders before looking up, tilting her head, and letting that roguish half-smile fill her face. Sandra's eyes briefly strayed to the bar stool where the back of a woman with shoulder-length auburn hair sat. There was something vaguely familiar about the woman, but since Sandra could not see her face, she shoved aside her discomfort. It was a very nice backside. Not that she was here to meet anyone, but that didn't mean she couldn't appreciate the view. Waving Sandra over, Geri greeted her old friend as she stood in front of the woman sitting at the bar.

"Well, I guess hell has frozen over after all." Geri chuckled. "What brings you to my little slice of heaven? I thought you said you didn't want to give the press anything to wag their tongues about."

"I got thirsty, and this place always had the best lemon drop martinis in the state of California," Sandra answered.

8

"Of all the gin joints…"

Sandra knew that voice. She put the pieces together while berating herself for the decision to stop at Lavender Lips for a quick drink and to commiserate with Geri at the same time. The woman turned slowly, and Sandra lost her carefully engineered poker face for a second. She risked direct eye contact.

"Governor Murphy, are you following me?" There was that smoky voice. The voice which had not so long ago asked that pointed question. However, regardless of how upscale and discreet Lavender Lips was, Sandra couldn't figure out why Wynter would be in a lesbian bar.

"You two know each other?" Geri asked, while grinning and winking at Sandra.

"Not like that," Sandra corrected and immediately regretted that response. "We've crossed paths before. Ms. Holmes is a member of the press. She works for TRU."

Geri had the good sense to cringe. "Oh, that's right. I almost forgot you were a reporter for that propaganda machine and a major thorn in Sandra's side."

Wynter shrugged and glibly replied, "Good thing it's irrelevant to my desire for a good microbrew, and you've never held that against me. Sit, Governor Murphy. I promise I won't bite. At least not in this safe space. I presume Lavender Lips is a safe space for you? What will you have? I'll buy. It's the least I can do for always giving you fits at your press conferences."

"Thanks, but I'd prefer to purchase my own drink. Unfortunately, I can't have the press misinterpreting your generous offer. Next thing I know, I'll be part of a trumped-up scandal exploited by your network."

Wynter grabbed her shirt and feigned an expression of hurt. "I may ask tough questions, Governor, but I have never reported or repeated any falsehood. So don't lump me in with some of my colleagues who are entertainers, not reporters. There is a difference in the programming."

Sandra scoffed. "Perhaps, but you work for a network that gleefully sidesteps the ethics of reporting without bias. While entertaining to some, opinion pieces are a real danger to others. You're an intelligent woman, Ms. Holmes, so frankly, I believe that network is beneath you and your talents. But what I'd really like to know is why you are here. I haven't been to this bar in years. Were you hoping to glean a salacious tidbit about me by sidling up to one of my closest friends? You do your research. I'll give you that."

"Hm, so much to unpack in your series of statements peppered with, dare I say, insulting questions." Wynter grinned. "Why does anyone frequent a lesbian bar, Governor? I'm not at all afraid of my queerness. Avoiding queer venues is your schtick."

So Wynter was queer. Now that was an interesting piece of information. Sandra opened her mouth to defend her decision to avoid public places that generated gossip and innuendo, especially within the right-wing media. At the last minute, she stopped, not wanting to come across as defensive.

"If you'd bothered to take a breath rather than jump to conclusions, you would have learned that I've been coming to Lavender Lips for a very long time," Wynter continued. "I found this bar about a month after moving to the area and have been a regular ever since. Geri is one of the few individuals I would call a genuine friend, especially in the overly pretentious southern California crowd. How about if we declare Lavender Lips a safe space? I promise I won't use anything I learn about you in this bar in any segment I choose to write. You have my word." Wynter stuck out her hand.

Sandra tentatively accepted Wynter's hand and shook. Glancing at her friend, who had watched the exchange with apparent interest, ending with a single arched eyebrow, Sandra said, "I'll take one of your famous lemon drops, Geri. You can put Ms. Holmes' beer on my tab."

Wynter chuckled. "Ah, now who is trying to bribe whom? Hoping that my future questions will be softballs like the ones you receive from the network that shall not be named? If I admit the network I work for leans right, you must acknowledge our competition practically falls all over itself to ensure they don't tarnish your golden image."

"Perhaps," Sandra agreed. "But at least they don't tell outright lies. I would think the rampant homophobia would have sent you packing long ago." Sandra shook her head. "I just don't get it."

Wynter shrugged. "I'm merely invested in the truth, Governor. Unfortunately, your favorite place to give interviews already had a token lesbian. Since they weren't interested in hiring me, I went to their competition. TRU gave me a chance, and they treated me well. I don't have to agree with all my colleagues to do my job. How about if we pivot to another topic? What took you so long to come out? Strictly off the record," she added.

Sandra schooled her expression lest she appear irritated. It wasn't the first time, nor would it be the last that she'd gotten this question. Smiling, she gave her pat answer. "Although this question has been asked and answered many times, I'll humor you. Because, Ms. Holmes, how I identify is irrelevant to my qualifications to do my job."

"I beg to differ. Besides, if that were the case, why reveal that about yourself at all? You didn't answer my question about why it took you so long. It isn't like you have a partner or wife who might be irritated that you don't love them enough to make your relationship public. Or do you?" Wynter grinned.

"No, I don't have a special person in my life. But I am extremely curious about your first statement. Why do you believe it is relevant information?"

"We have our first black woman as a supreme court justice and vice president. That milestone gives hope to all those little black girls who now know it is possible to reach those heights. Don't you think it would be nice for all those little queer girls to know this is achievable? Rumor has it you will be the Democratic nominee for president. If you win, you'll be an important role model. But if there is any hesitancy, such as keeping your queerness secret for so long, how do you think that will land? All those little queer girls will believe that how they identify is something to be ashamed of. Just because we can hide our queerness, unlike persons of color, doesn't mean we should."

Wynter wasn't wrong about that. Sandra briefly entertained telling the young reporter the real reason, but she didn't trust her, settling on the next best answer. "You make very valid points, Ms. Holmes. Can I perhaps get away with 'better late than never'?" Sandra nodded her thanks to Geri, who had slipped the lemon drop in front of her without interrupting their conversation.

Wynter smiled and answered, "Only if you stop calling me Ms. Holmes. I honestly don't want to be enemies with the first lesbian president of the United States. Contrary to what you might believe about me, we are not on opposite sides of most issues. Truce?"

A genuine smile erupted from Sandra's mouth. "Of course. One thing I am quite sure of is that every vote counts. Who am I to offend a potential voter?" Sandra lifted her drink, and Wynter followed as the two women clinked their glasses together. "To fresh starts."

"To amelioration." Wynter tipped her glass and took a generous sip of her drink. "I'm not sure I want to give up on our sparring. You make a worthy opponent, but I am amenable to making things better, or at least tolerable for you. I'll continue to seek the truth, but I suppose I could alter my tone and act less aggressively when digging through the political muck. It probably won't make my bosses happy, but that was never my primary concern."

CHAPTER TWO

When she walked into her house, Sandra was still thinking about Wynter as she greeted her mother. Rose Murphy was a powerful woman that very few had the guts to cross. However, the bombing had affected her legendary strength, and she seemed oddly vulnerable to Sandra. Since the bombs had destroyed everything but the panic room at Rose's house, Sandra had invited her mother to stay with her until the contractors could rebuild her home. She must have smiled as her mother's eyes narrowed, adopting that same level of scrutiny when young Sandra snuck out of the house to meet her girlfriend in high school.

"What has you so happy? The press was brutal today. We'll have to do some damage control with that nasty upstart asking questions about the permits for the panic room. I told you that would come back to bite us." Rose lifted the teacup in the most ladylike manner and took a small sip.

Sandra sighed. "Yes, Mother, you did. And yet, here we are, alive today because of that decision. The FBI informed me of the many breaches in security. That would have been public record had I chosen to request a permit. With that knowledge, Karl Schmidt would have rigged the room with explosives, and neither of us would be alive today to have this argument. I hardly think this minor blip rises to the same level of scandal as a former president leading an insurrection. Or grabbing a woman's pussy," she added dryly.

Rose's face failed to mask her disgust. "Must you be so crass in your defense? Perhaps you are correct, but the far right is winning the media war. When their politicians make a gaffe, their voters don't care one bit. However, any minor mishap by us or even an innocent comment creates a significant dip in the polls." Rose frowned, showing her extreme displeasure.

"I don't even know if I want to make a presidential run. The polls are notoriously incorrect. Why they insist on polling candidates who haven't declared their candidacy seems ludicrous to me. Everyone wants to plan my future, but what if that isn't my dream? Governing the state of California is enough for me. So why isn't it enough for you, Mother? You know, a reporter asked a question today about why I waited so long to come out, and I gave my pat answer, but I was so tempted to provide the real reason."

Rose furrowed her brow. "I didn't see that in the press conference. You'd think the reporters would get tired of that same old line of questioning. Hasn't it run its course yet? If not, it won't get more traction than it already has. It's not like that small percentage of extremists would vote for you anyway, regardless of if you were a straight soccer mom, fashioned in the perfect model of what they believe should be a woman."

"I ran into the reporter you seem to abhor quite by accident. She had an interesting take on my decision to wait until after I'd won to reveal I am a lesbian." Sandra decided to sit and enjoy a cup of tea with her mother. She wanted another drink, but perhaps the tea would help relax her. After her brief time with Wynter, Sandra felt more invigorated than she had in a long time and she buzzed with unusual energy. Lifting the teapot, she poured herself a cup and added one teaspoon of honey, stirring thoroughly to avoid the sweet nectar pooling at the bottom.

"I certainly hope you kept to the script. That woman is a viper. She's been poised to strike ever since you declared your candidacy for governor," Rose stated with confidence.

"I believe Ms. Holmes may be less acidic in the future. We agreed to a sort of truce. I suppose I understand why she's been so harsh with her questions. I don't think she wishes me any ill intent at all. However, her quest for the truth makes her a potential ally."

"How in the world did you come to that conclusion?" Rose frowned as she set her cup of tea on the table.

"Wynter, um, Ms. Holmes," Sandra quickly corrected, "is motivated by a desire to uncover the truth and demonstrate her talents as a reporter. I should hire her to do opposition research for me. She would be quite good at that. Who knows, down the road, if I'm fortunate and she is still engaged by my campaign, she may make an excellent press secretary."

Rose lifted one eyebrow. "Are you out of your mind? Anyone working for TRU is a despicable human being whom we cannot trust."

"We'll see," Sandra responded. "When a person has more options to choose from, suddenly the world looks different. I suspect my life of privilege does not track with what Ms. Holmes might have endured in her young life. She's bright, focused, ambitious, and takes the initiative to drive her career rather than let her chosen occupation chew her up and spit her out. I admire someone with those traits enough to want them in my inner circle. If I make a run for the presidency, I will need all the talent I can get my hands on. The fight will not be easy. As you've already noted, the right is winning the media war."

A tiny smile formed on Rose's face. "So, you haven't eliminated the idea of running for president? That's wonderful, honey. Harry will be happy to hear that. He's insistent that you may be the only person to take on the far right."

"Mm," Sandra grunted. "Politics is a dirty business, Mother. Are you sure you're ready for what will surely be a war? I'd like to hire my own security because I am not naïve enough to believe there won't be another attempt on my life. And they don't care who is collateral damage. In fact, I believe they'll call it a victory if they also manage to take you out. Your influence in politics is legendary."

"You could reconsider the Dignity Protection Section."

Sandra shook her head. "I'm not opening that can of worms. I'm just thankful the press did not choose to go down that path again. Even Wynter Holmes let that slide."

"What about those nice young women who took charge so effectively?" Rose inquired. "The war heroine could still be a potential match for you. Everyone can get behind a love story, especially if both women are powerful and accomplished in their respective fields."

Sandra shook her head vigorously. "No, Mother. I never appreciated your attempts to find me a suitable partner after realizing it would never be a man. Besides, you obviously did not see what I observed. Those two women are very much in love with each other. I doubt I'd have a chance with Emma Schmidt. It's a pity, really. She was my type."

Wynter Holmes's arresting eyes flashed in her unconscious mind with the irritating thought that she was also just her type. Perhaps a bit young since the woman couldn't possibly have reached her thirties yet. But along with those penetrating eyes, her perfectly proportioned mouth verged on pouty, but not quite. Definitely kissable. Sandra shook her head. The last thing she needed to think about was how attracted she was to Wynter Holmes.

"Now, for the last time, I am perfectly capable of finding my own dates," Sandra stated with authority.

"Very well, dear. Besides a stable relationship looking better for you as a candidate, I genuinely wish to see you happy," Rose noted with sincerity.

"I know you do. However, I do like your idea of seeing if those women are available to join my security team, especially while Karl Schmidt is still at large."

†

After Governor Murphy left Lavender Lips, Wynter remained at the bar and decided to have one more drink. She didn't want to admit that she found the governor attractive. What red-blooded lesbian wouldn't want to swim in her ocean? Perhaps she was too hard on the governor, but it rankled Wynter whenever someone powerful and influential failed to admit their queerness. It wasn't like it was 1952. Granted, with the rise in extremism, there was a genuine fear that rights the LGBTQIA+ community had fought so hard for might slip away, while everyone sat back and let it happen.

Wynter had very few friends who stuck by her after joining TRU. She tried to argue that changing views from the inside was a legitimate strategy, but even she knew it hadn't worked like she'd planned. Geri was one of the few women who never judged anyone's choices, which was why Wynter frequented Lavender Lips. She enjoyed talking with the owner. Geri was better than a therapist—a stable wall Wynter could bounce ideas on. Wynter thought she'd been the perfect journalist, never taking a side, but maybe she should take sides. The far right was winning. Unfortunately, she might be contributing to their narrative. Although, her questions were equally pointed to the political royalty on the right.

"So, how long have you known Governor Murphy?" Wynter asked before taking another sip of her drink and looking up slyly from her second drink.

Geri laughed. "Oh, no, you don't. You aren't roping me into spilling any gossip for that two-bit network you work for."

Wynter set down her glass and gave Geri direct eye contact. "I promise I would never divulge any secrets about her private life. Contrary to popular belief, I am not trying to torpedo the governor's career or get all up in her business. While I'm disappointed that she waited so long to come out of the closet, I still respect her right to maintain a modicum of privacy. Even political figures deserve to keep the public away from their bedrooms. I was simply curious. Are you an ex?"

Geri chuckled. "Curious, huh? Bullcrap. I know that look, Wynter. You've been coming to my bar for years, and you're not exactly stealthy about your interest in a person. Now that would be a story I would read." Geri waved her hand in an arc, simulating a carnival barker showing a spectacular marquee. "Lesbian reporter from right-wing network in a steamy affair with the presumptive Democratic presidential nominee."

"Fine, be that way." Wynter laughed at her not-so-subtle attempt to glean more information about the charming governor. Yeah, she could admit to herself that, given different circumstances, she would have gone hard to get the lovely governor to return to her place for the evening. "Who wouldn't be interested? I'll bet she has men and women clamoring for her attention. I am surprised she isn't married, though."

Geri smiled. "Sandra has a knack for attracting the wrong people. For all her intelligence, that soft heart of hers leads her down the wrong path again and again. That's all you're getting from me. If you decide to make a play for Sandra, don't jerk her around. Okay? She's one of the good ones."

"I believe that." Wynter sighed.

"Then why do you always go all nuclear on her when she gives a press briefing?" Geri held up her hands. "Look, I'm not judging. Just curious." Geri grinned.

"Because I'm an out and proud lesbian reporter. If I tossed softball questions her way, everyone would disregard my reporting, thinking I was giving her a pass because she's part of our big LGBTQIA+ family."

"What family?" Geri scoffed. "The divisiveness in this country is not limited to those outside the community. There are plenty of radical members tearing one another apart over transgender issues. And more and more LGBTQIA+ are admitting to their affiliation with the Log Cabin Republicans. I don't recognize the same level of kinship I used to see ten or twenty years ago. No offense to you if you're one of those Log Cabin Republicans."

Wynter relaxed her elbows on the bar, leaning forward slightly. "I'm not, but I respect their right to choose whichever political party they wish to associate with. That's democracy. My job as a reporter is to uncover hypocrisy wherever it grows, exposing those that tend to those gardens. It is not to pass judgment on either party. So if the public has no idea who I would vote for, I've done my job of impartial reporting. And just between you and me, I'm planning on voting for Governor Murphy, not because she's hot, but because I agree with her stance on most issues. The ones I might disagree with are not important enough to vote for her opponent, no matter who they are."

A large group entered the bar, and Geri saluted Wynter before turning her attention to the new patrons. Wynter swallowed the rest of her drink in one gulp and exited the bar, wondering when she'd have the pleasure of running into the alluring governor again. She preferred interacting with her in a social situation versus at one of her press conferences.

CHAPTER THREE

Sandra grit her teeth, barely resisting the temptation of throwing her phone against the wall. She rarely lost her cool, but her patience had been depleted long ago after an entire week without a word on Karl Schmidt. That maniac was out there, undoubtedly planning her downfall. If that wasn't bad enough, she'd tried to get ahold of the two brave women who had saved the day when Karl blew up her mother's house, but both were in hiding. That seemed out of character for the confident women she'd personally witnessed display a great deal of bravery in an impossible situation. Even Sandra had refused the offer to lie low in a safe place until they caught Karl. She could not let her foes know Karl had rattled her. If that occurred, her political career was over. She'd had to settle for the two agents the

FBI had recommended and sent to provide temporary security until she employed her own security team.

Taking a deep breath to center herself, Sandra continued her brief discussion with Adam Carter, Special Agent in Charge at the local FBI office. "Will you at least keep me posted? I want to know the minute they capture this terrorist. I presume that when you have him in custody, he will suffer the consequences of his actions to the full extent of the law."

"You have my word, Governor Murphy. We've attempted to follow the money trail. I believe we're close and should have a break very soon. His picture is all over the news, and tips are coming in daily. Every available agent is working the case. We will have our man soon enough," Adam Carter assured her.

"Thank you for all you do," Sandra praised. "I know you are a busy man, so I'll let you go."

Sandra leaned into her comfortable leather office chair and began twirling her pen, a bad habit she had picked up when she was particularly anxious. Her former campaign manager had brought that to her attention, and she had worked on stilling her hands while interacting with prospective voters. However, in the privacy of her own home, she didn't give a rat's ass if her mother noticed the nervous habit. It was this or alcohol.

Her mind wandered to a week prior when she'd made a rash decision to stop off at Lavender Lips and have a drink. Knowing that the bar was Wynter's favorite watering hole made it difficult for Sandra to avoid the place. Not a good idea. No, it was a terrible idea. But that didn't stop Sandra from popping from her chair and stalking over to the large bodyguard standing outside her front door. She rationalized that Wynter probably wasn't there, anyway. Of course, the young woman had a life that presumably did not include spending all her time at Lavender Lips. Running into her the prior week was a fluke. An unbelievable freak occurrence.

Since Sandra had a knack for remembering names, she quietly addressed the large man, startling him in the process. "Good evening, Frank."

"Good evening, Governor Murphy." He chuckled nervously. "You startled me. If you ever want to change careers, I'm sure the FBI would hire you in a heartbeat. I didn't hear you approach."

Ignoring his confession, Sandra pressed on. "I was hoping to get out of the house this evening. Staying inside is becoming incredibly claustrophobic for me. I don't suppose you're allowed to have a drink while on duty."

"No, ma'am. And I would not recommend you go for a drink. There are still very credible threats on your life."

Sandra sighed. "The place I plan on visiting is very discreet. I doubt any members of the domestic terror cell bent on erasing my existence will dream of setting foot in this place."

Frank raised one eyebrow. "Where are we going?"

"Lavender Lips. A good friend of mine owns the place."

Frank nodded. "Ah, the lesbian bar. My older sister loves that place. Very low-key. That should be easy enough to determine whether someone out of place enters. All right, Governor. You may want to call your friend because I suspect I'll get a few strange looks if I enter the bar with you."

Sandra smiled at his response. No wonder this man, who looked like the military had just honorably discharged him, had treated her respectfully. When he mentioned his older sister, there was affection in his voice, along with the softening of his eyes. Clearly, he loved his sister.

Sandra was glad they hadn't sent a homophobe to provide security. She'd had that happen to her before. That was the real reason she chose not to accept the security detail provided by DPS, the Dignity Protection Section, typically assigned to the governor's office. The man had barely held his contempt hidden beneath the grim line on his face. Sandra had finally had enough and fired him without explanation. That had angered him even more, and she wouldn't be surprised if the man had joined a fringe group. Perhaps he was even one of Karl Schmidt's foot soldiers.

Frank remained quiet as all those thoughts quickly filtered through her brain. Sandra was sure she hadn't masked her emotions as she recalled the unpleasant exchange she'd had with the homophobe.

Grabbing her purse, Sandra addressed the perplexed man who watched her closely. "Let's go. I'd rather not be there when it's busy and overrun with thirsty patrons. I doubt there will be many people in there at this time."

"Yes, ma'am." Frank dutifully followed her to her Honda plug-in hybrid.

Sandra was acting recklessly. She knew that, but the chance of running into Wynter a second time was just too tempting to pass up.

†

How could Wynter forget that alluring scent? The minute the combination sweet, citrusy smell reached her nose, Wynter turned around to find Governor Sandra Murphy strolling into Lavender Lips like she owned the place. Only this time, she had an enormous bodyguard practically glued to her side. Wynter wondered if he would join her at the bar or remain at a respectable distance.

Swiveling on the stool, she addressed the governor. "Are you following me, Governor Murphy?" Wynter grinned.

Governor Murphy threw her head back and laughed. A glorious sound to Wynter's ears. "No, Ms. Holmes, but I am glad I ran into you."

The large man kept rotating his head, casing the place before taking a seat at a discreet distance from the governor, who grabbed the empty stool next to Wynter. After thoroughly checking the bar, the man kept his eyes on the front door. Presumably, he was looking for any threat to Governor Murphy. Wynter winced when she thought of how harsh she'd been with her questioning, knowing there was still a risk to the governor's life. She wasn't sure she would have been as poised after an attempt on her life and the life of her mother.

Geri grinned as she set a napkin in front of Sandra. "A lemon drop?"

Sandra nodded.

"Wynter, remember? I feel like I'm back in high school when you address me as Ms. Holmes. And since I had a miserable experience in secondary school, I'd rather not travel back to that time in my life."

"Very well. How about I call you Wynter while we are both in a social gathering? But for a press conference, I must insist on remaining more professional, lest the public believe I'm playing favorites. And you can drop the governor title and simply call me Sandra."

Wynter looked at Sandra with what she assumed was shock and realized her mouth hung open. Unattractively, she presumed. Deciding to recover from her surprise, she asked, "So, why are you glad you ran into me? I would think you've labeled me the dreaded press piranha."

"I've done no such thing. While I'll admit I believe you are wasting your talents at TRU, your questions reveal your ability at reduction, bringing forth the essence of the issue. It hasn't always been pleasant answering your pointed questions, but I appreciate the fact that you have a job to do. I was wondering, Wynter, if you've given much thought to your future and if you see yourself doing anything different from covering the political beat?"

Wynter laughed. "I'm still stuck on reduction. Are you saying I create a brilliant sauce with my questions?"

Sandra shrugged. "Sure, why not? Food analogies are delicious, don't you think? Your future," Sandra prompted.

"To win a Pulitzer, of course." Wynter grinned.

"Would you ever consider dipping your toes a little more into politics? Perhaps involvement in the news from a different perspective? Such as press secretary?" Sandra asked.

"Are you offering me a job, Governor?"

"Sandra, remember?"

"I can't call you Sandra while we're talking business. Unless you aren't serious about the possibility of working for you."

"Oh, I am deadly serious. The other networks that failed to gobble up your talent made a colossal mistake. If I decide to make a run for the presidency, I'll need someone on my team who is bright, ambitious, and able to think on their feet. I believe you fit those requirements." Sandra nodded her thanks when Geri set her drink on the napkin.

Wynter paused while she took a sip of her beer. She needed a few minutes to respond to the surprising offer. A significant part of her wanted to jump at the chance, but something held her back. Not that she would ever have a chance with the attractive and accomplished governor, but accepting a job with her would make that an impossibility. The press would have a field day with the governor dating her younger press secretary. Of course, she'd never consider dating her in her present position with TRU, either. So, what the hell? Maybe a career change was precisely what she needed at this point in her life. It was becoming increasingly difficult to work for TRU. She'd lost most of her friends over it, which made her reassess who her real friends were.

"All right. Let's say, for shits and giggles, I take you up on your offer. I'm going to need a lot more details before I consider it," Wynter finally responded.

A wide smile blossomed on Sandra's face, and Wynter had never seen a more beautiful sight. "How about if I take you to lunch tomorrow and provide those relevant details?"

Wynter lifted her glass. "It's a date." She smirked and pointed to the large man sitting uncomfortably a small distance from Sandra. "Will he be our chaperone?"

"I'm afraid so."

Sandra seemed to ignore her subtle flirtation, and that impressed Wynter. This might be a fun challenge for Wynter. Could she get the delectable governor to crack? Maybe even encourage Sandra to try her hand at innocent flirtation? Now that was a task Wynter would relish getting behind, among other less PG things she could conjure in her mind.

Wynter held out her hand, palm side up. "Give me your phone."

Sandra furrowed her brow. "Why?"

"So I can type in my digits."

"Oh, okay." Sandra dug inside her bag and produced the phone for Wynter, placing it in her outstretched hand.

Wynter's thumbs flew over the tiny keyboard, and she entered her phone number in record time. Grinning, she handed the device back to Sandra. "Send me a text on when and where to meet you tomorrow. I expect you'll need to get reservations because I deserve to be wined and dined if you're going to convince me to join your team."

Sandra arched one eyebrow, then answered, "I didn't take you for someone who is high maintenance, but very well, I will find a place suitable for our negotiations."

"Does that mean you're going to try to lowball me? How misogynist of you. As a fellow feminist, I expect you to offer a fair wage comparable to what you've paid men in a similar role. At least you provided me forewarning so I could do my own research. Don't expect a pushover." Wynter knew she had shot Sandra a cheeky grin and was probably coming off as incredibly arrogant. But from her observations, that didn't seem to bother Sandra.

"I would expect nothing less." Sandra returned Wynter's cocky smile with one of her own. Sandra finished her drink, setting it down on the bar as she nodded almost imperceptibly at her bodyguard. When she stood to leave, she addressed Wynter. "I look forward to our lunch meeting tomorrow, Wynter. I am delighted I ran into you today."

"Well, if you ever want to run into me again, by sheer coincidence, I spend a fair amount of time at this bar. It's a place I feel comfortable. Low key, but mostly a lesbian clientele." Wynter held up her glass. "Cheers. Have a good evening, Sandra." Using the governor's first name felt unfamiliar, but Wynter wanted to try it out. She had rolled the name around in her head many times, but it sounded just a tad sultry to her when it burst from her lips. Another attempt at flirtation, she supposed.

Sandra nodded her goodbye and left without another word, her loyal lapdog following.

When Sandra returned home, her mother looked up from her tablet and asked, "Where were you off to this evening? I would think you'd need to lie low until they find the man responsible for blowing my beautiful home to bits."

"I felt claustrophobic and needed some air. I don't know why I've been avoiding the bar that Geri owns. It is certainly discreet enough, and I've missed Geri. Although we haven't talked much with one another lately, I need to call her so we can catch up properly." Sandra walked to her expensive custom couch and sat. "I ran into the reporter again and floated the idea of her working for me. I need a savvy press secretary, and I believe she fits the bill."

Rose frowned. "Are you sure that's a wise idea? She works for TRU. Their politics do not exactly align with yours."

"Theirs might not jibe, but for some reason, I believe her personal views track perfectly with mine," Sandra responded.

"What is the matter with what's his name as your press secretary?"

Sandra chuckled. "The fact that you cannot remember his name tells the story quite nicely. Walter is like a blob with a mouth talking to the press. Unfortunately, his pontificating is not helping us."

Rose nodded. "Right, Walter. I suppose the man is a little stiff."

"That's putting it lightly. Sometimes Walter is so boring that I feel myself nodding off, and I'm sure I've seen members of the press roll their eyes on numerous occasions when he makes the rounds to spread my message to the various talk shows. I'd be better off without a press secretary. But if I must have one, I'd prefer someone like our current president's press secretary. She's got fire, and so does Wynter Holmes. Mark my words. She'll get her own moniker after she puts a reporter in their place."

"Walter came so highly recommended." Rose shrugged.

"By whom, Mother? Some old white guy that has been in the political game for over fifty years? Things are rapidly shifting. We are losing the messaging war, and that blood loss needs to stop now. I take that back. It needed to stop six years ago. If our party does not grow some balls and tits, we will die a horrible death in the midterms, setting up a brutal campaign in the future."

"The pendulum is swinging the far right's way at this moment in history, but surely it will turn back once it's gone too far."

Sandra scoffed. "It went too far several years ago, and now there is open support for racism, sexism, and conspiracy theories. Every time I believe they've gone to the extreme, the US collectively shrugs, and the outlandish becomes the new normal."

"Darling, we need to talk about your personal life and how it will impact your campaign. A stable relationship with the right person who has a specific pedigree will help your brand."

"My brand? Mother, I am not a grocery item that needs marketing."

Rose waved her hand in the air. "Pish posh, yes, you are. Marketing is a crucial part of every campaign. How do you think that unqualified buffoon got into the office? It was certainly not due to his talents in business or politics. For goodness' sake, the man had several bankruptcies and never held a single political office. Instead, he marketed himself in a way that caught on. Everyone ignored his glaring deficiencies. We must get people to look the other way on your lesbianism."

"Throwing a fake relationship in their face seems like it would have the opposite effect." Sandra laid her head on the couch. Suddenly, she felt exhausted. This same conversation played out far too often these days, and it drained all her reserves.

"It worked for Michael Douglas," Rose noted. "People love to follow a good love story."

"You are not seriously hanging your hat on a movie? Besides, he was a widower and a straight man, as I recall. I believe those are relevant facts you're forgetting." Sandra shook her head. "Oh. My. God. I can't believe you have me talking about a fictional romance."

"James Buchanan was the only president to never marry while serving as president. As a result, he's consistently ranked last when comparing all the presidents. Buchanan comes in lower than the buffoon. I don't think that's a coincidence. Even Grover Cleveland married during his time in the White House, and his ranking is middle of the pack. The public prefers a married leader."

Sandra held her hand up. "Enough. I am done talking about this."

"Very well, darling. Don't take advice from your well-connected, politically astute mother." Rose crossed her arms over her chest and pouted, looking very much like a small child that wasn't going to get her way.

Sandra burst out laughing because seeing a woman in her sixties sulking had seriously touched her funny bone.

"What are you laughing at?" Rose asked, the derision dripping from her lips.

"How ridiculous you look pouting like a five-year-old."

"Fine, I'm heading to bed. This old woman needs her beauty sleep."

CHAPTER FOUR

Sandra stretched in her big, lonely, king bed and yawned. She glanced at her clock and noted the time. No matter how tired Sandra was or how late she had stayed up the night before, Sandra normally woke right before sunrise. She could always blame the chirping birds, who seemed to know when the sun was about to rise, but her internal clock was robust. Mornings were her moments of peace before she started her day. A time to reflect.

She hoped Wynter would enjoy her lunch today at Mister A's. Calling in a favor, Sandra had snagged a reservation at noon. She'd even secured a primo table with a view. Last-minute reservations were nearly impossible ever since the COVID restrictions had loosened. It seemed everyone in the city was eager to eat out after months of being cooped up in their houses.

She had decided not to text Wynter the prior evening, wanting to wait so she wouldn't seem too eager. Sandra pondered whether Wynter was an early riser like herself. Five in the morning was an absurd time to text a person. She knew she needed to wait a few more hours. Certainly, seven in the morning was reasonable enough, she argued.

Throwing on her silk robe, Sandra ambled to the kitchen to start the coffee. Her mother always had tea, but Sandra never could get used to what she considered an anemic replacement for her needed morning jolt. She could admit to her persnickety nature regarding a robust coffee. The popular chain stores were not to her liking as Sandra preferred the small, independent, organic growers who roasted small batch beans.

Once Sandra had prepared her coffee with a splash of heavy whipping cream, she sat at the breakfast counter with her hands wrapped around the warm cup and pondered her upcoming date with Wynter. Her brain backtracked to the word date as if a train had screeched to a stop on the tracks. No, this was not a date, even though Wynter had cheekily referred to it as such. This was a business lunch. She planned to present a job offer that, hopefully, the lovely Wynter would not refuse. Thinking about Wynter's clear blue eyes brought a small smile to her face.

Deciding it was ridiculous to wait until seven to text Wynter, she grabbed her phone and typed a simple text.

What she didn't expect was a response almost immediately after sending the message.

Reservations were made for noon today at Mister A's.

Ooh, Mister A's...Trying to impress me, Governor? LOL. Good call because I don't come cheap.

What are you doing up at six?

I could ask you the same question. You really should get back to your hot date from last night. She'll wonder why you slipped out of bed and left a cold spot behind.

Ha ha, nice try. I didn't realize you wanted to write gossip pieces. I'm sure you know I am not seeing anyone at the moment.

I'm not aware of that, but good to know. After learning about our lunch date today, I'd hate to have an uncomfortable interaction with a jealous lover. LOL.

Go back to your in-depth research on me, Wynter, and I'll see you at noon.

Looking forward to it.

"Why are you smiling?" Rose interrupted.

Sandra's body jumped in her chair, startled by her mother, who had walked into the kitchen. "Damn, you shouldn't sneak up on someone with a piping hot coffee in her hands."

Rose wrinkled her nose. "You don't have coffee in your hands. You have your cell phone. Who in the world are you talking to at six in the morning?"

Choosing to ignore the question, Sandra responded, "You're up awfully early. Is there a specific reason?"

"Actually, there is. I have an early morning meeting with the Speaker of the House. She was hoping you would join us."

The smile slipped from Sandra's face. She hated all the behind-the-scenes politics. The planning and plotting always appeared disingenuous as to why she'd entered politics to begin with.

"I'd really rather not. Hard pass. I told you, you would be the first to know when I am ready to make a final decision about my candidacy." Sandra held up her hand to keep her mother from interrupting. "Before you say anything, I know I've been sending mixed messages, and my vacillating over which direction I plan to go has given you, and everyone else, whiplash, but I still have more soul searching to do."

"She's prepared to put the full weight of her considerable influence behind you, Sandra, but I cannot keep putting her off. Blowing off the Speaker is not in your best interest."

Sandra sighed. "I will need a lot more than the Speaker's backing if I have a sliver of a chance. Before I commit, several open positions on my team need filling. However, I may feel more confident if I manage to secure Wynter Holmes. I'm meeting her for lunch."

Rose narrowed her eyes. "Please don't tell me you're interested in that smarmy little rodent. That's who you were texting so early in the morning. I'm surprised she was up this time of the day."

Sandra busted out in laughter. "Smarmy rodent? Surely you could think of a more sophisticated taunt. Something about her is intriguing to me. What's that old saying? *Keep your friends close and your enemies even closer.*" Sandra shook her head. "Or something like that. Besides, I believe Wynter could be a friend, and a helpful one at that, versus an enemy."

"I prefer the saying *trust no one.*" Rose smiled.

Sandra laughed again. "Oh, good lord. I didn't think it was possible, but you've turned even more cynical than during my formative years. It's a miracle you couldn't mold me better into your likeness."

Rose scoffed. "Murphy women are bred to be strong independent powerhouses. The fact that you have a soft, empathetic side that relates to all types makes you the perfect candidate. Since the Democratic Party has no one who stands a chance against this new movement which insists that we travel back in time one hundred years, it is no wonder they are putting pressure on me to convince you to run."

"I don't respond well to pressure. You know that."

"Very well. Have your little meeting, and let me know how it goes. If this Wynter Holmes is the key to getting you to decide, I will be the first to welcome her to the team."

"Sure you will. Don't you have to get ready to meet with Nora?"

"I do, but if Frank accompanies me to my meeting, that will leave you unprotected." Rose frowned. "I hadn't really considered that. You haven't heard an update on Karl Schmidt, have you?"

"I'm not as worried as the rest of you. I suspect Karl is too busy hiding from the authorities to take another shot at me."

"These nutcases never operate in a vacuum, dear. I don't believe I'm at risk as much as you. I'll tell Frank to stay with you. Besides, Nora has her own security detail. That should suffice for me."

"Let me make a quick call to my contact in the FBI. Perhaps they have news," Sandra responded.

Rose nodded and then left the kitchen. Sandra wrapped her hands around the mug and sipped her coffee. She wasn't in any hurry to start her day. It seemed there were always fires to extinguish. She laughed as she thought of what she might look like in a fire uniform. Would Wynter like that?

†

Not wanting to hassle with parking, which could be tricky, Wynter had called for an Uber and arrived at the restaurant ten minutes before noon. She hoped that wouldn't suggest she was too eager for the lunch date, even though she was. She wasn't sure what had possessed her to needle the governor into making a reservation at an upscale place. Wynter was the furthest thing from someone who might be impressed with a five-star restaurant. In reality, she was more of a burgers-and-brew kind of gal.

41

Wynter climbed from the Uber and made her way slowly to the elevators. If she timed everything correctly, she'd arrive closer to noon. After Wynter pressed the elevator button, she swiveled her head toward the large man who had accompanied Governor Murphy and the governor herself. It was as if she had sensed their approach. Although Sandra had said the bodyguard would be present, Wynter masked her disappointment that it wouldn't be just the two of them and greeted Sandra.

"Hello, Governor. I see that you also would rather be slightly early than late." The elevator doors slid open, and she entered the small space.

"Always," Sandra responded as she followed Wynter into the elevator. "I thought we had established that you should call me Sandra."

Wynter pressed the button for the twelfth floor. "I don't believe that was ever agreed to. In fact, I distinctly remember you stating that if we were to discuss business, I should address you more formally." Wynter arched her eyebrow. "We are going to discuss a job offer, correct?"

Sandra laughed, and Wynter found she enjoyed that sound a little bit too much. "Yes, we are, and I am confident you will join the team. Nobody on my team calls me Governor Murphy." Sandra turned to Frank. "Isn't that right, Frank?"

"Yes, ma'am," Frank responded.

Sandra rolled her eyes. "I suppose, like with you, I am still working on Frank. However, I assure you it's one of my few hard and fast rules. So, I insist you call me Sandra. Please."

"How can I resist, with you using please and all? Is Frank joining us for lunch?"

"Oh, no, I've reserved a separate table for Frank. Not that I don't trust him, but I thought it might be awkward for him to be a part of the negotiations."

Wynter couldn't help the smile that quickly blossomed on her face or the rapid increase of her heartbeat. If she ignored Frank, who would probably sit at a table next to theirs, she could pretend this was more than a business lunch.

The elevator doors slowly opened, and Sandra led Wynter and Frank to the restaurant's entrance. The maître d' immediately greeted the small group and beamed at Sandra. If Wynter didn't know better, she would think they were an item.

"Sandra, it is so good to see you. It's been too long. I saw your name on the reservation list and was delighted to learn you would be arriving for lunch. I was so worried when I heard about the bombing."

"Not one of my better days," Sandra responded wryly. "But I suppose I am a very hard person to kill, as is my mother," she joked.

"Oh my, Sandra, you shouldn't joke about things like that. I hope you can put that nastiness out of your mind and enjoy a good meal today."

"That's the plan."

"Right this way, I have your tables ready."

43

"Thanks, Peter."

Once Peter had led them to their table, Wynter grinned at Sandra. "Not bad, Sandra," Wynter said as she forced herself to use the governor's first name as requested. Their view of the beach and the city was nothing short of spectacular.

"Peter and I actually go back a long way. Believe it or not, we went to high school together. He always makes sure I have the best table. Not that he needs the money, but every time I attempt to tip him, he refuses my gesture of appreciation."

Wynter tilted her head in confusion. "I didn't realize maître d's earn robust salaries."

"Oh, they don't. Peter has a wealthy husband. But since he's quite the extrovert, he actually loves being a maître d' and meeting and greeting people. He believes his job is important."

Wynter chuckled. "Okay, that's different. I've never heard of anyone in this profession feeling like they make a difference. Sure, teachers, nurses, doctors, but a maître d', really?"

"Don't be a snob, Wynter. Why shouldn't every single individual believe their job is important? Do you actually know what a maître d' does?"

Wynter felt her face heat in embarrassment. "Not really."

"Not only does Peter make reservations and greet all the patrons, but he is also responsible for the ambiance at Mister A's. He controls everything from the temperature to the volume of the music. He takes his job seriously. Not only that, but all the waiters and waitresses report to him, and he makes sure the waitstaff is efficient."

"Okay, wow, call me properly chastised. If only the entire world approached their careers in the same manner."

"Indeed. Good segué. Now, let's talk about your career, Wynter."

Wynter nearly swooned at how Sandra elongated her name, making it sound almost sexual. Before she had a chance to answer, the waiter appeared.

"Good afternoon, Governor Murphy. It's good to see you again. Would you like your usual?"

"Good afternoon, Ralph. No, I think I'd like to shake things up today. I'll take the Zen And The Art Of cocktail."

Ralph turned to Wynter. "And you, miss. Would you like a drink to start?"

"Who am I to argue with such an inventive name for a cocktail? I'll have the same."

The waiter nodded. "You won't be disappointed. I'll be back in a jiffy with your drinks and to take your lunch order."

Wynter leaned in and whispered, "Do you know every person at Mister A's, and what did I just order?"

Sandra laughed, and that beautiful throaty sound went straight to Wynter's nether regions. "Roku gin, lychee, yellow chartreuse, and mint," Sandra answered. "And, no, I don't know everyone here. They have some new waitpersons I haven't had the pleasure of getting to know yet."

Wynter leaned back in her chair. "Mmhm, I suppose this is your hangout. Well, the drink sounds delicious. Why isn't that your usual?" Wynter asked.

"Burnt orange old fashioned. I'm very partial to anything with orange, but strangely enough, I don't care for orange juice. I prefer grapefruit juice at breakfast. Fresh squeezed orange juice has a kind of consistency I don't enjoy. I'll drink it if it's the only choice and not be rude to a host offering it."

"And you call me a snob?" Wynter joked.

"Big difference between dissing someone's job and stating a preference." A tiny smile appeared on Sandra's face.

"I didn't exactly diss his job. I was merely surprised."

Sandra raised an eyebrow. "You don't think questioning the importance of Peter's job displayed a tiny bit of elitism?"

"Touché. Okay, I'll admit I have more to learn." Wynter leaned in again, and even though she knew she shouldn't, she couldn't resist flirting. "I'd especially love to learn more about you, Sandra."

†

Sandra didn't know what to do about Wynter's subtle attempt at flirting with her. She quickly searched her memory, trying to think of what messages she'd been sending to the young woman. Was it a mistake to insist Wynter call her by her first name? No, she was honest about urging everyone on her team to address her less formally.

46

Where was that quick wit and ability to think on her feet that she was known for?

The waiter returned with their drinks, and Sandra had never felt more relieved in her entire life. Setting down the beverages, he inquired, "Are you ready to order? Can I answer any questions about the menu?"

Sandra glanced at Wynter, who answered, "I'm so sorry, I haven't had a chance to study the menu. What are you having, Sandra?"

"The White Sea Bass. It's to die for. I usually get that or the salmon. Mister A's is one of the few places I don't need to state that I would like my salmon cooked medium rare."

"Okay, I'll have the salmon, and I'm sure that Sandra will allow me to taste her White Sea Bass," Wynter answered.

Sandra grinned. "I'll do better than that. If you enjoy the sea bass, I can share the dish with you, and you can share your salmon."

Wynter's mouth turned up in a crooked smile. "Sold."

"I know the Planca Grilled Spanish Octopus is part of the dinner menu as a starter, but I was wondering if you could ask the chef to prepare that for us as well?"

"I'm sure Chef Williams can accommodate you," Ralph answered.

"Thank you, Ralph."

He nodded and bowed. "My pleasure."

After Ralph left, Wynter had a mischievous look on her face. "What if I didn't eat octopus? Isn't that presumptuous of you?"

"Oh, would you have preferred a different appetizer?"

"Did you know octopi are one of the most intelligent creatures in the sea? Didn't you ever see that documentary, *My Octopus Teacher*?" Wynter asked.

"I'm afraid I don't have a lot of time to watch television. Is that why you're opposed to eating delicious octopus? Because I am telling you, it's the best item on the menu." Sandra leaned forward, looking Wynter directly in the eye.

"Well, then, I suppose I will have to try it just to ensure you're a woman of integrity." Wynter relaxed into her chair again.

"A woman of integrity?" Sandra didn't even try to mask her confusion.

"Yeah, do you always tell the truth, or are you one of those politicians that use alternate facts or insist that your opinion is always fact?" Wynter challenged.

"So cynical for one so young."

"Don't think I didn't notice how you've deftly avoided answering my question. And for the record, I'm not that young. I simply take good care of myself and appear younger than I really am."

"Okay, humor me and answer a question one should never ask another person. How old are you?"

Wynter smirked. "Thirty-eight. And I've made sure to live each year to the fullest. Now answer my question."

Sandra was far too interested in the answer to her question to backtrack and respond to Wynter's query. "You haven't been working for TRU that long, making it seem like it was your first job after college. That does not compute."

"Hmm, have you been keeping track of my career? TRU is not my first job in journalism. I worked for several smaller stations before landing the job at TRU. Plus, I told you I've lived life to the fullest. I didn't go directly to college after high school. I felt like I needed to experience the world first, to give me a greater appreciation of formal education. Besides, I didn't want to have a mountain of debt. Working and saving afforded me the opportunity to pay for my education without owing some smarmy financial institution for the rest of my life."

"Isn't that a bit of an embellishment?"

"I don't suppose you've ever had to worry about paying for school, given your family's wealth. Surely you realize the seriousness of the rising education costs in our country. At some point, the politicians will need to address the issue, or we'll fall even further behind other countries who have figured it out, along with universal healthcare."

"I agree, Wynter. Hopefully, I can impact those important issues, but I am also realistic. Baby steps. Unfortunately, few people understand the intricacies of politics. With such a divided nation, I'm surprised we get anything done. Our state has worked hard to have both a trifecta and a triplex, with Democrats controlling the offices of governor, secretary of state, attorney general, and both chambers of our state legislature. While the US also has control of both chambers, without a sixty-vote majority, everything is stalled in the Senate. I don't see that changing anytime soon." Sandra sighed.

"Then why do you want to run for president?" Wynter asked.

"Honestly, I don't know that I do. And yet, I am sincere about wanting to make a difference. Although that road is littered with danger and disappointment, the office of the presidency does have some power. Not as much as the American public believes, but as we all are painfully aware, the nomination of supreme court justices is one of the most important powers. Of course, that also depends on senate confirmation, which can be tricky. I'm lecturing you. Sorry."

Wynter grinned. "No problem. I love talking politics. Let's circle back to my original question, which you've yet to answer. Serious consideration of the job you'd like to offer depends on your answer."

Sandra placed her hands on the table and clasped them together. "Very well. Here is the messy, unvarnished truth. I suppose it depends on one's definition of honesty. As you already know, I've kept some things about myself private until recently. For some, that was interpreted as dishonesty. What the public is entitled to know versus what politicians share is often up for debate. For example, do you believe the public should know if I've ever been in love? Or is that none of their business?"

"Hm. Good point. Have you?" Wynter stared intently at Sandra, patiently waiting for her answer.

Sandra chuckled. "I thought I was. Once. But while I loved her, I don't believe I was ever in love with her. And you?"

"Same. I've loved many women but never been in love. You know, like the kind of love for which you would sacrifice almost everything." Wynter placed her elbow on the table, propping her head in her hand. She momentarily stared off into space as if remembering something or someone.

"I don't believe sacrifice is necessary for a stable, loving relationship. Compromise, maybe, but never martyrdom to the point of changing who you fundamentally are. That would be selfish to even ask."

Wynter's attention returned to Sandra. "Wow, that's deep. Besides keeping certain important facts about yourself from the public, have you ever intentionally misled them?"

"Intentionally misled, no. Willfully spun a few facts, absolutely. Like on a date or in a new relationship, politicians will present certain facts about themselves that shed them in a positive light. I've definitely done that. I have never told an outright lie. And as you are already aware, sometimes I've bent or broken a few rules."

Wynter cringed. "Yeah, I wanted to apologize for how hard I was on you at the press conference. You'd just experienced a significant trauma, and I went right for the jugular. I'm glad you didn't apply for that permit. If you had, I suspect that psychopath would have blown up your safe room. I understand why you didn't, but I hope you realize I had to ask the question."

51

"Thank you for that apology. I did wonder why you failed to bring up the whole DPS controversy. Did you sense my subsequent guilt over that decision, considering my mother was affected by it? You have a heart after all," Sandra teased.

"Maybe. Why did you dismiss DPS?"

"Subtle homophobia. I meant to hire my own security team, but never quite got around to it. I'm assuming this is off the record."

"It is," Wynter assured.

Sandra smiled. "Back to the main topic of discussion today. Since honesty is so important to you, I will depend on you to keep me honest, including sharing details and facts that you believe the public is entitled to know, regardless of whether they are beneficial or flattering to my candidacy. Whatever they are paying you at TRU, I will add ten percent to the salary. Full healthcare benefits and a retirement plan also come with the offer."

Wynter's eyes widened. "Are you serious? You don't even know what I make."

"I know it's not what you deserve, nor is it at the same level as your male colleagues. Am I right?" Sandra looked expectantly at Wynter.

"I don't exactly know what my colleagues make. I've never asked. That would be rude," Wynter answered defensively.

Sandra shook her head and rolled her eyes. "You're a reporter. I doubt it would be much of a challenge for you to dig out that information." Plucking her phone from her bag,

Sandra quickly typed a query into her favorite search engine. She turned the phone to Wynter. "Here are the salaries for the top news anchors at TRU. I didn't even have to dig for the information. Do you see a pattern here?"

"Fine, TRU is a sexist, racist, homophobic network. Are you happy now?"

"Not yet. When you agree to resign from that horrible excuse for a news station, I'll be overjoyed. I'm sure it's frustrating to make less than those a-holes at TRU who spout all that ridiculous conspiracy theory bull. I'm offering you a chance to use your intelligence and talents while compensating you what you're worth. And, if TRU is paying you what I think they are, a ten percent raise may not even come close to appropriate remuneration for your skills. Name your price."

Wynter grinned. "Okay, let's say I'm interested. What would be my job and title?"

"Communications director. You would be responsible for all communications between my office and the public, including interactions with the media. And, if I decide to run for president, I'll want you on my campaign trail in the same capacity, including helping me write speeches and prepare for debates. Does that sound like an interesting enough challenge for you?"

"You don't want me on opposition research?"

"I have individuals for that, but knock yourself out if you can't resist digging around. Once a reporter, always a reporter, I suspect. You'll have free rein to decide what to focus your energy on. As long as you're by my side, helping me be a better politician and person, I don't care how you spend your time."

"You're not making it easy to turn down your offer."

Sandra laughed. "Why in the world would I want to make it easy, and what is your hesitancy?"

"Oh, I don't know. Whenever something seems too good to be true, it always is just that."

"Again, with the cynicism. Someday I'll want to understand the origins of your skepticism. Is it just me, or do you distrust most people?"

The waiter returned and set the octopus in the middle of the table, along with two small plates. "Enjoy, ladies."

Wynter closed her eyes and appeared to murmur a prayer, although Sandra did not know what she was saying because her voice was so soft. When she finally opened her eyes, Sandra had to know what she was doing.

"I didn't exactly take you for the religious type."

Wynter laughed deeply. "Oh, I'm not. I was speaking my mantra to help me try to ignore that I'm about to eat this intelligent creature. I apologized to the universe for my weakness because it looked delicious. Forgive me for being a weak, weak woman. I'll admit that I'm a foodie and would have struggled to resist any delicacy from Mister A's. Although, I generally tend to gravitate to hole-in-the-wall establishments. Let's just see if it is as good as you say."

Sandra cut a small piece, pointing to the delicacy. "Go for it."

Wynter jabbed her fork in the tiny morsel, then popped it into her mouth. "Mmm," she moaned. "Fuck me, if that isn't out of this world good. God, I'm so sorry, Mr. Octopus, but intelligent or not, I might have to order this whenever it's on the menu. With that twenty percent salary enhancement you're going to give me, I'll be able to come to Mister A's more often."

Sandra shook her head and smiled. "I believe I just got played. Nice negotiating tactic. Twenty percent it is. I'm going to squeeze every single cent of that salary out of you." She held out her hand. "Welcome to the team, Wynter."

CHAPTER FIVE

Toni wiped her bleary eyes. She'd given up on getting a good night's sleep ever since Em, Jimena, Hank, and Steve had decided on the plan to set a trap for Karl Junior. Each night Toni watched the monitors, waiting for Karl to make his move. Although Karl had almost assassinated the governor, catching Em and Jimena in the crossfire, Toni wasn't worried about their plan going sideways because The Organization had directed Sophie and Val to provide backup. Val could probably handle the job with one hand tied behind her back, but Toni's wife, Char, had insisted it was always better to send agents in teams of two.

The Organization had been following Em's undercover assignment closely. Unfortunately, they were caught off guard by Karl's plan to blow up Rose Murphy's house while Governor Sandra Murphy was having tea with her mother. Hank had provided The Organization the perfect opportunity to become intimately involved when he had called. Hank had asked Toni to hack into the FBI and check on a colleague he suspected might be one of the many moles they were trying to root out after the assassination attempt on the governor's life. Now, The Organization was working alongside Em, Jimena, Hank, and Steve without the FBI's knowledge. Hopefully, it would stay that way. Char trusted the small team would not betray them.

Finally, Karl Junior was making his move. Toni watched her screen as five men descended on the safe house where Em and Jimena had laid their trap. Toni smiled as she saw Val and Sophie quickly immobilize three of the men, leaving Karl Junior and his right-hand man for Em and Jimena.

"You sure you don't want us to take out Karl and Smitty?" Val's voice crackled in Toni's ear.

"No, let Em take care of her brother," Toni answered.

"You trust their skills?" Sophie asked.

"Yes, Char has wanted to recruit Em for some time now. Jimena only recently appeared on her radar. It was pretty impressive how they handled the situation with the governor." Toni's eyes moved back to the screen as she caught movement.

"Gunfire inside. We're going in," Val stated.

Toni sighed in relief when she saw Em take out Smitty, and then Jimena dragged him to the side, placing a gun at his temple. Like a Ninja, Em had snuck into the room where Karl ranted and let a string of cuss words fly from his mouth after discovering the empty closet he assumed Em would be in. When he turned around after shoving a new magazine into his AK-47, Em already had a gun pointed at him. The scene unfolded quickly after that, and Toni wondered how Em would feel after shooting her brother. From what Toni saw, Em didn't have a choice, but Toni knew that didn't matter because events like this weighed heavily on a person, no matter how strong they were.

Toni watched and waited. As soon as Val and Sophie exited the house, she clicked on her commlink and said, "Nicely done. See you back at our temporary base. I'm going to contact that reporter, Wynter Holmes. I know she still works for TRU, but I'd like to re-establish with her so that we can control the narrative. She can be the one we feed information to as soon as we capture Bridget and Mikhail. Char is still concerned about protecting the governor. At least Karl Junior and his terror cell are no longer a threat."

"You sure this reporter is the best person to give the story to?" Sophie asked.

"Yeah, there's something very likable about Wynter, despite her choice of employer. Although I haven't convinced Char of that yet," Toni answered. "This morning will be a small test for Wynter, and I hope she passes."

"Me, too. Char can get grumpy when things don't go our way. On another topic, when will you tell Em about her mother and father?" Sophie asked.

"Soon. Char wants to meet with Jimena and Em in person before we provide them with more information. Based on my interactions with Em and everything that's happened over the last few weeks, we're confident Em isn't some double agent. She won't be happy to learn that her parents are Russian spies. She's never even met Mikhail. Bridget wasn't much of a mother to Em. Even so, learning she's a Russian agent will definitely shock Em. Plus, Em still believes Karl Senior was her father." Toni stretched in her chair and yawned. "I'm going to go to bed for twenty-four hours straight after all this is over."

"I know you're still monitoring chatter with the Russians, but you can't continue hanging out in your lab twenty-four-seven. You should try to get some sleep today," Sophie suggested.

Toni's phone buzzed, and she spied the number before answering. "Maybe. Hey, gotta go. Em is calling, and I also have to contact Wynter. See you guys soon."

†

Wynter's police scanner crackled to life at the same time her phone buzzed on the nightstand. Rubbing her eyes, Wynter grumbled to herself. "Aw, come on, you couldn't wait until at least seven."

She picked up her phone and saw a cryptic message directing her to an address. Wynter grinned as she read the text from T, her mysterious angel of information. She had wondered if she would ever hear from the woman again since T hadn't contacted her in a while.

Rushing to dress, Wynter barely brushed her hair and found matching clothes before running out of the house. She phoned her favorite cameraman on her way to the address, hoping he wouldn't balk too much at the early hour. Generally, he was good-natured about early morning calls, knowing that when Wynter phoned, there was always a breaking story to cover.

When Wynter finally screeched to a stop in front of the address T had provided, there was already a line of police cars and several ambulances. Wynter muscled her way to the edge of where the police had sectioned off the area. She recognized Emma Schmidt and Jimena Aguilar talking with two men she assumed were fellow FBI agents. Jimmy, her cameraman, was already pointing his camera at the line of police vehicles and panning the entire area.

Wynter tried to get some answers, but the authorities weren't releasing any information. Taking a chance, Wynter called the number for T.

"Wynter. What can I do for you?" T asked.

"Hey, T, want to give me a little more detail on what's happening at this address?" Wynter inquired.

"You're a reporter. I'm sure you can dig out the story," T answered.

"Police are very tight-lipped right now. Looks like a shooting, and someone didn't make it. Come on, tell me what you know."

T sighed. "Karl Schmidt Junior is the person who died."

"Sting operation?" Wynter asked.

"Yeah. Something like that."

Wynter watched closely as Emma Schmidt interacted with one man she assumed was an FBI agent. Since Em looked upset and handed her gun to the man, Wynter surmised Emma was the one who had shot her brother.

"It was Emma Schmidt, right?" Wynter blurted. "Come on, I just need you to confirm my suspicions. I won't ask for any additional details."

"Okay, yes. The FBI will probably release that information later today, anyway," T answered.

"Thanks, T."

Wynter ended the call and kept her eyes riveted toward the scene as Jimena and the other male FBI agent re-entered the house while Emma waited by the SUV. Wynter noted the blood dripping down Emma's arm. She hoped the heroic agent hadn't sustained a severe injury. It didn't appear so, but what did Wynter know about gunshot wounds? When the male agent and Jimena returned, Jimena began to clean the wound. Wynter was too far away to hear what they were saying, but Emma seemed almost in shock. In Wynter's mind, that could be the result of her injury or the fact that she'd shot and killed her own brother. She didn't envy what Emma Schmidt was going through or had gone through in the last few weeks. The woman must be made of steel.

After Emma, Jimena, and the male agent left, there wasn't much else to see. So Wynter told Jimmy to keep shooting film while she found a quiet spot to call Sandra. She needed to know what had happened. Maybe that news would put her at ease to know that Karl Schmidt Junior was no longer a threat.

†

Sandra tried to remain patient, waiting to hear from the FBI about Karl. She also needed to practice the same tolerance for Wynter's need to give her current employer a month's notice before she could officially join Sandra's team. Another week had passed with no word from anyone on Karl's whereabouts. It was now coming up on over two weeks since her mother's house had blown to tiny bits.

It was barely six in the morning, but Sandra wanted to start her day, and there were a few things she needed from her San Diego office. Working from home had been mostly suitable, but being unable to venture outside her house was driving her batty. The last time she'd been out was when she'd had lunch with Wynter. An involuntary smile appeared as she sat at her breakfast nook, sipping her coffee. Screw the time of the day; Sandra needed to know what was happening with the FBI's effort to capture Karl. She vowed to call after she settled into her office. Frank wouldn't be happy that Sandra had grabbed the night shift man to accompany her to the office. He preferred to be the one to escort her when she left the security of her home.

Pushing open the French doors, she found the quiet man, nearly immobile, on her patio. "Coffee, Pete?" she asked.

"No, thank you, ma'am. Frank will be here in another couple of hours, and I'd rather not have something that will keep me awake during the day."

"What did I say about you calling me ma'am? Would it be an imposition if I asked you to escort me to the office this morning?"

Pete's face scrunched in discomfort. "So early? You don't want to wait for Frank? He usually accompanies you when you need to go out."

"I'll text him to meet us at my office. It's downright exhausting hiding in my home, and I usually start the day early. I refuse to act like a scared rabbit anymore. There are things I need at my office."

"Very well, ma'am."

Sandra shook her head. "I'm not going to break you of that habit, am I?" Like Frank, Pete had refused to address Sandra by her first name.

A slight smile formed on Pete's face. "No, ma'am. My mother would bring out the wooden spoon if she thought I was ever being disrespectful to you. She voted for you, ma'am. Loves what you've brought to our great state. She thinks a woman should have been in the White House years ago. She's hoping you announce that you're running so she can cast her vote for you again."

†

Pete dutifully followed Sandra into her office and sat quietly on her couch. She wondered how Pete and Frank didn't go bananas with nothing to do all day but make sure some unhinged white nationalist didn't try to kidnap or off her.

Sandra decided to wait until eight to call Adam. *Hopefully, he will have an update.* She could easily spend the next hour on the new bill to address the homeless problem. She'd been following the political wrangling and everyone expected her to sign the new legislation, but Sandra took nothing for granted. Before signing the document, she wanted to read every word.

Reaching for the thick sheaf of papers, she had barely reached the second page when her phone buzzed on top of the desk. It surprised Sandra to see Wynter's name appear on her screen.

"Hello, Wynter," Sandra answered. "I didn't realize you were always an early riser?"

"Listen, Sandra. I thought I would give you a heads-up. Emma Schmidt shot and killed her brother, Karl, early this morning. I need to head to the press conference the FBI is having shortly, but in case you haven't heard, I thought it might make you less anxious. Although, the mother is still in the wind."

"How did you hear about this?" Sandra asked.

"I'm a talented reporter and have a vested interest in this particular story. My police scanner and a confidential informant that I assume has connections with the local police department or FBI. She gives me an advantage with stories like this one. And, for the record, this story is a biggie. So many layers. I was hoping to get a break and complete my reporting on this before giving my notice. That's why I asked for a month."

"Thanks for the call, Wynter. I appreciate the information. It must have been hard for the undercover agent to shoot and kill her own brother."

"Yeah, that's what I thought, too. I'd love to interview Emma Schmidt, but the FBI is corralling around her and won't give anyone access to the undercover agent."

"You might want to give it a rest. Emma and Jimena have gone through a lot, including serious injuries from the bombs. I doubt they'll want to give an interview to the press. I have access to classified information, and the FBI didn't even trust me with their whereabouts. I was unable to contact them to thank them for their bravery. Perhaps now that Karl is no longer an issue, I'll be able to reach out to them."

"I don't suppose you'd let me talk to them at the same time?"

"Not if you're going to harass them," Sandra teased.

"I'm wounded you think I would harass them. You said it. Emma and Jimena are heroines who saved your life. The interview would be very flattering. Besides, I'm almost positive they're both lesbians. Makes me want to go easy on them."

"You didn't go easy on me, and I'm a lesbian."

Sandra's phone lit up, and another call rang out. "Can you hang on? I think this might be the FBI providing an update."

"Go ahead and take it. Call me back after you've talked with the authorities."

Sandra laughed. "Okay, but I'm not giving you any juicy information."

"Spoilsport," Wynter said before ending the call.

Sandra pressed the button to accept the new call.

"Governor Murphy," she answered.

"Hello, Governor Murphy, Adam Carter here. I know it's a little early, but I wanted to let you know that Karl Schmidt is dead, and we have several of his associates in custody after a successful sting operation this morning. As a result, we believe this specific domestic terror cell is now disbanded without its leader."

"Thank you, Mr. Carter. Yes, I heard. What about Bridget Schmidt?" Sandra asked.

"How did you hear about it already? Damn press," Carter muttered. "There is a nosy reporter who somehow gets wind of everything before we can shut it down."

"Bridget Schmidt," Sandra prompted.

"Oh, yes, sorry, Governor. We haven't found her yet. We are following up on a few leads, but it sounds like she wasn't as directly involved in the group, or at least not their most violent ideologies," Carter answered.

"I wouldn't be too sure about that. Bridget befriended my mother for a very specific reason. I'd say Bridget Schmidt may be a crucial person of interest. My gut says there is more to that woman than we are aware of. How is Emma Schmidt doing? I understand she was the one to take out her brother."

"Taking a well-earned rest."

"And the other agent?" Sandra inquired.

"Her, too."

"Thank you, Mr. Carter. I wonder if I could meet with them to express my gratitude?"

"I'm sure they would both say they were just doing their jobs, but I'll let them know. I would like to give them a few days of peace and quiet, though."

"Of course, of course."

"To be safe, I recommend keeping the security detail in place."

Sandra sighed. "I'll take your recommendation under advisement. While Frank and Pete have been excellent, I wonder if it would be possible to have Emma and Jimena take over that detail after their rest?"

After a long pause, Adam responded, "Well, um, Emma's skill set is undercover work, and Jimena is a Border Patrol Field Agent. I don't believe that would be the best use of their talents."

"Perhaps you should let them decide for themselves, but we can talk about that after they return to their positions."

"Have a nice day, Governor. We'll call with any updates on Bridget Schmidt. Stay safe." Adam ended the call.

The senior FBI agent in charge had decided not to respond to her snarky comment. Sandra looked at her phone and smiled wryly. She would have probably done the same, simply failed to respond. *There is more than one way to crack an egg.* Perhaps she would put Wynter on the job of finding a way to contact Emma and Jimena directly. Wynter was an extremely talented investigative journalist, creative at excavating information. Considering Wynter had scooped the story about Emma shooting her own brother, it wasn't a stretch to figure she might already know how to get ahold of them.

Sandra settled into her comfortable leather chair and smiled, thinking of those calculating opaque blue eyes. Yes, Wynter was ambitious and brutally obsessed with digging out the truth, but Sandra suspected there was much more to Wynter. The obsession ran deeper than merely catching some politician with their pants down. Wynter might wish to uncover certain secrecies, yet Sandra had her own need to unlock the mystery of Wynter Holmes. She prided herself on reading people. Although Wynter proved a more significant challenge than most.

Sandra had almost forgotten about Pete, who shifted on the couch. He remained quiet, not indicating he'd heard her end of either conversation. She decided to address the unanswered questions he might have.

"Karl Schmidt's associates were apprehended. Karl was shot and killed in an altercation with the FBI. His mother is still at large, so Adam Carter has recommended that you and Frank continue to follow me around until they get a handle on whether she was an integral part of the attempt. I hope you did not take offense to me exploring other options. I'm sure you're bored out of your mind playing babysitter to a middle-aged woman."

"No, ma'am. No offense. I don't know Jimena, but Emma is top-notch at everything she does. If my daughter were at risk, I'd want Em to be the one to watch over her."

"Well, that's an even better reason for me to find a replacement. Twelve-hour shifts must play havoc on your family time. How old is she?"

Pete's smile lit up the room. "Five, and she's very precocious. A bit of a challenge for my wife."

"This is a special time, Pete. Don't miss too much of her life, because you won't ever get that time back. How about if I send you home? I honestly don't think I am in imminent danger with the news I just received. I'm sure you would rather spend time with your precocious daughter. I'll make sure I still compensate you. My gift to you for your sacrifice over the last few weeks."

"I don't believe my supervisor would approve of that. It's no problem, ma'am. This is my duty, and I take it seriously."

"You let me deal with Adam Carter. If I'm completely honest, I would really prefer to have some time for myself. Not that you've ever overstepped your role because you're so quiet. I sometimes forget you are even here, which is an enormous problem. There are some things I'd rather not share with others." Sandra smiled to soften her next words. "Respectfully, you and Frank are both fired. Now, go and spend time with your daughter." Sandra waved her hand toward the door to her office.

CHAPTER SIX

Not realizing it was close to noon, Sandra had been chugging along on the work piled up on her desk. A tentative knock on her door caused her to look up into the anxious eyes of her assistant.

"I was going to ask if you wanted me to order lunch for you, but apparently, you have that covered."

"Huh?" Sandra responded. She was genuinely confused.

"Oh." Carla looked horrified. "I am so sorry, Governor. I thought you had approved this. She brought lunch. I'll get rid of her for you."

"Get rid of who?"

"That pesky reporter from TRU that always gives you a hard time. I should have seen through her ruse."

Sandra waved her hand in the air and began laughing. "No, no, send her in. I wasn't expecting her, but I've asked Wynter Holmes to join our team, which she will do in approximately four weeks."

"Am I being replaced?" Carla's voice quivered.

"Absolutely not, Carla. Don't worry. Your position is safe. Wynter will be our new director of communications."

"We don't have a director of communications," Carla answered.

"We do now." Sandra smiled. "You can send her in."

Wynter bounded into the office, holding a white bag. "I come bearing gifts. After hearing about Karl Schmidt, I thought you might be in a celebrating mood." Wynter cringed. "Not that I think celebrating any person's death is the right thing to do. I just meant you probably feel relieved." Wynter swiveled her head around the office, and then her nose wrinkled. "Where's your shadow?"

"I sent him home to spend time with his daughter."

Wynter made herself comfortable in the chair, slightly off to the side of the enormous desk. "Was that wise? I mean, Bridget Schmidt is still out there. She could also be a threat. Maybe not as big as Karl Junior, but still." She set the large white bag on the desk.

"I'm touched that you're worried about me. Looking for a scoop, Wynter?"

The shocked expression on Wynter's face had Sandra reassessing her joke.

"Goddess, no. This lunch is strictly off the record. I would not want to make my future job any harder if you say

71

something I'll need to rewind later," Wynter teased, apparently regrouping after her initial reaction.

"Funny. I was only joking, you know."

"Yes, I figured that out, but at first, I was a little hurt that you thought I had some kind of angle for bringing lunch today. Honestly, I *was* worried about you. Plus, I wanted to thank you for the job offer and lunch the other day."

"No thanks are necessary. I pulled out all the stops to get you to join our team because I think you're worth it. If you are really that worried about me, maybe you can help me track down Emma Schmidt and Jimena." Sandra paused. "Shoot, I forgot her last name."

Wynter quirked her eyebrow, then answered, "Aguilar. That's her last name. They're a couple, you know."

Sandra leaned forward. "Yes, I picked up that vibe in the short time they were inside Mother's home. I'm surprised you learned something that private about them. So, you've done research on them already?"

"Of course I have, but why do you want to track them down?" Wynter asked.

"I want to wine and dine them like you and offer them positions on my security detail," Sandra answered.

Wynter chuckled. "You know, you'll be making my job a lot harder. I can hear it now. Governor Sandra Murphy only hires lesbians, passing up qualified men and persons of color. Although Jimena would tick that box. What was wrong with muscles one and two?"

Sandra grinned. "You mean Frank and Pete?"

"Yeah, them. They looked like former Navy Seals or some other military elite."

"So is Emma Schmidt," Sandra answered.

"Oh, yeah, that's right. Former Army Ranger. That was certainly very impressive. I'm sure you two would have made a very handsome couple. Too bad she's already taken."

"Are you jealous?" Sandra knew she shouldn't have said anything to Wynter's comment. Still, the words simply slipped out, sounding far more flirtatious than she had intended. Or was her libido completely taking over any rational thought?

Wynter grinned and shrugged. "Maybe just a tiny bit disappointed." She demonstrated the measurement with her thumb and forefinger. "I mean, both are exceptionally hot. Story of my life, either all the attractive lesbians are taken, or I become their subordinate, and apparently, my boss has ethics."

"Are you flirting with me, Ms. Holmes?"

"Ooh, we're back to last names. That does not bode well for my volley back to your flirtation."

Wynter caught Sandra's eye and would not break contact. It was a challenge that Sandra was not prepared for.

"So, does that mean you know how to contact them? You've clearly been busy with research," Sandra redirected.

"Maybe," Wynter hedged. "But I have a price for that information."

Sandra smiled. "Name it."

"Join me for dinner tomorrow night. I'd like to take you to one of my favorite places to eat. Don't expect a Mister

A's experience because it's quite the opposite. But, I don't think you'll dislike the food. In my humble opinion, it's every bit as good, without the exorbitant prices."

"I don't think that's a very good idea, Wynter."

"Why not? I'm not asking you to share my bed, just a meal. Work colleagues do that sometimes," Wynter insisted. "I brought lunch today, and that hasn't seemed to send you in a tailspin. Best dim sum in the city. I hope you like it."

Sandra leaned back in her chair, mainly to provide a bit of distance between Wynter and herself. "I do enjoy dim sum. Jasmine Express? Can I give you money for lunch?"

"Absolutely not, and by the way, always go to Hong Kong BBQ for the real stuff."

Sandra chuckled. She couldn't believe she was about to agree to this. Of course, she shouldn't, but something about Wynter was so appealing, and Sandra couldn't help herself. "All right. It sounds like this is not a fancy place. Will I be okay in jeans?"

Wynter grinned as if she'd just won the lottery. "Jeans are perfect. Plan on getting a little dirty."

"What?"

"Now, Governor, get your mind out of the gutter. I just meant the place has delicious food you eat with your fingers. And if you want to lick said fingers, perfectly fine with me, but they aren't totally barbaric and do provide bibs and napkins." Opening the white bag, Wynter pulled takeout containers from inside and set them on the desk. "I didn't know what you might like, so I got a wide variety. Hom sui gok, steamed pork bun, sweet rice cake, chicken pot stickers, pork and shrimp shiu mai, shrimp dumplings, and xiao long bao."

"That is a lot of food," Sandra noted.

"Yeah, but you'll be hungry again in like one hour. You have a microwave in these ostentatious offices, don't you?"

Sandra nodded. "I think we have one in the break room."

Wynter laughed. "You don't know, do you? Probably never been there."

Sandra flushed red. "No, I usually eat at my desk after my assistant orders from the deli around the corner. This is quite a treat."

"I'll bet you get the same thing every single day. You need to live a little, Sandra, and get out of that self-contained rut you've put yourself into." Wynter opened one container and then ripped open the paper holding the chopsticks. She grabbed one of the pot stickers and popped it into her mouth. "Dang, I forgot the sauce. Potstickers are not the same without the sauce." She opened the small plastic container with the dipping sauce and pointed her chopsticks at Sandra. "Eat up before I gobble them all down."

†

Wynter nearly skipped along the sidewalk. She couldn't believe she had enough moxie to actually ask the stoic governor out on a dinner date. Relishing how flustered the ordinarily unflappable woman had become, Wynter smiled before climbing into her car. She had at least five hours to kill before swinging by Sandra's home to pick her up for their date. Granted, Sandra probably did not consider it a date, but that could change. Wynter was intuitive enough to see her own attraction reflected in Sandra's eyes.

The governor had wanted to meet her at whatever restaurant Wynter planned to take her, but Wynter had insisted she come pick her up. She didn't even need the address because that had been plastered all over social media. A nasty group of white nationalists had discovered the private information and gleefully posted it, cajoling their members into protesting outside her home. The group had taken issue with Sandra's stance on lax gun laws and dove into action when Sandra had signed the sweeping gun regulation bill a few months back.

Wynter thought now might be an excellent time to track the address for Emma Schmidt or Jimena Aguilar. She didn't want to approach either just yet. She could be as ruthless as the rest of the reporters looking to get the scoop first, but knowing what both women had gone through in the last few weeks, she thought the least she could do was give them a few days to themselves. Holding onto a sliver of humanity was vital to her. Perhaps her new job wouldn't be as brutal regarding her constant fight to remain a decent human being. Admittedly, there were occasions when she'd danced far closer to oblivion than she would have thought possible. She wasn't proud of those times, even when she was the first reporter to dig out the story.

Before easing from the parking space, Wynter pulled her phone from her bag and pressed the number for her mysterious contact. She hoped to glean more information from the woman after her brief conversation earlier.

T had provided her very first break, even though it had only got her an insignificant spot on a news team as a research assistant. The mysterious woman had continued to contact her over the years, providing sensitive information about various political heavyweights. Unfortunately, that contact stopped when Wynter began working for TRU. That didn't surprise her because most of the information was about individuals who were either connected to TRU in some way or politicians TRU promoted heavily. Wynter figured she might finally be out of the doghouse with T.

The phone answered on the second ring. "Hello," T answered hesitantly. "What's the emergency?"

Wynter only knew the voice on the other end as T. "No emergency, T. I just wanted to thank you for the tip this morning. I don't know what prompted you to call again, but you'll be happy to know that I'm leaving TRU within the next month. I'm going to take a new position with Governor Sandra Murphy. I suspect her politics align more with yours, and maybe you'll stop being angry with me."

"Angry?"

"After I started working for TRU, you kind of ghosted me until this morning."

Wynter heard the long sigh on the other end. "Contrary to popular belief, I have a life, and it's been a bit hectic lately. Don't worry. There is something large coming down the pike, and you'll be the first reporter I turn to when I have something to share. By the way, I'm happy to hear

that you're getting away from that cesspool. Governor
Murphy is a good person. And, frankly, a small hope for the
future. So, what do you need?"

"Contact information for Emma Schmidt and Jimena
Aguilar," Wynter answered.

"Nope. You will not harass either of them. That's a
new low, even for you, Wynter. I've fed you information
over the past few years because I thought you were one of
the good ones. Clearly, I was wrong. I should have listened
to my wife," T mumbled.

"You're married? With a wife? I knew it. A fellow
sister. But you've got it all wrong. I'm not going to harass
either of them. Although, I will admit an exclusive interview
would be quite a boon. Sandra needs the information because
she wants them to consider a job with her security detail. She
was very impressed with both of them."

T chuckled on the other end of the phone. "Sandra?
You're on a first-name basis with the governor? Now, that's
an interesting piece of information. Well, you can tell the
governor to get in line. They're both being courted for
different work. The security detail is way below their talents.
It would be a waste."

"Aw, come on, T. Why don't you get me the
information and let them decide for themselves," Wynter
implored.

"Sorry, Wynter. Not this time. You're a talented
investigative reporter. I'm sure you'll find a way to track
them down so you can impress your latest crush. But I'll tell
you what I am going to do. I'll make sure the governor

remains safe. Your interests and ours are not mutually exclusive."

"Yeah, wouldn't it be incredible to have an out lesbian as the next president of the United States? That's why I agreed to join her team. Finally, I'm working for something I can get behind one hundred percent. Of course, that doesn't mean I won't be trying to uncover corruption wherever it sprouts. I believe that doing that will help Sandra. I've no doubt her enemies are up to their fat white necks in dirty business."

"You have no idea. I promise I'll have something for you soon, but you might have to pitch it to a different network because I doubt TRU will agree to air the story. You need to give me your word that no matter what, you'll make sure one of the major networks picks up the story, or I won't give you the information."

"Fine, fine. You have my word. I promise. I'll go to the competition if TRU doesn't run the story. I'm leaving there, anyway. It's not like that will torpedo my career. News can be a nasty business, and my loyalties definitely do not remain with TRU even though they gave me a job when the other networks turned their nose up at another out lesbian. Hypocrisy at its finest," Wynter said.

"Not to be rude, Wynter, but I have to go now. I'm working on something more important than tracking down a few addresses that can easily be obtained with a scant amount of research. Don't get lazy." T ended the call without so much as a goodbye or see you later.

"I am getting lax," Wynter mumbled to her phone. "Where did my killer instinct and relentless pursuit of the next big story go?" she asked herself.

†

Wynter had driven back to her condo. After covering the big news about Karl Schmidt, she'd asked for a few days off. Initially, Wynter thought she would do some follow-up because there was much more going on than the FBI released to the public. She knew it in her gut. Wynter could almost taste the story's magnitude, especially after T had let slip the cryptic message. She'd bet her last dollar it was all tied up in this recent plot on the governor's life.

Grabbing a bottle of water from her refrigerator, she settled into her favorite chair and began rocking. All the puzzle pieces floated around in her head. She had more than one reason to track the contact information for Emma and Jimena. They had several missing puzzle pieces in their possession, and she wanted them to complete the picture forming in her mind. She'd been honest about waiting a few days before she did that. She could be relentless when tracking a story, but she wasn't a heartless bitch. It had to sting to be the one to kill your own brother, even if he was a worthless piece of shit. *Well, no time like the present to obtain that information.*

Jumping from her swivel rocker, Wynter hurried into her office to start doing the research that T had suggested. Emma Schmidt was far savvier with hiding her address than Jimena. Although, the only reason Wynter was able to track

80

down Jimena's address was through records on her deceased parents, who were not as careful as the Border Patrol Agent. She had recently researched both women and learned of the mugging when Jose, Jimena's father, had lost his life. Wynter thought Jimena might have inherited the house after her mother passed, and she had been right.

"Bingo!" she exclaimed and punched the button to print off the information. Then, glancing at her watch, she noted the time. "Shit on a shingle," she grumbled. Wynter had let the time fly by, and if she didn't jump in the shower, she'd be late for her date.

After exiting the steamy shower, Wynter wiped the glass and looked at her reflection. While she didn't necessarily look her age, signs that she wasn't getting any younger appeared in the corner of her eyes when she smiled. The dreaded crow's feet barely made an appearance on her face. They would be entirely visible in ten years, even with the heavy make-up she had to wear when on camera. She didn't really mind because being in front of the camera had never been a lifelong goal. Wynter preferred the investigative work, mainly in the background, but TRU had insisted she take a more front-facing role, and because it gave her access to the political stories, she had agreed.

Although the place Wynter planned on taking Sandra was a small hole-in-the-wall barbeque, she wanted to look nice. Selecting a pair of jeans she bought specifically because they had not flattened her ass like most pants, she tossed them on the bed as she considered what blouse to wear.

Fashion had never been in her repertoire, but whenever she'd forced herself to buy new clothes, the salespersons had said she'd probably look good in a potato sack. Of course, she'd brushed off those compliments as the speaker wanting to make a sale. Aside from her nearly non-existent ass, no matter how many squats she did, Wynter had to admit her trim body didn't look horrible in most clothes.

Finally, she settled on a casual blue pullover that brought out her ice-blue eyes. Wynter glanced at her watch again and cursed, knowing there was a good chance she would be late. San Diego traffic was brutal at this time of the day.

CHAPTER SEVEN

When Wynter pulled up in a new BMW electric car, Sandra wasn't surprised. She had figured her for someone who probably had strong feelings about climate change. What astonished her was the choice of one of the higher-cost electric vehicles. She hadn't asked how much TRU was paying her, but she suspected her offer of twenty percent over her current salary might be much larger than she had planned for. Not that it mattered much since the universe had blessed Sandra with a wealthy family who had connections to donors with deep pockets. She didn't doubt she could afford Wynter, and she would without question be worth every penny.

Wynter was also more casually dressed than Sandra, and she almost ran back to her closet looking for something other than the silk blouse she'd chosen to go with her designer jeans. But Sandra couldn't think of a top that would be casual enough for dinner without pulling out one of her T-shirts or sweatshirts from one of the various fun runs she'd participated in over the years.

Sandra opened the door before Wynter pushed the doorbell. Not wanting her mother to begin her twenty questions and cause Wynter any discomfort, she rushed outside with her purse slung over her shoulder.

Wynter's twinkling blue eyes sparkled with mirth. "I told you the dim sum would leave you hungry after a scant amount of time."

"What?" Sandra answered distractedly.

"I assume you're starving by the way you practically shoved me to the side to leave your house," Wynter joked.

"Oh, no. I would have invited you in for a drink, but I have a nosy, meddling mother, and no one should be exposed to that until I've eased them into it. You'll have plenty of time to spend with her after officially joining the team. She can't help herself."

"Can't help herself from what?"

"From getting involved in my campaign or frankly anything remotely political, including weighing in on policy decisions."

Wynter raised an eyebrow. "Your mother is like a political advisor?"

"Oh, heavens no. But I let her think she is." Sandra winked. "Trust me. If you knew her like I do, you'd do the same. It's simply easier that way."

Wynter chuckled. "Then I can't wait to meet her."

Sandra shook her head. "Be careful what you wish for. You might just get it, then not know what to do with it."

"Oh, I've never regretted getting what I wish for," Wynter replied.

†

Wynter wasn't joking when she had suggested casual attire. The place looked like it was about to fall, with its severely weathered wood slanting dangerously to one side. Sandra believed a strong wind might just blow the thing down. She got a ridiculous picture of a gigantic wolf blowing and the structure tumbling into a heap of rotted wood with just one breath.

"Um, is it safe to enter?" Sandra asked.

Wynter chuckled. "Your white privilege is showing. Of course it's safe. And when you have your first bite, you'll never go to another barbeque hut again. Trust me, these hole-in-the-wall places you've yet to explore are in a whole other stratosphere. Jimmy's barbeque sauce will make your taste buds dance the jig and sing an aria simultaneously. Come on, follow me." Wynter gestured to the gray, rotting wood door.

The small parking lot was full, so Sandra suspected it was a popular place to eat. She shrugged and followed Wynter inside after Wynter pulled open the door as it creaked like an old lady emerging from a shabby leather recliner. The inside was marginally better, with long wooden tables that looked stable enough, although worn by years of use. They reminded Sandra of her grandfather's farmhouse table, sturdy wood, built to last. Sandra would have preferred spending more time at the farm, but after her mother had married her second husband, the heir to a Hollywood legend, they rarely visited. Even though her father died in her teens, Sandra had insisted on changing her last name to Rose's maiden name in honor of the grandparents she loved so dearly. That had been a massive fight with her mother, which she'd won through pure obstinance. Ironically, her mother had returned to Murphy after her second husband died. When Sandra had successfully entered the political arena, her mother wanted to ensure people made the link between mother and daughter.

Wynter didn't seem put off by sitting next to a large family chowing down on an enormous plate of ribs. A young girl had a massive bib placed around her neck with barbeque sauce smeared all around her mouth. She beamed a smile at Wynter.

"Hey, half pint. How are the ribs today?"

"Good. Uncle Jimmy says I can eat more ribs than anyone in the whole state of California." She pointed to her protruding belly. "I have a food baby growing inside me."

Wynter chuckled. "Where did you hear that expression?"

"Mama said it one day," she answered.

The attractive African American woman shook her head. "She got those big ears from her daddy. I gotta watch what I say."

"How you doing, Charise?"

Charise sucked her teeth. "Can't complain, and even if I did, no one would listen." She smiled, and sparkling white teeth appeared. "Who is your date?" The large man sitting next to Charise continued to eat while the women conversed, only glancing at Wynter and Sandra once as he nodded a greeting. Another little boy and girl remained quiet, peering cautiously at Sandra.

"I can't believe you don't recognize your own governor. I hope you voted for her," Wynter answered.

Charise wrinkled her nose. "Hmm, she looks different in them jeans. What y'all doing bringing her to Jimmy's? Ain't you got enough money now to take her somewhere fancy?"

Wynter leaned in and whispered, "I wanted to impress her, and everyone knows this is the best food in the city."

Charise nodded. "Mmhm, girl, you got that right. You gonna have your usual today?"

"Nah, I thought we would get a little bit of everything so she can sample all of Jimmy's brilliance."

Charise raised her hand and waved toward the busty woman clearing the table. "Shondra, Wynter wants to order everything on the menu. Better bring out the bibs, too."

The woman's eyes widened. "Everything?"

Wynter chuckled. "Yeah, like a sampler platter, not full dinners," she amended.

"We don't got no sampler platter. This ain't Burger King, ya know. So you don't get to order things your way." Shondra rolled her eyes.

"Don't be a bitch, Shondra. Wynter is one of our best customers. Just tell Jimmy she wants a variety to share with the governor."

"What you goin' on about?" Shondra asked.

"She brought the governor to Jimmy's, and you're acting like a low-life with no manners. Mama taught us better," Charise chastised.

Shondra narrowed her eyes at Sandra and Wynter. "You look different in jeans. Didn't know you rich people wore jeans."

Sandra chuckled. "I guess I need to work harder at getting out more and showing a different side. It smells heavenly in here. I am very much looking forward to tasting the food. I may never go anywhere else for barbeque."

Charise grinned. "That's a fact, sure enough." She sucked her teeth again and lifted her curvy body from the wooden bench. "Never mind, Shondra, I'll give the order to Jimmy. You'll probably mess it up."

Shondra huffed but turned around to continue bussing tables as Charise walked to the back of the restaurant, opening the door and revealing the barely visible smoker. A plume of smoke curled and eventually dissipated under the cloudless sky. Sandra couldn't hear what she was saying to the big man tending the smoker and large grill but assumed she was giving him their order. Shondra deposited the dirty dishes into a large bin and returned with placemats, bibs, and utensils.

"You gonna have what's on tap?" Shondra asked.

"Sure, do you have any pale ale?" Wynter asked, then turned to Sandra. "Do you drink beer?"

"Not for a very long time." Sandra leaned close to Wynter and whispered, "Would I be offending Shondra more if I just wanted a glass of water?"

Wynter shook her head and turned to Shondra. "Just one beer and some water, please."

"Well, surely I can handle getting the drinks," Shondra grumbled and ambled over to the bar. With practiced ease, she tipped a glass under the tap, filling it to the rim with the perfect amount of foam at the top. After grabbing a bottle of water from the case, she walked to Sandra and Wynter's table and placed the drinks in front of them.

Sandra hesitated before opening her bottle of water. She wasn't about to ask for a glass and risk irritating Shondra. Lifting her bottle in the air, Sandra touched the plastic bottle with Wynter's foamy mug of beer and said, "Cheers."

†

Wynter had caught Sandra looking at her bottle of water like it was the enemy before uncapping the drink and making the dullest toast ever. She enjoyed seeing the usually buttoned-up woman out of her element. Wynter suspected that Sandra rarely voluntarily entered into a situation where she didn't have complete control. Wynter looked forward to more times when she could cause the prim and proper governor's world to tilt just enough to have a little fun.

89

Wynter chuckled. "Cheers? How ingenious of you," she remarked as a smirk overtook her face.

"You're enjoying this, aren't you? Probably figured out that I rarely step outside my comfort zone. However, I have a feeling I am going to enjoy every last minute of this adventure. I'm even going to don the bib, just to prove you wrong about your impression of me." With a flourish, Sandra grabbed the bib and tied it around her neck. Then, pointing to the second one lying on the table, she said, "Your turn."

Wynter threw her head back and laughed for several seconds. "Can I please take a picture? You never know when I'll need something to convince all your constituents you're someone us common folk can actually connect with."

Sandra spread her hands out and answered, "Be my guest. Of course, I'll have to get used to taking your advice as director of communications. But I will assume you always have my best interests at heart."

Wynter locked eyes with Sandra and answered with a level of seriousness she wasn't sure she possessed. "Always, Sandra, always."

When platters of food kept coming, Sandra's eyes bugged out. Wynter assumed she'd never eaten at one of the more colorful hole-in-the-wall eateries that specialized in good food and plenty of it. The fancier restaurants couldn't compare to the volume of food at Jimmy's Barbeque. Sometimes she would leave one of the five-star restaurants still a little hungry, but that never happened at Jimmy's.

"I swear, I cannot eat another bite. If I do, my stomach will explode like Ripley in *Alien*. I'm too old to birth a food baby. Any chance we can pack this up and take it with us? I can bring my mother a small container. She will definitely gush over the food. I am not exaggerating when I say this is by far the best barbeque I've ever tasted. I'm definitely coming back here now that I know about this place."

Wynter grinned. "Told you so." She pointed at the large stain on Sandra's bib. "I'm glad you decided to protect that elegant silk blouse. I doubt the barbeque sauce would have come out, no matter what fancy laundromat you take your clothes to."

"I'll have you know I do most of my laundry. But you are correct; this blouse requires dry cleaning."

Wynter squinted at Sandra in disbelief before recognition set in, and then she smirked. "Got it. You're a control freak who does not trust anyone else to properly separate her clothes. I am quite sure you would never let me near your clothes."

"I had an awful experience in college," Sandra defended.

"With laundry?" Wynter burst out in laughter.

"My roommate offered to do the laundry. She said she had loads that were way too small, and I should just combine my clothes with hers. I thought she would at least separate the whites from the colors. I ended up with dull gray panties. I hate the color gray. It isn't even a proper color. Never again." Sandra shook her head.

Wynter caught Shondra's attention and mimed packing the food into small, to-go boxes. "Not that this conversation isn't riveting, but I thought we could hit up this ice cream place with the most unusual flavors."

The look Sandra gave Wynter was almost comical. "Where in the world do you pack your food? Even with hollow legs and arms, I don't see how you could fit in one more bite of anything. I sure can't. It's why I turned down dessert."

Wynter waved her arm in the air. "We'll walk around the cute neighborhood where the ice cream shop is located, and by the time we're ready for ice cream, I think you'll be able to convince your stomach to make some room for the sweet, creamy goodness that will have those taste buds of yours dancing the Macarena."

Sandra got a twinkle in her eye. "I do love ice cream. But I have one condition."

"What's that?"

"Since I am sure you will insist on paying for the barbeque and earlier brought me lunch, let me get our ice cream. I think I also owe you another lunch."

Wynter stuck out her hand. "Deal, but you know I'm not keeping track, and I wish you wouldn't either." When Wynter grasped Sandra's hand, it surprised her how soft her skin was. Although she shouldn't have been astonished by that simple fact. It wasn't like the governor performed manual labor. And, coming from money, Sandra probably received regular manicures, complete with nourishing hand massages. Nevertheless, Wynter couldn't help imagining how soft other parts of Sandra's body might be. After seeing Sandra give her a strange look, Wynter realized she hadn't let go of Sandra's hand, absently caressing it as if Sandra were her lover.

Wynter let go of Sandra's hand and cleared her throat. "Well, it seems like you can teach an old dog new tricks. I thought you would surely fight harder and try to pick up the check."

Sandra narrowed her eyes. "Are you calling me an old dog? And, just for the record, I'm not really keeping track. I'm just not used to someone, um…never mind."

Wynter laughed. "Will it help if I amend that to beautiful old dog?"

"No," Sandra deadpanned.

Charise brought over the to-go boxes and laid the check on the table. "Here ya go, sugar. Don't be a stranger and come back and see us sooner than letting another six months go by. And don't tell me you've been too busy with your fancy job." Charise shook her head. "Never thought you should accept that job. They spout all them lies, ya know."

"Good thing I won't be working with them much longer. I'll be joining Governor Sandra Murphy's communications team." Wynter jerked her head in Sandra's direction before pulling her credit card from her pants pocket and setting it on the bill.

Charise nodded, grabbed the credit card and bill, and said, "Good. I approve."

Wynter laughed and responded, "Whew, now that I have your approval, I can sign the contract." She winked at Charise to take the sting out of her sarcastic response.

Sandra leaned in and whispered, "You are the luckiest person alive. It seems like you just got saved by Charise with her perfect timing."

Wynter smiled. "Well, let me say, for the record, that I am surprised you haven't had droves of women attempting to impress you with takeout dim sum and hole-in-the-wall barbeque to die for. A woman as exceptional as you should definitely be used to someone fawning over her and trying to do everything in their power to impress."

"Trust me, Wynter, you've absolutely succeeded in your ability to astonish me. In a good way," Sandra added.

CHAPTER EIGHT

Sandra had enjoyed her dinner a lot more than she wanted to admit. She wasn't used to going to an eating establishment without the owners fawning over her as if she were some A-list movie star. Shondra and Charise could have cared less that the governor of their state was sampling their cuisine. Could a person call barbeque cuisine? Or was that saved for the fancy restaurants she usually frequented?

However, it wasn't the spectacular ribs that had delighted her. Instead, Wynter proved her conversation acumen and in-depth understanding of politics, albeit a bit on the cynical side of the equation. When a small portion of sauce gathered at the corner of Wynter's lips, it took all of Sandra's self-control not to wipe it off, or even worse, lick it off and then finish with a toe-curling kiss.

By the time they had reached the ice cream place, Sandra had somehow found room in her stomach after eyeing the vast array of flavors. She'd never heard of ice cream flights before, but Wynter had insisted that was the only way to go. That way, they could try many different flavors. Sandra had always wanted to try lavender ice cream, and when she saw lychee and passion fruit as additional options, she chose those three for her flight. Wynter decided to try Azuki bean, sweet potato, and a dragonfruit sorbet. Sandra had wrinkled her nose at the sweet potato flavor until she tasted it and had to check her first impression of the novel treat. After that, she would never again question Wynter's choices for any type of food.

When Wynter had driven her back to her home, Sandra wasn't ready for the evening to end, and against her better judgment, she had invited Wynter inside. She knew her mother would subject Wynter to at least twenty questions. That was her mother's modus operandi whenever her mother visited and Sandra had invited a woman inside. Which wasn't often because it always sent them packing. But Sandra justified her decision because Wynter was a future employee, certainly not a love interest. At least, she shouldn't think of her in that way. Unfortunately, her rogue heart wasn't cooperating with her head.

Sandra set her purse on the small table in the foyer and entered the parlor where her mother sat rigidly on the couch, reading a book. Although she knew her mother hadn't gone anywhere this evening, she had dressed to the nines. Sandra wondered if one of her political allies had sought an audience earlier in the evening, or was Rose shrewd enough to wait around, hoping Sandra would invite Wynter inside for an after-dinner drink?

Rose would never let an opportunity pass to interrogate a woman who could be a potential love interest. Rose was a lot of things, but stupid was not one of them. Sandra was sure she recognized her attraction to the younger investigative reporter. Rose had torpedoed more than one of her budding relationships when she hadn't approved of who Sandra was dating. It wasn't even about Sandra being a lesbian. Rose had decided long ago to accept Sandra's identity. But she wanted to be the one to pick out the perfect partner to complement Sandra and, with the right woman by her side, make her more appealing to the public.

Rose looked up from her book, setting it promptly on the table. She stood and offered Wynter her famous smile. "Well, hello, you must be Wynter."

Sandra wasn't fooled by her greeting. She was sure Rose had already had one of her minions create a complete dossier on Wynter Holmes. She probably knew more about Wynter than Wynter knew about herself.

Wynter returned Rose's smile with one of her own. "And you must be Mrs. Murphy, Sandra's mother, although if I didn't know for a fact that she has no sisters, I would have guessed you were Sandra's sister."

"Aren't you the little charmer? Is that how you get all your targets to spill their secrets?" Rose smiled in what Sandra recognized as her way to draw first blood without being obvious. She could always feign innocence, claiming it was a joke.

Sandra gritted her teeth and hissed, "Behave, Mother."

"What?" Rose's eyes widened in an attempt to portray innocence. "It was a joke, my dear. Although I have followed your career, Wynter. You are quite accomplished for someone so young. No wonder my daughter wishes to steal you right from under TRU's enormous and distorted noses."

"I'm a lot older than I look. I'm also very excited about working with Sandra. I believe in her candidacy for president and will do everything in my power to ensure the media positively and fairly represents her. Yes, I've been as hard on her as every other politician I've covered, but that has never affected my sincere belief that she might be the only one to beat the unhinged Republican alternative. He still has quite a following. If he is allowed to steal the next election, I fear for our democracy. We need an absolute blow-out."

Rose narrowed her eyes, then pasted on a smile. "Why don't you come and have a seat and tell me all about your plans for Sandra," Rose directed. "Do you drink wine, my dear, or would you prefer something stronger?"

"I have to admit to knowing nothing about wine. I usually have a beer or hard cider with my meals. I tend to gravitate to the more casual pub fare or comfort foods unless someone picks up the tab and drags me to a fancy place." Wynter winked at Sandra, adeptly avoiding Rose's scrutiny as she followed Rose into the parlor with Rose's back to her. "My food pyramid consists of burgers and fries, pizza, ice cream or cookies, and barbeque with all the fixings. Sometimes I add potato chips, just to liven things up," Wynter joked as she sat on a chair that looked just as stuffy as her mother, who had wrinkled her nose in obvious distaste for Wynter's preference for food and drink.

As Wynter tried to adjust her rear in the uncomfortable chair, Sandra rushed into the room and attempted to play traffic cop. "Wine isn't for everyone. I agree certain foods go especially well with beer. I could also make you a mixed drink," Sandra offered.

Wynter waved her hand in the air. "Oh, I'm not picky. If you have a bottle of wine, I'll give that a go. I'm always ready for a new adventure. It's about time I developed a more sophisticated palette. No one person can be an expert at everything. You can teach me about wines, and I'll share my expertise in other areas."

The innuendo was not lost on Sandra. Nor did it escape Rose's inspection, as evidenced by her perfectly arched eyebrow, which Sandra assumed Rose practiced in the mirror daily.

"I believe the bottle of port should make a nice after-dinner drink," Rose suggested.

Sandra nodded and left the room to pour three glasses. She only felt mildly bad about leaving Wynter alone with her mother, but she'd seen how Wynter was either oblivious to Rose's subtle digs or could easily hold her own with her calculating mother. Before returning to the parlor,

Sandra gulped one glass of port and then filled her glass again. Unfortunately, she'd probably need more than two glasses to make it through the evening. It was a mystery to Sandra how she could adeptly handle any cancerous or overzealous reporter, but her mother seemed to find that button that reduced her to a compliant adolescent. She didn't relish being anyone's puppet, but her mother came damn close to being the consummate puppet master.

As she walked back into the parlor, she heard the tail end of her mother's question.

"...and proud lesbian?"

When she heard Wynter's response, Sandra nearly dropped the three glasses of port she carefully carried in her hands.

"I sure am. Is that a pre-requisite for a partner for your daughter? Or for someone taking on the role of communications director? I'll keep that in mind as we traverse the country."

Sandra simply handed the glasses of port to her mother and Wynter, rather than get into the middle of the discussion. She had no interest in adding her two cents.

A small smile appeared on Rose's lips. She looked up at Sandra. "I like this one. I believe she will keep you on your toes." Rose turned toward Wynter. "To answer your question, yes, I suppose it is. I saw the toll it took on my daughter's life, and I won't be happy if they force her to hide again because of someone else's discomfort with the truth. Believe it or not, I am not the one who pushed Sandra into the closet. I only wanted to carefully navigate the announcement for optimal effect. We were almost too late. The window was closing rapidly with the recent uprising of puritanical rhetoric around sexuality." Rose sighed. "And to think that a mere five years ago, it was almost in fashion to be a lesbian."

"I don't believe it has ever been in fashion, but I did have higher hopes for the trajectory until that bubble burst quite spectacularly. That's why I would never agree to work for someone who insists on hiding that part of themself. While I don't believe in outing anyone, I also maintain we do more harm than good when we remain in the closet. Who will all those budding baby dykes have to look up to if we all remain hidden, like being a lesbian is something to be ashamed of?" Wynter asked before taking a sip of her port.

Rose's expression turned serious as her lips formed a straight line. "Is that why you were so hard on my daughter? Did it upset you that she waited so long to come out? You mustn't blame her. I miscalculated the timing of the announcement. I should have let her do it when she first entered politics. Of course, Sandra believes I was putting politics before her personal well-being, but she was wrong about that. I knew how cruel the press could be." Rose glared at Wynter. "I wanted her ready to take the heat. Sandra is not as cutthroat as your average politician. I didn't wish to see her hurt. She has a much thicker skin now."

Wynter's eyes lost their sparkle when she responded. "For what it's worth, I am sorry to have directed my OCD in your daughter's direction. I made some assumptions that do not appear to be accurate. Sandra has labeled me a cynic, and she isn't all wrong. I'm afraid I haven't had a favorable opinion of most politicians. Your daughter is changing my mind. If I didn't believe she was inherently a good and honest person, I would not have even considered her offer. Perhaps you will see it in your heart to forgive me. I have a sneaking suspicion that I will work as closely with you as with Sandra. It wouldn't be good for the campaign to have an acrimonious relationship with one of Sandra's key advisors."

Rose laughed. "You are good. Fine. Water under the bridge. I'll confess to labeling you a smarmy little rodent when you went after her at the press conference."

"I had a little white rat when I was a kid, and he was the cutest, sweetest thing. So, I'm not going to take offense." Wynter chuckled.

"Well, it seemed particularly insensitive after almost losing our lives," Rose added.

"It was, and I'll admit I felt a small amount of guilt. Sandra should have tackled the red tape on permits before building that room. We will need to make sure she is squeaky clean in the future. The opposition will grab at any straw to discredit her candidacy. They are quite good at making even a minor point seem catastrophic to the masses."

"Are the two of you done pissing all over the floor, trying to establish your dominance?" Sandra took a large sip of her port.

"Must you be so crass, Sandra? We're just exploring the edges of this new political relationship you've thrown us into. I believe we're both acting with considerable restraint."

"Agreed. It seems your mother and I reached an understanding and have common ground—doing what is necessary to achieve success with your candidacy. Within reason," Wynter amended.

Sandra smiled. "Well, that's a relief because I honestly believe the two of you will make a formidable team. Mother has the ruthless instincts to advance anyone in the political arena, and Wynter, I will count on you to keep her within the bounds of ethical practice. You can be our Jiminy Cricket."

"Somehow, I don't believe you'll need that from me. You seem to differ greatly from most politicians I come across."

"Both of you need to remember that politics is dirty business sometimes, and occasionally, the mud is unavoidable to bathe in. But, I will attempt to remember not to cross the line and add too much excrement to the pot because every time someone stirs that pot, it stinks to high heaven. Personally, I prefer to avoid the smell," Rose wryly noted.

Wynter and Sandra laughed in stereo before Sandra added, "Now who is being crass?"

"Neither of you is what I expected. It's been a delightful surprise. For the record, I don't mind getting a little dirty." Wynter grinned.

Rose sipped her port, then returned her hands to her lap, smiling serenely at the two women. Sandra wondered if Rose was also viewing Wynter in a whole new light.

"Well, I think I'll turn in and let you two finish your after-dinner port. I hope you enjoyed it, Wynter." Finishing her port, Rose set the glass on the table.

"It's nice. Different from my usual choice for an after-dinner drink, but not awful," Wynter answered.

"Well, I should hope so. While not the most expensive port one can purchase, I suspect this bottle costs nearly as much as a month's salary at that horrible place where you work." Rose stood and, before leaving the room, placed her hand on Sandra's shoulder. "Good night. I hope you enjoy the rest of your evening."

After Rose left, Wynter whispered, "How much do you think your mother believes I make? I think she underestimates the deep pockets of the TRU network."

"Doubtful. Mother is nothing if not thorough. I imagine she has a full dossier on you, including how much you make with TRU. Not that I can't afford what I offered as compensation, but I probably would have been more prepared for the negotiation had I gone to my mother before our lunch the other day."

"Holy crap, just how rich are you?"

"Not me, my mother. I don't even know, but I suspect it is in the vulgar territory. Hopefully, you won't hold that against me. You don't have to finish the port if you don't want to. I'm sure I can rustle up a beer for you."

"No, no, this is growing on me." Wynter took another sip and smiled. "Hmm, whatever shall we do now? Did I imagine things, or did your mother leave us alone on purpose?"

Sandra sighed. "One never knows with her. She still surprises me occasionally."

†

Wynter didn't know what to think about Sandra inviting her inside for a drink. Earlier, Sandra had shared that she had not wanted to subject Wynter to her mother's interrogation, so the invite had surprised her. However, that didn't stop Wynter from eagerly accepting. She also wasn't expecting to like Rose Murphy, but the woman was a force, and Wynter couldn't help respecting her strength. It took a bit, but she thought she had finally received Rose's stamp of approval. In fact, if Wynter hadn't misread the situation. Rose might even try to encourage something more than an employer-employee relationship between Wynter and her daughter. She was sure the shrewd woman had not missed the double entendres. But Wynter was eager to learn where Sandra might land on the possibilities.

Wynter pinned Sandra with a questioning gaze. "Why did you invite me in for a nightcap? You had to know that might encourage something you aren't prepared for."

"I was having a good time and wasn't ready for the evening to end. It's been a long time since I had a night out, complete with good food and conversation." Sandra appeared to answer honestly. "Besides, I knew I had to get the interrogation with my mother over sooner rather than later, lest you decide to renege on your agreement to become my communications director. I suspected you would hold your own with her, and I wasn't wrong."

105

"Can I be honest with you?" Wynter asked.

"Of course."

"I'm wildly attracted to you, and nearly all I've thought about all night is what it might feel like to kiss you. Dinner tonight may not have been a date in your mind, but I hoped that might change. And then you invited me inside for a nightcap, and well, that was confusing to me. Am I wrong to think you are sending mixed messages?"

Sandra scrubbed her face with her hand and sighed. "No, you're not wrong. I haven't quite figured out what to do with my own attraction. I only know that hiring you and starting something, um, more personal is probably a horrible idea."

"Why?"

"You were the one that said I need to remain squeaky clean. Unfortunately, having a torrid affair with one's communications director is about as far away from squeaky clean as one can get."

Wynter grinned. "Torrid affair? I like the sound of that, but I don't understand the issue."

"Surely you comprehend the dynamics of a power imbalance? While the 'Me Too' movement has primarily been limited to powerful men taking advantage of women, I am sure my opposition would jump at the chance to bring such a titillating story to the surface while screaming hypocrite at the top of their lungs."

"First, I would not be an unwilling participant. I believe I just confessed to my attraction well before you indicated any interest. And second, I don't see our working

106

relationship as having a power imbalance. I envision our business association in the same manner as a music producer or talent manager becoming involved with one of his or her musicians. Everything I plan to do for you as your communications director is to further your political career. You won't be ordering me around nearly as much as I plan to do with you." Wynter stood and made her way to the couch. Sitting close to Sandra, she felt particularly emboldened to take her hand. When Sandra didn't pull back, she jumped in with both feet and caressed the side of her face.

Wynter wasn't sure who moved closer to whom first. And it didn't matter, really. All Wynter registered was the soft exploration of Sandra's lips as their tongues tentatively explored one another. Wynter felt, more than heard, the quiet hum of pleasure that Sandra emitted as the kiss intensified.

"For the record, my mother is the only other person I've allowed any amount of control. While my mother is a total pain in my rear end, she is also the shrewdest woman I know and a brilliant political strategist. I see a very rocky future between us. You ordering me around doesn't seem to compute. In case you have not picked up on this yet, I have significant control issues."

"Oh, I've gathered that, all right, but you must trust me on this. I understand the media probably more than you or your mother ever will. So, you'll have to let me direct things in that arena. However, I am not opposed to a role reversal in the bedroom. You can have complete control there," Wynter teased.

"Well, now, that's a deal too good to pass up."

"In all seriousness, I'm not sure I've ever been more attracted to anyone else. I really feel the need to let this play out without either of us placing restrictions on the exploration. Let's just see where it goes. I presume we are both adult enough to move on without drama if things don't work out. It's all about respect, and I believe I've shared that I have tremendous admiration for who you are as a politician and a person, despite how hard I have been on you."

"Thank you. That means the world to me. Not that I need my mother's permission, but she is rather astute at picking up on subtleties, and you haven't been all that restrained. She's been wanting me to pursue a romantic interest. It might be beneficial to have her perspective on this."

Wynter wagged her finger in the air. "Oh no, you don't. I will not reduce whatever we plan on pursuing to political theater. Whether your favorability increases or decreases with the news of your involvement with me will have no bearing on where we decide to go. I won't let my feelings be used in that way. Things will continue organically or not at all. No fake relationship or carefully engineered public announcement."

"I don't understand. So you want to keep this a secret?"

"No, I've never hidden my sexuality or relationships, and I don't plan to now. At the same time, I won't let this turn into a circus or, goddess forbid, some calculated political maneuver. If asked, we will be honest. If we treat this as no big deal, the press will eventually settle into that narrative. Even governors or future presidents are allowed to date." Wynter leaned in again to steal another quick kiss.

"I'm probably going to regret this, but since that horse is well out of the barn and into that lovely pasture, I'm all in," Sandra exclaimed and then gulped her port before taking Wynter's hand and leading her down a hallway that Wynter presumed led to Sandra's bedroom.

"You must think I'm easy," Wynter joked.

"Oh, I'm so sorry," Sandra stuttered as she abruptly stopped leading Wynter. "I thought we were on the same page."

Wynter quickly pivoted from her teasing when she saw the shock and embarrassment on Sandra's face.

"We are. I apologize. I *am* easy. At least when it comes to you. I don't have any stupid rules around how many dates we need to go on before making one another scream. I really hope you are a screamer."

"I'm not, especially with my mother just down the hall," Sandra answered.

Wynter grinned. "We'll see about that."

†

Sandra had caught a tiger by the tail. Now she wasn't sure it was prudent to continue holding on, but she'd made clear her intentions when she led Wynter to her bedroom. Sandra hadn't exactly told the truth about not being vocal, but she also had a healthy dose of self-control that allowed her to remain relatively quiet when the situation called for it. But Sandra wasn't sure she wanted to stay in control. There was something so hot about Wynter's more forceful side. She might even allow Wynter some dominance in the bedroom—something she normally would never consider.

Walking straight to the remote control on her nightstand, she selected a light jazz playlist, hoping the music would provide some cover. Sandra suspected Wynter would not hold back and might even scream louder to get a reaction. A big part of Sandra wanted that. She'd love to see this beautiful woman writhing on her bed and shouting her name in ecstasy. Vocal lovers always made her come harder.

"Nice choice," Wynter noted. "But I seriously doubt it will drown out my cries of pleasure. Just so you know, it doesn't take much when I'm wildly attracted to someone. A previous lover once joked that she could 'blow on me once and I'd come undone.' Granted, it's a bit of hyperbole, but not entirely untrue."

Sandra pushed the buttons on the remote to turn up the music, then set the remote back on the nightstand. "Hmm, well, that doesn't sound like much fun. I was looking forward to teasing you mercilessly. If you're bound and determined to be vocal, I want to hear you begging me to let you come."

Wynter laughed. "Did you just make a pun? Bondage, huh? I'm not opposed to that. Every minute I spend with you, I am more and more shocked. I can't wait to peel another layer. Speaking of that, do you prefer undressing your partner or finding them already naked in your bed? I'm down with either."

Sandra shrugged. "No preference. I'll let you decide while I freshen up."

"And she's back. Miss Prim and Proper. But, no fair. I hope you have a guest toothbrush because I'm not letting you be the only one with minty fresh breath. Not that tasting the port in your mouth wasn't delicious."

"I'm sure I can rustle one up. My dentist gives me a new one every time I see him, and I've honestly no use for them since I use an electric toothbrush. Dental health is essential."

"Ugh, okay, can we stop with the boring discussions about oral health? When you grabbed my hand, I thought surely we'd be naked, hot, and sweaty by now. I see glimpses of a woman who can relinquish control as easily as she commands. Time to let go, Sandra." Wynter removed her shirt, tossing it aside in one fluid movement before striding toward Sandra. She reached for the buttons on Sandra's silk blouse.

The feral look in Wynter's eyes had Sandra wondering if Wynter would rip them off or take the time to undo each one with precision. Sandra wasn't sure which she hoped for. The shirt was one of her favorites, but the buttons were easy to sew back on.

It pleased Sandra that Wynter had taken her time as her nimble fingers worked each button. Sandra's shirt wasn't the only thing coming undone. With each button, Wynter used her fingers to lightly caress her chest all the way to her stomach. Finally, those long fingers made their way to the end and reached the top of her jeans.

111

Sandra quickly removed her shirt, tossing it toward her antique chair. A slight quiver flowed over her body when Wynter reached the top button of Sandra's jeans. Wynter made quick work of unzipping Sandra's pants and pushing them down as Sandra stepped out of them, leaving her in her matching set of silky, light blue undergarments.

Wynter's eyes riveted to Sandra's body and remarked, "Nice, but these need to go, too."

"Happy to oblige as soon as you lose your jeans."

"Done." Wynter removed her pants in record time. The women stood before one another for a few seconds before Sandra pushed the straps down on Wynter's more functional, tan bra. Reaching around, Sandra found the clasp and set Wynter's well-proportioned breasts free. They were larger than Sandra had envisioned and not at all sagging like her own. Tossing aside the momentary fear that her older, more mature body would not compare favorably to Wynter's, Sandra removed her fancier bra, letting it fall to the floor. She reached out to move her hand over Wynter's collarbone and down her stomach, resting at the top of her boi shorts. They were the hottest thing Sandra had ever seen. Wynter didn't have a washboard stomach, but the soft curves on her trim body looked incredibly sexy in the tight underwear that clung to her bottom like a second skin.

Wynter pushed her boi shorts down her legs and stepped out, leaving her gloriously naked.

"Beautiful," Sandra whispered.

Wynter caressed Sandra's hips as she helped Sandra remove the last piece of clothing. "My sentiments exactly."

"I could push you onto the bed and then fumble with the comforter and sheets, but I'd rather not embarrass myself." Then, pointing to the bed, she invited, "Shall we?"

Each woman turned down their side and climbed into the king-sized bed with butter-soft bamboo sheets.

"What? No Egyptian cotton sheets with an 1,800 thread count?" Wynter quipped.

Sandra laughed. "I thought you, of all people, would appreciate bamboo sheets. They are much more environmentally friendly. They're also soft and have natural anti-odor and antimicrobial properties."

"Hmm, you're partially correct. But the sheets are only eco-friendly if the bamboo fibers are mechanically versus chemically processed. Oh, my goddess. What the hell are we doing? Are you sure you want this? I don't think things could be any more insane than having a conversation about the pros and cons of bamboo sheets as we lie on the bed in our birthday suits. Ten years ago, I would have had you naked and begging for release within thirty minutes."

Sandra half smiled. "I am naked," Sandra teased. "The price of maturity, I suppose. Although, I will say on the positive side, haven't you learned more about how to please a woman in the past ten years? There is something to be said about experience. Rushed entanglements are not necessarily the best I have to offer. Perhaps we are simply ratcheting up the arousal. Good things come to those who wait."

Wynter turned toward Sandra. "I think we've waited long enough." She rolled on top of Sandra and began a slow

113

exploration of Sandra's body, starting with an almost languorous kiss.

It had been a long time since Sandra had been with a woman. But it was all coming back—the softness of their skin, how their bodies seemed to mold together. The few times Sandra had attempted a physical relationship with a man had been a disastrous trial. She didn't appreciate their body hair, smell, rigid muscles, or the scratchiness of their trendy five o'clock shadow. Finally, in her early twenties, Sandra had given up on the notion of settling down with a man, no matter what they expected of a future president. She wasn't sure that had always been her dream, but it was undoubtedly her mother's vision for her life.

"It's been a while," Sandra confessed. "I have toys in my drawer," she added awkwardly.

Wynter lifted slightly from where she had been kissing Sandra's neck, which sent a glorious message to her clit, almost as if there was an invisible string tugging on the sensitive bundle of nerves. "Oh, we will definitely have to explore that at a later date, but for right now, I want to feel all of you without something impeding that experience."

"Okay." Sandra nodded.

"Anything off limits?" Wynter asked.

"No place on my body is off limits, but I prefer a more teasing, gentle approach," Sandra answered.

"Good, because that's my preference as well. I think we are going to be very compatible. At least in the bedroom," Wynter amended. "I see a future of major challenges regarding political strategy, and perhaps we can also test our limits a little in the bedroom. Now, if you don't wish me to tie your hands and feet to the bedposts, I'm going to need you to lie back and relax. Let all the sensations flow over you like warm water in a bubble bath."

That visual stuck so deeply inside Sandra's head that she could almost smell the lavender from her favorite bubble bath. Wynter's hands and mouth were magical as they moved over nearly every inch of her body. Wynter gave each part equal attention, including her toes. Sandra had never had someone suck on her toes before, and it was the most erotic experience she had ever felt, but she also needed some attention to her throbbing clit and only managed to squeak out one word. "Please."

Thankfully, Wynter was attuned enough to her body to know what Sandra needed. As Wynter crawled up Sandra's body and nestled into the apex, Sandra naturally brought her hands to Wynter's head, but Wynter was having none of that.

"Hands back at the headboard, or I will find something to bind them there. Don't worry. I read cues extremely well. You won't need to direct my tongue. It is like a heat-seeking missile. It knows exactly where to go."

Sandra began to laugh until Wynter's tongue flicked her clit, sending a wave of arousal through her body, causing her to buck slightly, seeking more contact. When Wynter's thumb stroked lightly over her vaginal opening down to her anus while her tongue continued to tease her clit, Sandra nearly came undone.

"That's, that's so incredible. You're very good at this," Sandra said through labored breathing.

Sandra moved to the rhythm of Wynter's touch until she felt herself reach the precipice. It was almost excruciating how close she was, yet whenever she thought she would tumble to the other side, Wynter slowed her tongue.

"You're killing me here," Sandra exclaimed.

"Mmm, but what a way to die," Wynter mumbled against her clit. The vibrations of her words sent a new wave of pleasure to her core.

"Please, don't stop. I'm almost there," Sandra cried out.

With a few more flicks of her tongue, Wynter finally pushed a finger inside and found a rhythm that allowed Sandra her release. The extended moan came out more loudly than Sandra had intended, but she was too far gone to care if her mother heard anything. She was only partially serious, anyway. There were plenty of walls between her bedroom and her mother's.

Wynter found her way to Sandra's mouth and kissed her tenderly. Sandra could not wait another second and flipped Wynter onto her back, determined to elicit an equally powerful response.

"My turn since I believe I've been more than patient. I remember you saying you had no problem relinquishing control in the bedroom, yet you've already topped me. We can't have that. Now, can we?" Sandra teased.

CHAPTER NINE

The light rapping on Sandra's bedroom door roused Wynter awake. At first, she didn't remember where she was when she awoke in the strange bed with surprisingly soft sheets. Then she abruptly lifted to a sitting position as the sheet fell from her naked body.

The knock returned, and Wynter heard Rose's unmistakable voice on the other side of the door. "Sandra, Wynter, something big is happening. Both of your phones are blowing up downstairs with calls and texts. I didn't look at Wynter's, but Mr. Carter from the FBI left a text for you to call him back as soon as possible."

"Shit, shit, shit. I didn't mean to fall asleep in your bed," Wynter whispered.

Sandra yawned and stretched in the bed. Repositioning her body to a sitting position, she blinked and then looked at Wynter. "I guess I must have worn you out," she joked.

"This isn't funny, Sandra. What about your mother knowing I stayed over?"

"What about that? Neither of us is underage." Sandra yawned again. "Would you like some breakfast? I'm fairly proficient at pancakes or French toast."

"Did you hear me? Are you two up yet?"

"Yes, Mother, we heard you. We'll be down in a minute," Sandra called out.

Wynter climbed from the bed and grabbed her bra, shirt, and jeans before quickly picking up her underwear and sniffing. Deciding she could go without underwear, she stuffed the panties into the front pocket of her jeans and then proceeded to dress quickly. "Didn't you hear your mother say something big is going on? Aren't you curious about that?"

Sandra shrugged. "It's probably nothing. She can sometimes be dramatic, and I'm sure she's simply gleeful about seeing your bag still here. Mother never passes up a chance to get all up in my business." After Sandra tossed the covers aside, she strolled into the bathroom and collected a robe. Returning to the bedroom, she secured the ties together. "I set a new toothbrush on the counter for you."

"Thanks, but I'd better retrieve my phone and see what's happening. The news never sleeps. This could be my big Pulitzer break. I'll brush after I find out what the hullabaloo is about. I should have brought my bag upstairs last night."

"I don't think either of us was worried about our phones."

"Maybe not, but it wasn't like we were so distracted we ripped off each other's clothes on the staircase because we couldn't wait one more second to make love," Wynter noted.

"True." Sandra grabbed Wynter's hand. "Come on. Time to face the music. I refuse to feel embarrassed in my own home. Mother is only squatting here until they rebuild her new house. I'll protect you from her pointed comments."

Sandra led Wynter down the stairs the same way she had brought her to her bedroom the previous evening. Only this time, Wynter's eagerness was for an entirely different reason. She avoided Rose's smirk and made a beeline for her bag. Sure enough, there were three missed calls and several text messages from T.

"Do you mind if I return this call in private?" Wynter asked.

"Not at all," Sandra responded. "Let me show you to my office."

After Wynter settled into the chair opposite the desk, she dialed T's number. She didn't have to wait long as T answered after only one ring.

"Where the hell have you been?"

"None of your business. What's got you all riled up?" Wynter asked.

"I promised I would offer you an exclusive story, and I have a doozy for you. How do three sitting congressmen and one senator colluding with Russian spies sound to you?"

"Are you fucking kidding? What proof do you have?"

"Recorded phone calls and corresponding phone logs to prove they're real. Can you get TRU to run the story?"

"I can't imagine they would turn this down. This is huge, T. But, even if they do, I have a contact at one of the other major networks. If TRU doesn't let me run with it, I'll resign on the spot and give it to someone else, stipulating that I'm the one to do the live report."

"Okay. I'm going to dump the information into your secure network. You need to get your ass home soon because there is a timeline on this. We need you to break the story before noon. Bridget Schmidt will lawyer up, and they won't be able to keep her in custody for long with all the high-powered people behind her."

Wynter pulled her phone away from her ear and glanced at the time. "Holy shit. She's a Russian operative?"

"Listen to the calls, Wynter."

"Okay, that might be tight, but I'll make it happen. Where are the phone records from?"

"Both T-Mobile and AT&T."

"Shit, I only have a contact at T-Mobile. I'll probably need to confirm the phone records with a friend who works there. That will have to be enough verification."

"I'll give you the number of a woman I know at AT&T. Just tell her that T gave you the information. She'll confirm the records for you, even though I didn't exactly go through her to obtain the data."

"Hacking the phone companies again?" Wynter teased.

"They make it far too easy. It wasn't even a ten-minute job." T laughed.

"Have I told you how much I love you, T?" Wynter joked.

"No, and don't say that too loud, or my wife will kick your ass."

"Right, you have a wife. I almost forgot about that. We really need to meet someday," Wynter said.

"Perhaps. Someday. Having a go-to news reporter might be very beneficial to our organization."

"Well, I won't be a reporter for much longer," Wynter reminded.

"As much as I would like to discuss this more with you, you're on a tight timeline. Talk to you later."

"Bye, T," Wynter said, but the line had already gone dead.

Wynter found both Rose and Sandra in Sandra's large kitchen. She noted Sandra was still on the phone but obviously winding up her call. Her eyes met Wynter's.

"Thanks, Adam. Please let me know about any further information you get from Mrs. Schmidt. I'll be eager to learn how far her reach is." After ending the call, she addressed Wynter. "I assume you already heard from your mysterious source that they've detained Bridget Schmidt."

"Yeah, but it's so much more than that. I have something much bigger on the line. Look, I know this isn't the best thing to do to you right now because it might leave the wrong impression, but I have to go. I'm on a deadline to report this latest story, and it's a whopper."

"Care to share?"

"Not yet. At least not until I've verified the recordings and phone records. If my suspicions are correct, this will be terrible news for some and excellent news for you."

"Okay. Cryptic. Shall I call you later?"

"Let me call you. Unfortunately, I'll be slammed for the next few hours."

"I suppose pancakes or French toast are out." Sandra nervously touched the ties on her robe, ensuring they were tight.

The frown on Sandra's face led Wynter to act impulsively as she approached her and quickly kissed her on the lips, not caring if Rose was a witness to her affection. "Sorry, yeah. I really have to go now."

Slipping on her shoes, Wynter practically ran out of the house. After scrolling through her contacts and finding the name she needed, she pressed the button and put the phone to her ear. Then, juggling her keys in one hand, she opened her car door while holding the phone against her ear with her shoulder. She cursed when the phone tumbled to the ground. "Shit."

Deciding it was better to put her phone on speaker, she quickly retrieved the phone from the driveway and was relieved when her friend answered. "Wynter, I assume you're calling because you need another favor."

"I do, Kari. I don't need you to pull phone records for me this time. I only need you to verify that the phone records I will send you in about thirty minutes are accurate. Can you do that?" Wynter placed her phone in her cup holder and started her car.

"I shouldn't," Kari hedged.

"Aw, come on. You know I would never reveal a source," Wynter pleaded.

"I could lose my job, Wynter. Don't you understand that? You promised you wouldn't ask me to do this again," she whined.

"But this is big, Kari. Like the story is Pulitzer prize-worthy. You'll be a part of history," Wynter encouraged as she checked her mirrors before backing out of the driveway.

"You owe me. But don't send the document to my work email. I don't want any record of this. Meet me at the Buzz House in an hour," Kari instructed.

Wynter glanced at the time on her dash and responded, "That should work. Will you be able to verify the document quickly?"

"Yes, it won't take me too long. I wish there was a way to wipe evidence of this phone call as soon as we hang up."

"Let me deal with that. I know someone who can probably take care of that for you. Thanks, Kari. You're a true patriot. Believe me, you're doing the country a huge favor by helping me out on this."

Wynter knew she would have to wait until she returned to her condo to get the name of the other contact at AT&T because T was too smart to leave a record of that communication. She suspected someone had conveniently wiped T-Mobile's historical record of the calls between the mysterious woman and herself. Of course, T was a master hacker, and something like that would be child's play for her.

Screeching into the parking lot, Wynter threw her car in park and pressed the button to turn off her car. She grabbed her phone and dashed to her front door while fumbling with her keys. Multitasking was her specialty, so once Wynter reached her computer, she fired it up, then began scrolling through her contact list on her phone. She placed the call on speaker while she searched her computer for the file she knew T had left for her. Her boss answered after two rings.

"Robert Moss."

"Bob, open up a spot for me because I've got breaking news that we'll want to run as soon as possible. I need another hour to verify the phone records, and then I'm coming in. I want Jimmy as my cameraman."

"Whoa, hold on there. What story? I can't just interrupt our program for something you haven't even verified yet," Bob testily replied.

"Fine, then I'll take the story to your competition," Wynter threatened.

"That violates your contract."

"Sue me or fire me, then. But, Bob, I wouldn't want to be in your shoes if the higher-ups found out that you passed on a story about three sitting congressmen and one senator colluding with Russian spies."

"Which congressmen and what senator?" Bob asked.

Wynter clicked on the file labeled Pulitzer and laughed out loud. "Funny, T," she mumbled.

"What?"

Wynter now had the names of the four politicians, but she wasn't prepared to share them just yet. "Does it matter who they are?"

"Yes, Wynter, it does."

"Are you saying that you won't authorize negative reporting on certain members of Congress because they're under the protection of this network? You've got to be fucking kidding me now. Forget it, Bob. TRU doesn't deserve this story. You better have talented attorneys if you plan on coming after me. I quit, effective immediately." Wynter plugged in a thumb drive and began moving the files over. The entire folder disappeared as soon as Wynter had saved all the files to her thumb drive. Simply blinked out of existence. *Nice, T.* As a measure of insurance, she copied the contents of the thumb drive onto a second drive.

Bob sighed. "Wait, wait, wait. All right. I'll hold a spot for you and take the heat when this all goes down. I was starting to hate my job, anyway. But if you-know-who gets wind of this, especially if the politicians involved are under his protection, he'll nix the story quicker than a fat girl gobbling up the last piece of pie."

"You're a pig, Robert. You know, after we break the news, I'll be handing over the information to the other major media outlets."

"Why would you do that?"

"Because they won't try to spin it later with a bunch of biased sycophants who protect the former president."

"Fair enough, as long as we're the news outlet that breaks the story," Bob answered. "Believe it or not, I want TRU to be viewed as a fair news network."

"Deal. Now, I have to go to get everything lined up."

Fortunately, the list of calls made through AT&T was much shorter, and when Wynter contacted the name T had provided, the woman quickly verified the information. Wynter printed the other list, yanked out her thumb drive, and ran into her bathroom. After a quick shower, she decided against blowing her hair dry and putting on make-up. Instead, she'd let the studio do their thing before she went live.

Wynter looked around her living room for a place to hide the second drive. With little time, she glanced at her juicer and lifted the plastic lid before placing the drive into the tube. That would have to do for now until Wynter could put the drive in her safe deposit box. With paper in hand and her thumb drive securely tucked into the front pocket of her tailored black pants, she ran out to her car to meet Kari.

†

While Sandra was relieved that Adam Carter had informed her they now had Bridget Schmidt in custody, she ruminated about how anxious Wynter had been to leave. Sandra didn't do meaningless affairs or one-night stands. Wynter had exited this morning as if her ass was on fire, and she needed to find a way to extinguish the flames. Had Sandra gotten it all wrong? She thought they were on the same page and heading to something that could turn special if given half the chance. Now she wasn't sure, although she took comfort in the fact that Wynter had quickly kissed her in front of her mother. That was something, at least.

Sandra must have had a frown on her face because her mother looked up from her morning tea and remarked, "Trouble in paradise already? Well, that didn't take long," Rose sniped. "And to think I was starting to like Wynter. She has spunk."

"Shut it, Mother. Honestly, I don't really know what happened." Sandra sighed.

Her mother must have seen her massive disappointment because she stood and placed her hand on Sandra's arm. "I'm sorry. You really like this woman, don't you?"

"I do, and I thought she felt the same. I can't believe I was willing to toss aside all my trepidations for something that wasn't even real. At least not to her."

"Don't be so quick to assess the situation. From my vantage point, something is definitely present between you, crackling with energy that I don't think I've ever seen in you before. I get the sense that Wynter's job is important to her. Are you sure it's prudent to take her away from what she is clearly very good at? Yes, she would make an excellent

communications director, especially if she can uncover all
the dirty little secrets of our opponents and spin them in a
way that provides us a distinct advantage. Still, I think her
heart is in investigative reporting."

"Well, that is a conundrum, isn't it?" Sandra slumped
on the stool. "Perhaps it would make things far easier if I
didn't hire her. Although, there would still be a conflict of
interest, as I am certain TRU would tap her to follow the
campaign trail. That might present even further difficulties in
a budding relationship. Provided that is what transpires after
this morning's quick exit," Sandra added.

"You'll figure it out," Rose answered.

"Really? You've never held back your wise advice.
What gives?"

Rose waved her hand in the air. "Oh, you know that
old saying, 'the definition of insanity is doing the same thing
repeatedly, yet expecting a different result.' Clearly, my
meddling in your personal life has not worked out very well.
You're in your forties and still not settled with a wife."

"If you expect me to find one before I announce my
candidacy, I believe that ship has sailed."

"I realize that, but we have time before you actually
take the oath of office." Rose grinned. "I have a good feeling
about things to come. Mother's intuition."

"That's probably hunger pangs. I'll make you
breakfast. Pancakes or French toast?"

"Neither." Rose patted her stomach. "When a woman
gets to be a certain age, simply looking at fatty foods
translates to several unwanted pounds. I'll have some fruit."

Rose eyed Sandra. "Lucky for you, you got your father's constitution. That man never lost his trim figure."

"That's because he died before the middle-aged paunch could set in."

"Not true. I know plenty of men who gained weight in their thirties. Your father never did."

"I miss Dad."

"So do I, dear, so do I." Rose looked away, and Sandra felt a rush of emotion for her mother's loss. In an uncharacteristic gesture of affection, Sandra approached her mother and offered a comforting hug. She could count on one hand the number of times they'd shared this level of intimacy, verbal or physical. It felt right. Perhaps they were entering a new era. One where Rose would meddle less and support more.

Rose cleared her throat and awkwardly patted Sandra's back to indicate an end to the hug. "Thank you, dear. Now, do you want to fill me in on the call from Adam Carter?"

"Apparently, your former friend, Bridget Schmidt, is a Russian operative. At least that's what the FBI believes…"

†

Eager to listen to the files T had provided, Wynter fished the thumb drive from her pocket and stuck it into the USB port in her car. Since she recognized the voice in the first file, she couldn't help her verbal outburst. "Holy shit." The House minority leader was talking with Bridget Schmidt about the growing popularity of Sandra Murphy. Bridget reassured him that she or her colleagues would deal with the issue. She continued to snap at the congressman to worry about shutting down the negative press around the former president. They needed to control his rhetoric before they lost more ground, or they would go to plan B and start backing another candidate. Russia had as much a stake in this as the far right.

Wynter hadn't listened to all the files before she finally found a parking space one block from the Buzz House. She glanced at the time and noted she'd made it with a few minutes to spare. Kari had taken a table in the back and looked around furtively. Her nervous energy seemed to bleed into the atmosphere all around her. She looked so out of place that Wynter marched to the counter to order two coffee drinks.

When Wynter reached the table and slid the coffee in front of Kari, she whispered, "Vanilla latte with two shots of espresso. That's still your favorite, right?"

"Can we just get this over with?" Kari hissed. "Do you have the call logs? I only have fifteen minutes before I need to get back."

Wynter reached into her bag and pulled out the paper she printed, nudging Kari's knee as she slid the paper into her hands. "I'll have my friend wipe any evidence that I called you this morning. I'll also have her wipe the phone record when you call me back with verification. Thanks, Kari. I promise no one will know of your involvement in this story."

"You better make good on that guarantee because if I lose my job, I'm crashing at your place until you find me a new one."

"You got it." Wynter smiled.

Wynter heard rustling as Kari tucked the paper into her purse and stood to leave, grabbing her coffee before exiting the coffee shop. Wynter took another sip of her coffee and waited a few more minutes before leaving the Buzz House on her way to the studio. Robert wasn't going to like what she was about to report on. All four members were close allies of the former president, and the owner of TRU was also a staunch supporter.

Wynter desperately wanted to be the one to break the news, but even more critical, she wanted this story to get out there before the machine had a means of shutting it down. She decided to call T and tell her to send the information to another major network if she didn't see the story break on TRU by noon.

After sliding into her car and before resuming her review of the audio files, Wynter gave the voice command to call T.

"How'd you like the files I sent?" T chuckled.

"Loved them, but listen, if you don't see the news break on TRU by eleven-thirty today, I need you to send the information to another network, probably CNN. Ask for Liz. She won't ask questions and will know who to give it to. You can let her know I gave you her name. I have a bad feeling that TRU will try to kill the story. I can't let that happen, even if I don't get the credit for breaking it."

"Okay, I can do that, but don't you want credit?"

"I do, more than anything I've ever wanted in my life, because I feel it in my bones that this will be the story of the decade, but country before person. Besides, I want these bastards held accountable for going after Governor Murphy." Wynter's voice was pure steel.

"Got it. I may have a way of crediting you down the road. If TRU proves they are the asshole network I think they are, the new story will be that you are the anonymous source and broke the story only to have it killed by TRU," T answered.

"I like it. That's brilliant, T."

"Anything else?" T asked.

"Yes, I need you to wipe the call logs between Kari Nash at T-Mobile and me. There will be two calls for you to get rid of. I made one earlier today; the other will be when she verifies the information in the next hour. Kari is taking an enormous risk, and I don't want her caught in any destruction that might happen after this story breaks."

"Understood. No problem. I already got rid of the evidence of your call to my friend at AT&T."

"Thanks, T. I appreciate your thoroughness. I really hope to meet you someday."

"We'll see. Obviously, in my line of business, we must be vigilant about keeping the group under the wire. Not to be dramatic, but in the wrong hands, discovering our identities has life and death consequences."

"I understand and would never want to put any of you at risk. I have to go now."

After hanging up, Wynter began listening to the other audio files, which were even more sensational. This was going to blow up the airwaves. She suspected the story would take on a life of its own, and Wynter wanted to be a part of it all. Suddenly, she was second-guessing her decision to work for Sandra. But Wynter had made a commitment, and she would never go back on that. Maybe she could find a way to keep her toes in the pool of investigative journalism. CNN and MSNBC often had experts weigh in on various issues. But would they tap her knowing she was working for Sandra? She'd cross that bridge when she came to it. For now, she had another month to follow through on this once-in-a-lifetime story. Suddenly Wynter didn't want to wait for the call log verification to call Sandra. She felt a mild panic as her mind scanned how she'd left this morning. A quick kiss wasn't exactly a way to soften her exit. *Shit. I need to call and give her a heads-up. She probably thinks I abandoned her, or worse, that I only want a casual affair.*

Wynter briefly took her eyes off the road to find Sandra's contact information, but that was enough to nearly cause an accident as she swerved back into her lane, narrowly avoiding the truck. The driver stuck his middle finger up and laid on his horn to express his displeasure at her self-imposed distraction. After her heartbeat returned to normal, Wynter decided she better engage the hands-free system to phone Sandra. For whatever reason, she'd always been reluctant after learning the system had a few quirks and sometimes made a call to the wrong person.

"Call Sandra Murphy," she directed.

Sandra answered after three rings. "Wynter. Is everything all right with you?"

"Yeah. I'm sorry I ran out on you this morning. I didn't want you to get the wrong idea. I didn't have all the details before, but now I have more information, and I wanted to give you another heads up."

"Okay," Sandra hesitantly answered.

"A bombshell landed in my lap this morning that I had to run with quickly to get the news on air before noon. I'm hoping TRU won't kill the story, but even if they do, I have a contingency plan. I just listened to a tape of four of your biggest adversaries on the right colluding with Bridget Schmidt, who I'm betting is now a suspected Russian operative."

"Are you driving right now?"

Wynter's phone buzzed, indicating another call was coming in. "Yeah, and I almost got in an accident earlier. Listen, another call is coming in that I was waiting for. I have to go," Wynter answered.

"Please be careful. Cell phone distractions are a major factor in accidents. Call me later when you're not driving."

"Will do." Wynter ended her call with Sandra and answered the call waiting in her queue. "Holmes."

"The call logs are accurate," Kari said without preamble.

"Thanks, Kari. A friend of mine is going to wipe any record of phone calls. You should be in the clear."

"Good luck, Wynter."

"Thanks again. Bye Kari. I'll call later, and we can do something fun. My treat."

"Yeah, yeah. I want barbeque."

"You got it."

Wynter had everything she needed to go on air. Swerving in and out of traffic, she finally reached the studio and parked in her usual parking spot. Then, after grabbing the thumb drive, she ran to the front door, giving a small wave to the security guard, who gestured for her to go on through.

CHAPTER TEN

Sandra returned to her bathroom to shower and get ready for the day. She'd called her assistant earlier to relay her plans. Although she intended to work from home, she dressed as if she had to attend a press conference. This was deeply ingrained in her from the lessons her mother had taught her early on. One never knew when the press would come calling. She'd given Rose the basics of her conversation with Wynter, and Rose had promptly turned on the news. Sandra caught Rose's frown when she flipped to the TRU network channel. It wasn't the first time she had turned to that station, but Rose disliked the network so much that she usually only had it playing in a small corner of the TV while keeping the main view on CNN. Both recognized that keeping tabs on biased networks allowed them to know what the opposition was saying about Sandra.

As Sandra entered the den with the large flat screen TV mounted to the wall, Rose looked up and met her inquisitive eyes. "Nothing yet. Just the same old, same old bashing of the liberals. I can't believe they get away with calling us libtards in this day and age. What an offensive name. But they have no shame. It just makes my blood boil. Before that buffoon, it would have been unheard of to use that kind of language. Now it's considered 'woke' to challenge terms that are offensive to persons with disabilities or other minorities. And you know how the far right demonizes that word. Frankly, I'm surprised they haven't graduated to using the 'N word' with impunity." Rose shook her head in disgust.

"I'm going to grab my tablet and try to get some work done while we wait. I can't give one hundred percent of my focus to the drivel those hacks are spouting on TRU. Make sure you keep CNN running in the corner in case TRU decides not to run the story."

Rose nodded and picked up the remote.

As the minutes flew by, Sandra became increasingly concerned when no breaking news appeared on TRU. Her eyes flickered to the screen when she saw the Breaking News graphic appear in the corner, and Anderson Cooper began speaking.

"Mother, flip to CNN. It looks like TRU screwed Wynter over. I want to hear what they're saying."

Wynter's leg bounced up and down while the hair and make-up person worked on her. She wanted to get this over with so she could do more digging to fill in bits and pieces of the story. She knew she'd be able to find additional incriminating evidence.

"Stop that. You're going to mess everything up, and then I'll just have to start over, delaying your appearance in front of the camera." The make-up artist squeezed Wynter's shoulder.

"Can't you hurry it up?" Wynter complained.

"No, Wynter, I can't. You came in naked, with flat hair. It's not like this was a touch-up job."

Wynter stilled her leg, and finally, the woman removed the plastic bib, telling her she was good to go. She walked over to her cameraman, Jimmy, and whispered for him to record the footing and give her a copy immediately after the broadcast. Although Bob had assured her they were going live, she didn't believe him for one minute. He'd screwed others in the past to save his ass.

Jimmy grinned and nodded. "Fuck them if they fire me," he added.

"Thanks, Jimmy. Don't worry, you're the best cameraman they have. I've no doubt you could get a job anywhere. Besides, I hear Hollywood pays a lot more than TRU."

"It does, and a recruiter just contacted me the other day. I was considering giving my notice, anyway."

"If they try to sue you, I will make their life miserable."

Jimmy grinned. "I'm counting on it."

Wynter took a deep breath before strolling to the seat on the studio stage. Three cameras pointed in her direction, but Wynter focused on Jimmy's. Then, keeping her eyes on the countdown, Wynter began her broadcast when cued. She'd hastily recorded a rough draft of what she wanted written on the teleprompter, handing it to her favorite production assistant who could be trusted to clean everything up, make it flow, and sound more coherent than her quick ramblings.

"Good morning, I'm Wynter Holmes, and I have breaking news for you today, exclusively on TRU TV." A disturbance in the booth temporarily caused her to lose her spot on the prompter. She watched as she saw the head of the network, Daniel Goldstein's exaggerated gestures, indicating his irritation. That was not a good sign. No, not a good sign at all, especially when Bob eagerly nodded his head.

Wynter continued reading from the teleprompter, ad-libbing here and there to bring the news story more into focus. Finally, after finishing the short broadcast, she ripped the earbud out and made a beeline for the booth. By the time she reached the enclosed area, Bob was exiting, and Mr. Goldstein was nowhere in the vicinity.

"Want to tell me what just happened in the booth with Mr. Goldstein? And how in the world did he get here so fast?" Wynter hissed.

"Now, Wynter, you know I had to call Daniel. He's clarified that any major news event of a political nature has to be cleared by him before we go live. So I gave him the draft script. He went ballistic and told me to cut the feed and recycle an earlier taped program," Bob answered sheepishly.

"You promised."

Bob held his hands in supplication. "What was I supposed to do?"

"Fine. You'll have my letter of resignation by the end of the day. It's a good thing I have a backup plan, and you're not going to like it." Wynter brushed past Bob and marched over to Jimmy, who handed her a small memory card.

"I'll make a copy, just in case, and keep it in a safe place," Jimmy whispered.

"Thanks, Jimmy. I owe you."

"No, you don't. I've been looking for a reason to quit. These assholes just frayed my last nerve. Great broadcast, by the way. I hope it sees the light of day," Jimmy said.

"Oh, it will, Jimmy, and I'll give you credit for the great camerawork." As Wynter blew past Jimmy and headed for the door, she heard Bob ask Jimmy. "What the hell was that all about?" Wynter didn't listen to the rest of the conversation. She would worry about the legal consequences afterward.

Wynter grabbed her bag on the way out, smiling as she left the building. She felt giddy about her past decision to hire the best in the business to renegotiate her contract with TRU. The addition to Wynter's non-compete clause would keep her from losing everything. Her attorney had ensured that if TRU ever passed on a story she had uncovered, Wynter was free to shop the story to a new network. While the clause did not explicitly allow Wynter to air what the TRU produced using their resources, she felt confident she would prevail if taken to court. She also had a few other tricks up her sleeve regarding TRU's business that would more than embarrass the network if they wanted to play hardball. She'd make it her mission to uncover every slimy deal the network had made with various politicians. And she had the proof to back her up. Plus, she was sure T would be happy to add damning facts about the network to her treasure trove of incriminating data.

Glancing at her watch, she noted the time—just before 11:30. Wynter pulled her cell phone from her bag and scrolled through the apps until she landed on the streaming app for CNN live. She reached her car and tossed her bag inside before slipping into the driver's seat. Wynter sat there as the newsfeed loaded and waited, hoping that T had sent the information to CNN. After five minutes of listening to recycled stories and a short commercial break, it surprised her to see Anderson Cooper sitting in the chair. T must have sent Anderson Cooper a preview of the story before sending the actual files to her contact. *Nice.*

Wynter's phone buzzed in her hand, and she clicked on the text message, noticing there were three waiting messages she hadn't viewed yet.

Sorry TRU decided not to run the story, but at least CNN did.

Wynter thumbed a quick response. *It's fine. At least I have a copy of the broadcast they decided not to run. I'm going to try to get CNN to air it.*

Wynter was about to access the missed texts when she noticed several pending voicemails. She quickly thumbed another text to Sandra. *Gotta go. I have messages to answer. I'll call you later.*

Good luck.

After listening to the voice mail messages and reading her texts, Wynter replied to one and tossed her phone onto the passenger's seat. She plugged in the address for the airport. Apparently, there was a ticket waiting for her. She was heading to New York. She'd text Sandra after boarding the plane in case it was a tight timeframe to get to the gate. Wynter didn't even have time to go home, change, or grab an extra set of clothes. She'd worry about that later.

†

The news that Bridget Schmidt was a Russian operative unsettled Sandra. How could her mother not have known? She'd spent a considerable amount of time with the woman. Sandra wanted to ask Wynter who her anonymous source was. If it was someone in the government, why hadn't she caught wind of it before now? There had not been a whisper from any of her contacts. Knowing Wynter, she'd never reveal her source, but Sandra felt she had a right to know. She glanced at her mother, who sat stunned in her chair, undoubtedly trying to process the information that CNN had just reported. The network was still trying to confirm the story, but Sandra knew it was accurate. Wynter was not the type of reporter to air a story that wasn't fully vetted or from a very reliable source.

The dazed look remained on Rose's face as she almost whispered, "I brought the danger into our lives. I will never forgive myself if something happens to you. Wynter knows more about this whole mess, doesn't she?"

Sandra nodded.

"You don't think…" Rose left that thought hanging.

"Of course not."

"Well, what better way to protect her cover than to throw shade over another operative the FBI has captured?" Rose asked.

"Really, Mother?" Sandra huffed. "You've been watching too many spy shows. Wynter said she would call later. When she has time to talk, I hope to learn more. I need to find something to distract me while I wait. I'm going into my office to get some work done. Let me know if any of the news stations report additional details."

Feeling the buzz of her phone, Sandra hurried to take the call. "Hello."

"I assume you caught the news?" Adam Carter said without a greeting.

"Yes, I did. Did you know about this?" Sandra began pacing.

"No. We had no idea. I've been pressing my contacts at the CIA and Department of Homeland Security, and no one is talking. However, Homeland Security is now taking over the case. Bridget is being transferred into their custody.

Emma Schmidt is on her way. I have half a mind to let her talk to her mother, but I've been given strict orders not to let that happen. Bridget Schmidt informed us she'll only talk to her daughter."

"Then you should let her," Sandra answered. "I sure would like to talk with Agent Schmidt after she's done with her mother."

"I'll let her know, but I can't make any promises that she'll want to meet with you. This whole situation has rocked her to the core. I'm planning on sending her on vacation. She deserves the time off."

"Agreed. Maybe Agent Schmidt will contact me when she returns." Sandra glanced at her mother, who shot her a quizzical look. Sandra gestured she would fill her in later.

"Hey, you aren't thinking of poaching her?" Carter asked with a hint of irritation.

"Can I refuse to answer on the grounds it may incriminate me?" Sandra chuckled.

"I don't like the sound of that. We need her in the FBI. Her talents are far too great for her to become a glorified bodyguard. How about if we try to work something out where we can loan her to you until everything blows over? We can set her on a mission to uncover any additional plans the Russians might have for you. But only after she returns from vacation," Carter added.

"Thanks, Adam. I'll talk to you later."

"Stay safe, Governor."

After Sandra ended the call, she took a chair and addressed her mother. "Homeland Security is taking Bridget into custody. Unfortunately, no one seems to have known about her ties to the Russian government."

"Well, someone knew," Rose responded acerbically. "So, basically, the authorities have nothing. That's the first thing you'll need to change when you become president."

"What's that?"

"To fix the incompetence of the FBI, CIA, and Homeland Security," Rose stated.

"That's rather cynical of you. Where's that political savvy you're known for? Disparaging the good men and women in law enforcement and those responsible for the security of our nation, will not play well on national TV," Sandra noted.

"Well, somebody, somewhere, had information, and I intend on finding out who that was," Rose stated. "Do you think Wynter will reveal her sources to you?"

Sandra shrugged. "I hope so, Mother. I'll certainly ask her about it. But I'll need to promise never to disclose that information to the authorities. I imagine that Wynter takes her profession seriously and doesn't reveal her sources."

"Not even for the good of the nation?"

"Who says it would be for the good of the nation? As you've already said, if the FBI, CIA, and Homeland Security were all in the dark about this, I'm not sure Wynter should reveal her source."

Rose quirked one eyebrow. "Perhaps."

145

"I need to sit on all of this. I'll be in my office if more information comes to light."

Sandra wasn't getting any work done as she read through the complicated legalese of the latest draft bill the legislature wanted to tackle in their next session. Zoning off, she was startled by the buzz of her phone. When she spied who was calling, she eagerly answered. "Hello, Wynter. Are you okay?"

"Yeah. I don't have much time because the flight attendants are about to close the doors and prepare for takeoff."

"You're on a plane?" Sandra asked in shock.

"Yeah, CNN left a ticket at the airport for me. I'm going to hand over the tape that Jimmy, my cameraman, recorded and gave to me. My backup plan, with a little help from a friend."

"Would that friend be your source?" Sandra asked.

"I promise I'll tell you more about this shocking revelation, but I won't do it over the phone. I don't trust anyone right now."

"Fair enough. Please take care of yourself. You may have just put a huge target on your back. An even bigger one than is on mine."

"You, too. I don't think this is over. Not by a long shot. Can you get those massive guys shadowing you to come back and ensure your safety?"

"Probably, but I'm not sure that's needed just yet. At least not until the authorities learn more."

"I really wish you would. It would make me feel a lot better."

"I'll think about it. It's nice to know you care so much."

"I do, Sandra, I do. Sorry, they're telling us we need to shut off our electronic devices now and put them in airplane mode."

"Okay, bye Wynter." Sandra ended the call and sat there for a minute before making a last-minute decision.

Sandra decided she would travel to New York. She needed to have a serious conversation with Wynter. If both their lives were at risk, Sandra deserved to learn everything Wynter knew about Bridget and the endgame of the Russians. Were there already other plots in the works?

At least they had neutralized Bridget. But did they also have another operative waiting in the wings?

Sandra ran to her bedroom and quickly packed a bag. On her way out, she announced, "I'm heading to New York. Wynter is on her way to the CNN studios. I plan on tracking her down."

"You know they'll want to interview you if you show up at the studios. I'll bet whoever is there will practically salivate over an exclusive interview. Are you prepared for that?"

"I'll have a long flight to formulate answers to potential questions. Yes, I'll be ready."

When Sandra reached the end of her driveway and was about to open the security gate, she cursed and mumbled, "Damn, I do not have time for this." A row of media vans lined up on the road outside her home.

Knowing they would simply follow if she didn't stop and answer a few questions, Sandra gracefully put her car in park and exited.

The first question came from another TRU reporter.

"Governor Murphy, thank you for stopping and taking a few questions."

Sandra nodded. "Go ahead, Mr. Davis."

"What do you say to your critics claiming this is nothing more than a partisan hack job to discredit your political foes?" Mark Davis asked.

"Hmm, so that's the latest spin. Good to know. Honestly, Mr. Davis, I know as much as you about the recent shocking events. However, since I'm not on social media as much as many others, perhaps you can enlighten me on the latest conspiracy theories?"

"Rumors are that you hired actors who specialize in spot-on impressions, and those aren't really the voices of the Congressmen and Senator."

Sandra threw her head back and laughed. "Well, that's certainly creative."

"Governor Murphy, do you support a special counsel, commission, or committee to investigate the claims of treason that some believe goes as far up as the former president?" a young woman Sandra did not recognize called out.

"I support anything that will get to the bottom of this egregious assault on our democracy. I'm sorry, I don't know your name."

"Darla, from the Daily Beast. Aren't you more concerned that certain members of our government have conspired to assassinate a sitting governor, and our intelligence agencies failed to keep you safe? Is that why you refused DPS services? Do you question their competence?"

Sandra deftly avoided the question about the Dignity Protection Section, answering, "I have every confidence in the men and women in the FBI, CIA, and Homeland Security," Sandra responded. "I'm sorry, ladies and gentlemen, I have a tight schedule today, but if you send your questions to my assistant, I'll try to prepare a response." With that, Sandra slid into her car with the cacophony of voices calling her name. She only hoped none would follow.

Sandra smiled when she saw her mother approach the gate. She sent her silent thanks that Rose had checked the security cameras and noticed the press. Rose was particularly adept at keeping the press entertained. It would be easier to direct their questions at Rose versus attempting to follow Sandra, who had made it clear she was done answering questions for now.

Not wanting to involve a driver in what was essentially a personal mission, Sandra had decided to take her own car. The last thing she needed was a nosy reporter picking up on her interest in Wynter. Breathing a sigh of relief, Sandra rushed to the airport, barely keeping her speed at only five over the limit. She'd decided that was a calculated risk she was willing to take. Unless an officer was having a particularly bad day, none would chase down a car doing only five over the speed limit, especially if they noted the driver was a white, middle-aged woman. Sadly, she thought it might be quite different if she were a person of color. Unfortunately, white privilege was real. That was only one thing she was attempting to change in her state.

CHAPTER ELEVEN

Wynter could certainly get used to the platinum treatment. On her way to the airport, she'd called back the assistant who had left numerous messages to confirm that she was on her way. The airline tickets were waiting for her at the Alaska Airlines VIP check-in, and they'd put her in first class. The executives at TRU were cheap bastards and always arranged for coach, not even business class. Wynter made it to the gate with only a few minutes to spare, and once she settled into her seat, she made the call to Sandra.

She patted her pocket, ensuring she had the memory card of her broadcast. She didn't have time to retrieve her backup thumb drive from home with the shocking conversations between the slimy politicians and Russian agents. Her blood boiled just thinking about how far the opposition was willing to take things. It was one thing to work with Russia to discredit an opponent or dig up dirt on them and quite another to arrange for a hit. Losing their political clout wasn't enough. She wanted those bastards locked up for a long time, at the very least. Not necessarily an advocate for the death penalty, although Wynter certainly felt this high crime of treason might warrant that sentence, she preferred to see them rot in jail for the rest of their lives. And she didn't want to see any of those pathetic excuses for men end up in some cushy white-collar prison. Put them in with the general population of murderers, child molesters, and rapists.

When the flight attendant offered to bring Wynter a drink, she figured, what the hell. One drink wouldn't kill her. The flight was over five hours. She smiled and answered, "Sure, what do you have?"

"Would you prefer beer, wine, or hard alcohol?"

"I suppose you have fancy beer in first class," Wynter responded.

"Yes, we have a very nice Anchor Brewing West Coast IPA or a Full Sail Brewing Sesión Cervesa Lager."

"Hmm, do you have a favorite?" Wynter asked, smiling at the attractive woman.

The woman smiled back and answered, "I'm not really a fan of beer."

"Okay. I guess I'll have the IPA. Thank you." Wynter retrieved her tablet and began reading her latest mystery. She was far too excited to sleep.

Realizing she hadn't eaten anything all day, Wynter gobbled up the snack basket provided before departure and looked forward to what meals were available in first class. She hoped it would be tastier than the limited choice in the main cabin, even though she thought Alaska did an excellent job with their offerings. Wynter wasn't disappointed when the attendant came by shortly after delivering the beer and offered the meal. She was so hungry that she ate every morsel and smacked her lips after practically licking the Salt and Straw Ice Cream bowl.

Finally, the excitement of the day hit Wynter, and she fell asleep after all. The announcement to prepare the plane for landing interrupted her nap as her eyes blinked open. Momentarily confused before remembering the rapid evolution of events, she stretched and yawned, fluffed her hair, and readied herself for arrival.

Wynter thought she might have to catch a cab or call a Lyft to make her way to the studio, but the royal treatment continued. A massive sign with her name printed in large black letters met her just outside the security area after deplaning. She approached the man who inquired, "Ms. Holmes?"

"Yes."

"Do you have luggage?"

"Nope."

His face scrunched in confusion. "I've been instructed to take you directly to the studio and then I will be your driver for the duration of your stay. The studio has arranged for your hotel as well. Will that be to your satisfaction?"

"Hell, yeah. Lead the way. What's your name?"

"Jason, ma'am."

"Oh, please don't call me ma'am. I'm not that old. Wynter." She stuck out her hand in greeting, and the man took it with a smile. "I might need to do a little shopping after I finish whatever they have planned at the studio." Wynter shrugged and gestured to her lone sling pack.

Jason grinned and said, "You won't have a problem finding anything you might need in New York. I'll inform the studio, and I'm sure they'll arrange for any purchases you might require while you visit the city."

"How long will I be here?" Wynter asked.

"That's up to you, but they've arranged for at least two days at the hotel. Follow me."

"Perfect." Wynter walked alongside the man as they left the airport.

Wynter thought it was too bad that she'd agreed to take the job with Sandra. She could get used to this treatment, and depending on what happened with CNN, it would not surprise her if they made an offer to join their news team. Wynter sighed at the missed opportunity. Her ultimate goal had been to land a spot on either CNN or MSNBC, but she'd had to settle for TRU.

†

Jason weaved in and out of the lanes of traffic like a pro but could not avoid the famed New York traffic, and it

154

took them a fair amount of time to get to the studio. Once inside, a harried assistant greeted Wynter and led her to a chair where hair and make-up could give her a quick treatment. Liz briefly stopped by and gave Wynter the thumbs-up gesture. The studio was a hive of energy, even at the late hour.

Anderson Cooper himself approached with a warm smile. "Hello, Ms. Holmes. We're all very excited that you agreed to come on the air and fill in the blanks for us. Nice piece of investigative journalism. CNN was able to verify the recordings while you were traveling, but we were hoping you might shed more light on the story."

Wynter reached into her pocket and retrieved the memory card. "This is a copy of the TRU broadcast that the studio's head killed. It's the only one I have, so I'd really like it back. TRU has my thumb drive with the audio recordings, but I've hidden a backup. Fortunately, you have your own proof. I presume you won't need the backup."

Anderson grinned. "Are you still under contract with TRU?"

"Nope, I resigned right after they killed the story. Although I have a non-compete clause in my contract, my attorney wisely insisted on a tiny addition that should keep me from paying through the nose. I'm not worried about providing the truth to the American people. Let them come after me."

"Ms. Holmes, I can almost guarantee you have a bright future ahead of you. Therefore, I believe CNN is extremely interested in offering you a position."

"Wynter, please call me Wynter. Unfortunately, I had already planned on leaving TRU and agreed to another position."

Anderson's eyebrow rose. "It seems another network has beaten us to the punch."

"Not another network," Wynter answered.

Anderson tilted his head. "Will we be able to explore that tonight during the interview?"

"I'm not prepared to make an announcement on that just yet. Although my reporting is rock solid, there may be a perception of conflict of interest. I'm sure many will view this story as a political hit job. I promise it isn't, but the appearance will be there."

"That has definitely piqued my curiosity," Anderson remarked. "But I will trust your judgment. We're already labeled the fake media and enemy of the state by the alt-right. Nothing should diminish the power of this story. Just so you know, it is evolving fast. The DOJ already started its investigations, and the FBI seized several electronic devices. Thanks to your reporting."

The interview was a blur, and Wynter was glad Jason was waiting to take her to her hotel. On her way, she texted Sandra. She hoped Sandra had caught her interview and was pleased with her performance.

On my way to the Four Seasons. Did you catch the broadcast?

Wynter frowned when she didn't hear from Sandra. While it was late in New York, San Diego was three hours behind. Jason interrupted her mild panic, announcing their arrival at the hotel as he pulled to the front door. Popping the trunk, Jason retrieved a large bag and handed it to Wynter.

"What's this?" Wynter asked.

"I might have mentioned your lack of luggage, and the studio arranged for a small token of their appreciation. I'm pretty good at guessing women's sizes and preferences on style. I hope I wasn't overstepping, but I sort of took you for a more casual look. They aren't fancy, but at least you'll have a second set of clothes and new underwear. We can go shopping for more when you wake tomorrow." He handed her a card. "Just call this number, and I'll be here in a jiffy."

Wynter smiled as her gaydar pinged. She hadn't taken note before, but the excitement in Jason's eyes at the notion of shopping nailed her assessment, along with the use of the word jiffy.

"Wow! Thanks, Jason. You're a doll."

He beamed back at Wynter. "Have a good night, Wynter."

With her bag in hand, Wynter walked into the lobby and gave her name to the hotel clerk. Because of the late hour, the check-in process went quickly. Still wired from the whirlwind day, Wynter decided to have a drink at the bar before retiring to her room. She felt her phone buzz and smiled when she saw the text.

Sorry I missed the broadcast, but I have a surprise for you. Where are you right now?

Heading to the bar. I need a drink. I'm too wired to sleep.

Good, stay there.

Wynter frowned at the odd text. *What in the world is she up to?*

Finding a table in the dimly lit lounge, Wynter sat. She didn't have to wait long before a server approached the table and set a cocktail menu in front of her.

"Good evening. Welcome to the Four Seasons. Will anyone be joining you?"

"No, it'll just be me. Tell me your favorite cocktail. Normally I order a beer, but tonight I'd like to step outside the box and try something different."

The woman smiled. "I'd go with the Ty Chee Martini or For the Love of Roses. Both are quite different."

"Okay, but which one is your favorite?"

"For the Love of Roses," the woman answered.

"Sold."

"Make that two."

Wynter thought she heard an impossibility but turned her head to see a grinning Sandra holding on to a small rolling suitcase.

"Surprise." Sandra leaned in and pecked Wynter on the lips.

"Wha…what are you doing here?"

Sandra frowned. "I'm sorry. I thought you would be pleased."

Wynter reached for Sandra's hand and gently pulled her to the chair. "Oh, my goddess. I am. I have so much to share with you."

Sandra grinned. "I absolutely adore New York. There isn't a gaggle of reporters following me, hoping for a statement. I feel invisible here."

Wynter wondered how much the press had hounded her after the news broke. "I'm assuming there was a line of news vans waiting for you earlier today."

"There was. I answered a couple of questions, which was exactly the right thing to do. Otherwise, the vultures surely would have followed me all the way to the airport," Sandra answered. "Sorry, that wasn't a very nice comment, considering your chosen profession."

"Oh, we can be vultures. I don't hold that opinion against you. I can't believe you came all the way to New York." Wynter felt the need to physically connect with Sandra and stroked her arm until she reached Sandra's hand and clasped it to her own.

"Well, I wanted to share in this special moment of yours. I am so proud of you for breaking the story. Well, actually, Anderson Cooper was the first to announce it, but he gave you credit for the reporting." Sandra beamed with pride until her expression turned somber. "Listen, I also wanted to talk with you about something."

"Oh, no, no, no, please don't tell me you're ending things before we've barely had a chance to see where it goes."

"No, nothing like that. I had a lot of time to think while sitting on the plane. While I know you would be brilliant as my communications director, that isn't a job that will fulfill your passion, is it?"

Wynter looked Sandra in the eye, appreciating her intuition. She wasn't wrong. "It's a wonderful opportunity that you've offered me, but no, it probably wouldn't feed me as much as the excitement of the chase for that next big story. CNN offered me a position as a political contributor with the distinct possibility that I could have my own show in the future once I prove myself. I told them I had a position waiting for me."

"If I hadn't offered you the job, would you have taken the position with CNN?"

Wynter nodded. "Yeah. It's kind of my dream job."

Sandra squeezed Wynter's hand. "Then you should take it, but make sure you have an attorney review the contract. Don't let them lock you into something. You have a brilliant career ahead of you, and CNN isn't the only network that will heavily recruit you."

"Are you sure? They want me to spend a few more days in New York and think about the offer rather than turn it down immediately. How much time do you have? Want to play tourist with me?" Wynter asked.

"I'd love to."

"This will screw up whatever time off we might have together. I'm not exactly looking forward to that. I suppose I still need to think about this. I really don't want things to end before they've started," Wynter lamented.

"I have an idea that you can certainly feel free to shoot down, but…"

"I'm all ears."

"What if you convince CNN to follow me on the campaign trail? You can be the primary reporter to whom I would give total access. Then, if other stories pop up that you want to follow, you can still do that and fly back and forth to New York."

"Hmm, that might work, but then we would probably have to keep our relationship under wraps. I don't really like that. Goddess, this is all too much right now. I'm more than a little overwhelmed. For perhaps the first time in my life, I want to see where a relationship takes me, and I don't do well in the closet." Wynter slumped in her chair.

"Then be honest with them and see where that takes the discussion. If you don't want me to keep you a secret, I won't let that happen," Sandra responded. "I am more than a little enamored with you, in case you haven't noticed."

Wynter laughed. "I kind of figured that out since you flew all the way across the country to be with me during my big moment. I suppose it wouldn't hurt to lay everything on the line and see what they say. It's not like covering a campaign presents much of a conflict of interest. It's easy to do unbiased reporting on campaigns unless you do something controversial, like announce you have a girlfriend." Wynter grinned. "You know it'll probably be a long shot, right?"

"A long shot is better than no shot," Sandra argued. "If it doesn't land well, we'll figure something out."

"You sure about this?"

"I'm not sure about anything, including whether I want to become the next president of the United States. I might prematurely age, and then you won't want a dried-up old hag."

"Stop it. You aren't that much older than me. This country needs a young president again. A young, out and proud, lesbian president," Wynter added.

"That would certainly shake up the establishment."

The waitress approached the table and set the drinks in front of Wynter and Sandra. "Enjoy, ladies."

"Oh, we will."

"Hey, by the way, did you make hotel arrangements yet?"

"No, I didn't get the chance. I focused on finding you."

"Perfect. You can stay with me. I'm sure CNN won't mind if I have a guest. They'd probably drool over the possibility of having you on one of their shows. Should I pitch it to them?"

Sandra sighed. "I suppose I will have to get it over with because I doubt my mother wants to fend off reporters for weeks until I agree to an interview. Sure, go ahead and let them know I'm available."

"Brilliant, but I still want to hang out and have fun in New York. I'd love to take in a Broadway musical while I'm here. Maybe Hamilton?"

"You enjoy Broadway musicals?" Sandra asked.

"Of course I do. What's not to like about theater and music all rolled into one?" Wynter lifted the fancy drink to her mouth and sipped. "Wow! This is heavenly. Whoops, I forgot to make a toast."

Sandra lifted her drink in the air, and Wynter tapped their glasses together. "I'll make a toast. To the talented new CNN reporter."

"Thanks, cheers."

CHAPTER TWELVE

Bridget Schmidt smiled when the transport van came to a screeching halt, and she heard gunfire. It was about time the incompetent comrades came to set her free. She'd had to activate emergency procedures when they had caught the idiots with their pants down. That left only one more person with significant influence that she could depend on to carry out her primary mission. She had a theory about who was responsible for the leaked tapes, which did not please her. The mysterious Organization had been fucking up her own group's plans for years. That had to stop. Bridget suspected they had somehow placed a tracking device on her. Hopefully, that would play right into her plans to get rid of those pesky women once and for all. She wondered why they hadn't sent an assassin after her. Capturing her was merely a delay in the mission, not a permanent solution. Besides, the comrades had embedded more agents into America's fabric, ready and waiting for activation. Each one was hand selected to integrate seamlessly into society.

Although Karl Junior's plan hadn't worked and was contrary to what they had instructed her to do, it now might be their only option. The blasted woman was even more popular after the failed attempt on her life. They couldn't chance her announcing her candidacy. They needed a permanent solution for Governor Sandra Murphy.

Bridget calmly waited while the two agents assigned to the back of the vehicle pulled their guns from their holsters, readying themselves to engage. Bridget hoped they had sent the A team; otherwise, things could get messy, and she hated messy.

The back door flew open, and the overwhelming force was no match for the two remaining agents. Although one agent managed to get off a few rounds, it wasn't enough to stop Bridget's comrades.

"Have you prepared the bunker for unwelcome guests?" Bridget crawled from the back of the van, pushing aside one agent lying in her path. She lifted her arms, presenting her handcuffs, and one of her men searched for the key.

"We're ready," the man answered, then slipped the key into the lock to undo the handcuffs.

Bridget shook her hands. "We better be. These women are very proficient. I am eager to avenge Mikhail's death. What about our other target? Does she still have around-the-clock security?"

The lead man grinned. "No, after your capture, she sent them packing."

"So, business as usual?" Bridget walked alongside the leader of the strike team.

"Not exactly. The governor took a last-minute flight to New York." Opening the door to a black SUV, he gestured for Bridget to climb inside.

Bridget secured her seat belt and looked at the leader. "Hmm, that is an odd twist. Why?"

Shutting the door and crawling into the driver's seat, he turned his head and answered, "Unknown, but she met up with the reporter who broke the story on our allies in the American government. She and the reporter are staying at the Four Seasons."

Another man slid into the passenger's seat, and four others quickly climbed into the second vehicle.

"That's not a coincidence. We need to activate a team to take both women out tonight," Bridget stated. "It should be fairly easy to accomplish without security hanging around. I don't care how it's done because the mission is blown to bits, anyway. Frankly, I don't care about the American assets at this point. Let the press or the government put the blame on them. After this is done, I want a way out of this despicable country. I'm no longer useful here."

"Yes, ma'am. I knew Mikhail. He was a good man." The leader started the vehicle, eased back onto the road, and made a U-turn, leaving the carnage behind. The second vehicle pulled ahead, stopping less than a quarter mile down the road, quickly removing the roadblock with the help of two uniformed officers waiting in front of the barrier.

Bridget sighed. "Yes, he was."

"What about your daughter?"

Bridget shrugged. "Let her be. It's not like she is useful or problematic for us at this point. I had high hopes for her, but she always was a stubborn little girl, not easily manipulated."

†

Jimena could almost hear the wheels turning in Em's head. The little wrinkle in the middle of her forehead was prominent. Jimena wondered if the call from Toni had disturbed her more than she was willing to admit. Knowing that the women in The Organization had put out a hit on her mother had to be jarring for Emma.

They returned to their room after Em's marriage proposal, watching the sunset and the disturbing news from Toni that her mother, Bridget Schmidt, had escaped. Em had been quiet on the way back from the beach.

"Hey, future wife, what is going on in that brilliant head of yours?" Jimena asked.

The wrinkle in her forehead deepened. "You know they aren't going to give up. Even with Bridget out of the picture, I imagine Governor Murphy's life is still at risk. Toni didn't say that, but my gut says this is too important to their plans. They'll try again. I'm sure of it."

167

"Okay, say you are one hundred percent correct. Unfortunately, there is not much we can do about that. I'm sure Homeland Security, the FBI, or whoever will protect Governor Murphy," Jimena reasoned.

"Maybe, but what if she has a false sense of security thinking that we neutralized the threat with Bridget in custody?" Em asked.

"Why don't you call Carter and make sure the governor still has a protective detail assigned to her? Would that make you feel better?"

Em nodded. "Thanks. It's not paranoia if they really are out to get you," Em teased, then picked up her phone and hit the contact for Adam Carter.

"Carter," he answered.

"Hey, Adam—"

"How in the hell did you find out so fast?" Carter asked.

"What are you talking about?" Em feigned innocence.

"Four agents are dead, and your mother escaped. Isn't that why you're calling?"

"No, I'm calling because I wanted assurance you are still protecting Governor Murphy. My mother is just the tip of the iceberg. I don't think they plan to give up anytime soon."

Adam cleared his throat. "Um, she sent Frank home after they captured your mother."

"Carter, you better send someone to protect her. I'd offer, but I'm not even in the country right now."

"Homeland Security is monitoring the situation. It's doubtful they'll try something again."

"Are you out of your fucking mind? It's the Russians."

"Okay, okay. Relax, I'll run it up the line. Just enjoy your vacation, and we'll talk when you return."

Em growled after the call ended.

"You want to go back, don't you?" Jimena asked.

"Is it awful of me to think the FBI isn't well-equipped to protect the governor? I mean, it is the agency I work for, but there are a lot of incompetent agents. I guess I only trust a few of them to do the job right."

"Snob," Jimena teased. "Hey, why don't you call Toni and tell her your concerns?"

"Good idea." Emma dug through her bag to find the card for the special number Toni had provided her. She really needed to memorize the number and destroy the card.

Toni answered on the second ring. "Em? What's up?"

"I'm worried they'll make another assassination attempt."

"Jeez, woman. Do you have ESP or something?"

"Shit, I knew it. I never should have left on vacation."

"Hey, you aren't the only one taking care of business. We're on it. While Bridget figured out we had a tracking device on her, she didn't know we'd also been monitoring all of her conversations. Your mother has an elevated sense of her own intelligence. We know their intentions, and they plan to give it another go. We have agents assigned to Governor Murphy. She's in New York right now. We sent

Val and Ronda to intercept the team that took out the transport vehicle. Sorry, Em, but she won't survive the day. Val and Ronda are the best at what they do."

"Not that I'm sentimental or anything, but if you have eyes and ears on Bridget, maybe you should keep her alive long enough to uncover the other Russian assets still in the US," Em suggested.

"Hmm, you have a point. My bot is longer lasting but has an expiration date. I suppose we could wait until we're no longer receiving intel and then take her out. Of course, she's planning on leaving the country soon, so we'll have to ensure that doesn't happen. Now, go and enjoy your time off."

"Thanks, Toni." Em ended the call and turned her focus to Jimena. "I'm ruining everything with you, aren't I?"

"Not at all. Your sense of duty is only one of the many things I love about you." Jimena smiled and then leaned in to kiss Em. "Now, I think it's time we went back to bed. Rising before dawn isn't exactly my idea of a good time. Although, getting a proposal of marriage made up for being yanked from slumber." Jimena held out her hand to admire her engagement ring.

†

Val had found the perfect location to set up once the SUV hit Ronda's trap. The explosive devices were intended to stop the vehicles, and Val's job was to eliminate the threat. She heard a crackle in her earpiece and wondered what the hell was happening now. Ronda was the best person to lay down the trap, so she doubted that was the problem.

Toni's voice rang loud and clear in her ear. "Abort mission, copy?"

"What? Why? We're all set up. Ronda doesn't fuck up, ever."

"It's not Ronda. I've told her to abort as well. I just talked to Emma, and she believes there are other operatives out there that we need to worry about. Frankly, she's right, and we have the perfect opportunity to learn more intel before we act. I'd like to clean out the hornet's nest—completely. Char agrees. I just conferred with her. I wish there was some way to inject new bots into Bridget so we can extend the time where we have her under complete surveillance. Good thing for us that Bridget doesn't know about the surveillance bots. She only knows we found a way to track her. She believes she's leading you to a trap."

Val cackled. "Even if they've laid a trap, you know I can find a way inside."

"I was hoping you would say that. Do you think you can get a new bot inside of Bridget?" Toni asked.

"Maybe. How much time do we have with the current one?" Val asked.

"Four or five days, max," Toni responded.

"Okay, that gives me time to put together a plan and a team. Besides, Bridget won't be expecting us to wait. That might work to our advantage. Catch them flat-footed."

"Agreed."

"Don't agree with me, nerd. It makes me nervous." Val shifted to a sitting position and packed her sniper rifle. "Ronda, are you catching all this?"

"Duh, she contacted me first. I've already packed up and am on my way back to the temporary compound. Last one back has to clean all the firearms." Ronda laughed.

"You're an adolescent, but I will still beat you. Gloria is gonna lap that piece of shit you call a sports car," Val taunted.

"I still think it's weird how you named your car. And you call Toni a nerd."

"Shut it, or when you finally roll up, I'll shut it for you," Val warned.

"Stop squabbling, children," Toni teased. "See ya back at the ranch. Hey, your little munchkin asked if she could spend time in the lab with her Aunt Toni and Aunt Dani. Is that okay with you?"

"Where's Gina? Is she okay?" Val felt her heart race with panic.

"Yeah, grandma. She's out with Cindy getting a mani-pedi."

"What the hell is a mani-pedi?"

"You know, manicure and pedicure," Toni answered matter-of-factly.

"Cindy wanted one of those?" Val didn't figure Cindy for a girly girl. She'd only heard Cindy bark orders and threaten her and the other agents whenever they'd rolled in with injuries after a challenging mission. As the head of the medical team, Cindy was a force not too many argued with.

Her wife, Gina, on the other hand, was about as opposite to Val as one could get. She was definitely the type to get a mani-pedi. Val smiled, thinking about Gina and how they'd gotten off on the wrong foot. Val assumed Gina was high maintenance and not worth her effort, but something shifted, and she was now blessed with a wife and kid she adored.

"Hey, gotta go. The little munchkin just walked in," Toni interrupted Val from her thoughts.

"Don't be teaching my kid any bad stuff, and for fuck's sake, don't show her your nerd experiments."

"Why not? The kid obviously got her intelligence from Gina. I'm only encouraging her natural abilities. It's better than teaching her how to take out an enemy from three hundred feet away."

"Fine. Later, Nerd."

†

As their vehicles approached the other hidden compound, nearly one hundred miles away from the one the blasted Organization had destroyed, Bridget's driver deactivated the newly installed security measures. This time, they wouldn't stand a chance.

After the driver opened her door, she snapped, "When they come for me, and they will, I don't want you to eliminate all of them. We need to know more about this mysterious group, and I plan on getting that information out of them, even if I have to remove every one of their non-essential body parts. One by one," Bridget added. "The Americans are amateurs with torture interrogation." Her steely gaze pinned the muscular man to his spot as he vigorously nodded his response. "What's your name? I ought to know if we will spend the next few days together."

"Vladimir," he answered.

Bridget smiled. "Excellent name." She followed Vladimir into the plain cement building. After confirming her identity at the biometric access door, they entered the tunnels below. Bridget wondered if they would attack this evening or wait until tomorrow. The last time, they didn't wait, so she was more than prepared to receive guests.

Once they reached the final hallway, Bridget pointed to Vladimir, gesturing for him to sit in the large room equipped with a conference table, rows of television sets, and a wall of complicated electronics. "I trust we will not have a repeat of the leak of our communications to the media. Have they figured out how that occurred?"

Vladimir shook his head. "They are still working on it. The current theory is that the Americans were sloppy with their phones."

"Our voices, Mikhail's and mine were on those tapes. Are you saying we were careless?" Bridget asked with cold fury in her voice. "Does he believe we betrayed our country?"

"No, ma'am. But we could not control the technology the Americans used," Vladimir answered.

"I trust our communications are secure." Bridget pointed at the row of monitors.

Vladimir nodded. "We are secure."

"Who is closest to the location of the governor?" Bridget asked.

"We have limited resources that remain in the country, but there is a couple in Maryland. They are closest to New York."

"Very well. Use the back door channel to summon them. I would like this taken care of immediately while the women in The Organization are busy trying to take me out." A feral smile appeared on Bridget's face.

Vladimir began typing on the computer, activating a secure video channel. A woman with mousy brown hair and spectacles appeared on one monitor. She glanced to her right and jerked her head before a balding man joined her.

"We've already been contacted to clean up the mess you've made," the woman answered.

"Don't contact us again," the man added.

Bridget glared at the couple. "You have no idea who you are talking to."

The screen went blank, and Bridget seethed. She still had valuable connections and wouldn't hesitate to use them. Vladimir had assured her he didn't believe Bridget was a traitor, but now she wasn't so sure about that. Time would tell. Her contact had freed her from the American government. Perhaps he would also arrange for her extraction from the country.

She longed to return to Russia. She could barely remember her country because she'd lived so long in the US. Bridget thought quickly about what type of insurance might assure her safety if something happened to her contact. She suspected he was the only person keeping her alive right now. On top of worrying about the mysterious Organization, Bridget was increasingly concerned about what the Kremlin might view as a clean-up operation. She had access to the names of every single Russian operative assigned to the United States. It was time to use that information as leverage.

CHAPTER THIRTEEN

"Living in New York might not be the worst thing. I never realized how many food vendors there were in the city. That gyro was to die for." Wynter slipped her arm inside Sandra's as they entered the hotel. "I probably shouldn't have ordered that second one. What time are our dinner reservations tonight?"

"Not until six-thirty," Sandra answered

"Are you sure the outfit I bought for the theater is okay? I wouldn't want to embarrass you." Wynter grinned.

"It's perfect. I didn't pack formal wear, so I'll be more casual than you. I wonder if we have time for a quick power nap. Someone kept me up last night and then insisted on getting an early start to the day."

Wynter flipped her wrist to glance at her watch. "Yeah, plenty of time. I'm a little knackered myself, plus I think I've put myself into a food coma."

Neither woman noticed the nondescript couple sitting in the lobby, watching as Sandra and Wynter made their way to the elevators. Nor did they notice the two women on the opposite side who stood and quickly followed Sandra and Wynter.

Before the elevator doors closed, the women entered, and Wynter finally took notice because both pinged Wynter's gaydar. After the doors closed, Wynter pressed the button for the twelfth floor.

"Governor Murphy and Ms. Holmes, we don't have much time. Your lives are in imminent danger. Please let us accompany you to your room."

"What? Who are you?" Sandra asked.

"That isn't important. We would have taken the assassins out, but there were too many people around, and we prefer to stay in the background. Unfortunately, with you being in such a public place, we don't have a lot of options but to follow you to your room."

"Are you from the FBI?" Wynter asked. "How do we know we can trust you?"

"We work with your contact, T. She intercepted the intel," the taller woman answered.

Wynter grabbed her phone and quickly pressed the button to call T. "Hey, T, there's two people claiming you sent them, or something like that. What the hell is going on?"

178

"Yeah, you can trust them. Hey, sorry, but I'm a little busy here. Just follow their directions, and you'll be fine." The phone call ended abruptly.

"She hung up on me," Wynter huffed.

The quieter woman held her hand over her mouth to keep from laughing before the woman in charge shot her a warning look.

When the doors opened, Sandra calmly announced, "I figure if either of these women wanted to kill us, we'd already be dead."

Everyone exited the elevator and made their way to Wynter's room. After Wynter opened the door, she directed her question to the woman who had been doing all the talking. "Do we get to know your names? Or only letters, like T."

Ignoring her question, the woman answered, "Both of you need to go into the bedroom. I suspect there will be a knock on the door in the next hour. We'll handle it."

"I guess a power nap is out of the question now," Sandra whispered.

"Why are you so Zen about this?" Wynter asked with considerable exasperation. "Maybe you were a bit premature in sending Frank home."

Sandra shrugged. "I refuse to live my life in fear. That only gives them more power."

"Governor, please. Can you discuss this from the safety of that bedroom?" The woman pointed to the sliding doors separating the bedroom from the rest of the suite.

†

Candy had let Sophie take charge. She was the more senior agent, and it didn't really matter much to Candy. She was just glad to have a mission. It had been a little boring for her because she didn't get to go with Char, Toni, Val, Sophie, and Ronda when they captured the Russian spy. But with Char still recovering, Val and Ronda following up on Bridget's escape, and Toni monitoring the treasure trove of intelligence, that left Sophie and Candy to protect the governor and the reporter. The minute Toni got wind of Governor Murphy catching the flight to New York, Char had asked Sophie and Candy for their assistance.

"Hey, Soph, are you worried the reporter will try to dig into The Organization?" Candy took a seat on the loveseat.

"Not really. Wynter is good, but Toni's been helping her out. I don't think we're at risk, especially after we wrap things up here."

"What makes you think eliminating this risk will do the trick? It sounds like there are others to take on the mantle. I hate how deep their operatives have embedded themselves inside," Candy lamented.

"Toni and Dani are working on getting the names of all the operatives. Once we have the list, it's just a matter of time before we let the CIA or Homeland Security take care of them, or we do their job for them," Sophie answered.

"I certainly hope so. I'm not very good at playing the role of bodyguard." A knock on the door interrupted Candy.

180

"Showtime. You ready?" Sophie asked.

Candy nodded, and Sophie yanked open the door to the surprised man wearing a uniform and pushing a room service cart.

The man didn't have time to react before the dart hit his neck. Sophie quickly pulled him inside and swiveled to Candy.

"Find the woman," Sophie directed, already patting down the prone figure.

Candy nodded and made her way quickly down the hall, finding the nondescript woman with spectacles pushing a housekeeping cart. The woman pulled a gun from underneath a stack of towels, but before she could get off a round, Candy had sent a dart in her direction. The woman slumped to the ground, and Candy made sure no one else was in the hallway before dragging the unconscious woman into the suite.

"Easy peasy," Candy declared after laying the woman's gun on the table and propping her into an empty chair next to the balding man who was out cold on the love seat.

The women quickly zip-tied their hands and feet before Sophie lifted her phone to her ear. "We need a team to collect the packages."

Sophie paused, asking, "Can Hank and Steve lend a hand?"

"Okay, well, do you have an estimate on how long we have to babysit?" After a few more seconds, Sophie continued. "Okay, fine. We'll wait here."

Candy turned her attention to the bedroom door and noticed the small crack. "Shit."

Sophie followed Candy's line of sight and sighed.

✝

The minute Sandra and Wynter closed the doors to the bedroom, Wynter waited a minute before prying them open a crack and peering through the opening.

"What are you doing?" Sandra asked.

Wynter turned her head and placed her index finger against her lips. "Shh. Trying to find out what's happening. Aren't you curious about them?"

"Yes, I suppose so, but I don't have as much interest as an investigative reporter. If what they told us is true, I'm just thankful they're here. I'm not sure I could live with myself if you're caught in the crossfire of an assassination attempt. I keep putting the people I love at risk. First, my mother, and now you."

Sandra's voice was so low that Wynter almost didn't hear what she said, but her ears perked up at Sandra's use of the word love. She knew Sandra cared, but love? That wasn't possible. She certainly wasn't there yet.

"While I would love to unpack what you just said, can you be quiet? I'm getting gold right now. The leader is Soph, and I think T is Toni. Wait, someone just knocked on the door," Wynter whispered. "Holy shit."

"What?"

"Some bald guy just went down, and Soph dragged him into the room."

182

"Why?" Sandra asked.

Wynter shrugged. "I'm assuming he's an assassin. Oh yeah, I don't think room service carries guns, and this guy had two on him."

"You're serious, aren't you?" Sandra stepped close to Wynter, attempting to spy on the events unfolding in the other room. She gasped when the other woman pulled another person inside, setting down a gun with an extra long barrel before pushing the unconscious woman onto a chair.

Wynter jerked back, causing Sandra to stumble and fall to the floor.

"You might as well come out now," Soph called from the other room.

Wynter offered her hand and made an exaggerated guilty face. "I guess we're busted."

"You're joking about this?" Sandra asked.

Wynter smiled. "Too soon? Okay, I'll hold back on the jokes until we get more details."

The women shuffled out of the bedroom, both wearing sheepish expressions. Wynter addressed Soph, "I don't think we've been properly introduced. I know your name is Soph, and you work for some kind of organization, but I didn't catch your colleague's name."

"Candy," the younger woman offered.

Soph glared at Candy. "Sophie, but our names are unimportant, nor is any other detail you think you heard while eavesdropping. We'll be out of your hair soon enough."

"What do you plan on doing with these two?" Sandra pointed at the man and woman who remained unconscious in the suite's seating area.

"We have colleagues who will help us transport these two to the authorities."

"Who are Hank and Steve?" Wynter asked.

Sophie pinched the bridge of her nose. "Char is going to kill us," she mumbled. "Look, I know you're some hotshot investigative reporter Toni has been helping, but we need you to resist digging. We're not your enemy. Nosing around could kill many good people. If you wish for Toni to continue to feed information to you, then you have to let this go."

"I would never reveal my sources," Wynter defended. "What now?"

"We wait for our team to arrive, and until we learn more, Candy and I were assigned to protect you," Sophie answered.

"Hope you like doing touristy things," Wynter quipped.

A scowl from Sophie was the only response Wynter received.

Politics of Love

CHAPTER FOURTEEN

Toni remained glued to her computer, watching through Bridget's eyes. She was thankful her new and improved surveillance bot had made its way to her eyes versus an ear. This time the signal would penetrate any barrier, including the thick steel walls of an underground structure. Vladimir had left the room after Bridget barked at him to give her some space.

Bridget had fixed herself a drink and appeared to be stewing. When she began to tap her nails on the table in an irritating staccato, Toni turned down the sound. An abrupt movement startled Toni, who was so bored that she'd almost nodded off. Bridget began rummaging in the drawers of the cabinets against the walls until she found a thumb drive.

185

Returning to the laptop on the table, she lifted the lid, then plugged in the thumb drive.

Toni leaned in to get a better look at her monitor. Squinting, she tried to make out the name of the file that Bridget was accessing, but the writing was too small. It seemed like there were several security channels and password prompts which, fortunately, Toni could see as Bridget pressed the keys on the laptop. After copying the highly secure file from the computer onto the drive, Bridget added a password to the thumb drive.

Toni's phone buzzed, and she scowled when noticing it was from Wynter. She didn't have time for a distraction. Quickly answering the call and telling Wynter to follow Sophie and Candy's instructions, she returned her attention to her monitor. Bridget went through several more security gates until accessing a video link.

"What the fuck?" Toni exclaimed.

Char's sister and her tech buddy, Dani, looked up from her monitor and asked, "What? Candy's okay, right?"

Toni waved her hand in the air. "Sorry, yeah, Candy's fine, but I'm looking at a ghost right now."

"A ghost?" Dani's brows knitted.

Toni adjusted the volume and lifted her finger in the air. "In a minute."

Mikhail's face filled the screen. But that wasn't possible. Their team had taken him out when they captured Bridget.

Mikhail shook his head. "Bridget, you cannot contact me until things calm. They're watching me very closely now."

"I need a favor, Dimitri."

Toni wrinkled her nose, and then it hit her. Dimitri had to be related to Mikhail, maybe a twin brother. *He was her contact, the one that arranged for her escape, but why was she contacting him? To get her out of the country?*

"I cannot make arrangements for you to leave the country yet. Everyone is looking for you." Dimitri frowned.

"No, I understand that. This favor is something else. I'm going to send Vladimir to place a very important thumb drive inside the safe deposit box Mikhail and I used for our passports and other important documents. I'll have him hide the key under the statue."

"What is in this thumb drive?" Dimitri asked.

"Insurance. They won't dare touch a hair on my head with the threat of this list getting out. I know many people who would pay handsomely for the list," Bridget declared.

"What if he calls your bluff?" Dimitri asked.

"He won't. I'll make sure he understands what's at risk. Any word on whether the other team completed the mission?" Bridget asked.

Dimitri frowned. "No, not yet, but it shouldn't be long now. I have to go."

The screen went dark, and Bridget stood, making her way out of the room. Toni watched Bridget travel through the tunnel until she reached two armed guards.

"Will you please find Vladimir for me and send him to the conference room?" Bridget directed.

"Yes, ma'am," one guard answered.

Toni had heard enough. She pulled her headphones off and pushed back from the computer. "Dani, I need you to take over monitoring Bridget."

"Okay." Dani grabbed her crutches and made her way to Toni's station.

Toni plucked the earbuds from the desk next to her mouse and pushed them in her ears. She touched the left bud and said, "Hey, Val, where are you right now?"

"Not too far from the house. Why?"

"Can you turn back around and intercept something from a man who will be leaving Bridget's compound? He was the driver of the main vehicle. Big guy. Blond. He'll be heading to a bank to deposit a thumb drive into a safe deposit box. We need that thumb drive."

"Okay. Ronda, are you still on?"

"Yup, right here. I just made a U-turn. I'm already on my way back."

"Don't use explosives, Ronda. I know that's your go-to move, but we can't take the chance of blowing up the thumb drive along with the driver," Toni instructed.

"I don't need you to tell me how to do my job," Ronda sniped.

Val laughed. "You got to admit, Ronda, Toni has you pegged."

"If what I suspect is on the thumb drive, you both have the green light to take Bridget out. I know that may be difficult with only a two-person team, but Sophie and Candy are busy with Wynter and Governor Murphy. And Char is out of commission for the rest of her pregnancy. I'm not risking our baby's life again," Toni stated.

"Any chance we can pull in Jimena and Em?" Ronda asked.

"Nope, they are on a well-deserved vacation," Toni answered.

"Hank and Steve?" Val suggested.

"No, we need them staying put for now. The Russians must desperately want the governor dead now that the plan to turn her didn't work out for them. They'll keep sending people, and Hank and Steve are our inside team with the connections to round them up once we find them." Toni began pacing. "I just figured since you were on your way back and halfway there already, although we have time if you want to assemble a team. There are less experienced agents we can pull in, but you can't scare them, Val."

"Fuck that. Ronda and I can handle it. We'll go in tonight after we get your drive," Val declared. "Do you know how many are protecting their bunker?"

"Twice as many as last time, and we had a full team. Plus, I'm guessing this one is just as booby-trapped as the last one, maybe even more. You can't go in blind. Let me see what else I can discover before you infiltrate the bunker. I can send Dani as tech support." Toni stopped pacing and glanced at her friend, who had looked up when she heard her name. Dani grinned and shot both thumbs up.

"No," both Ronda and Val answered. "Char would kill us if something happened to Dani," Ronda added. "She hasn't stopped beating herself up after that undercover mission went to shit, and Dani ended up with a permanent injury."

"Can't you hack their systems from your lab?" Val asked. "We have all the other gadgets to help us out. I'm not a total incompetent with your prototypes."

Toni smiled. "Yeah, okay. Bridget practically handed me all the passwords and information needed to access their system from here. Just keep in contact—"

"I've got eyes on a black SUV that looks like the vehicle we tracked before," Ronda interrupted. "I do believe this is our man. Val, where are you at?"

"Right behind you, I see your dot on my screen." Toni could hear the screeching of tires through her earbuds. "Taking a side road and setting up for a shot to the tires."

"Got it. I'll take clean up."

"Don't blow the SUV up," Toni warned.

"I have finesse, you know," Ronda answered. "Don't worry. I'll get your precious thumb drive. Gotta go now…"

†

Bridget tried not to worry about how abruptly Dimitri had ended the call. She hoped she could trust Mikhail's brother. Bridget had known for some time how he felt about her, but she hadn't needed to leverage those feelings with Mikhail by her side. Now that Mikhail was dead, Dimitri was an important ally. She supposed she had loved Mikhail in her own way. He was an adequate lover and Emma's father. But if she were honest with herself, none of the men in her life mattered all that much. Dimitri needed to remain alive long enough to get her out of the States and hide her insurance until she found a way to sell the drive and disappear forever.

After realizing what a colossal mistake it had been to involve Karl Junior in their plans, Bridget had expected their government contacts would work with the authorities to obtain her release. However, it became clear that the Russian government had decided to cut its losses. She supposed she didn't blame them. She would have made the same decision. It had surprised Bridget when they allowed her to make a call. She'd taken a chance that Dimitri would not let her wither in some hole the Americans planned on taking her to. And he hadn't. Bridget knew she had to play things just right. Let Dimitri think he was a hero, and believe she was so thankful for his strength and cunning that it was only natural for her to fall for him. She would play on his feelings. If there was one thing Bridget was good at, it was acting a part.

She smiled at Vladimir's eagerness to run her errand. He, too, was enamored with her. She still had it. God had blessed her with the kind of beauty that appealed to many men and women. She had never used that advantage on a woman. Just the thought of being intimate with a woman disgusted her. How had a daughter of hers turned out that way? At first, she had been reluctant to use her daughter's affliction to turn the governor, but Mikhail had convinced her it was for the greater good. Perhaps that is when the shine faded, and now she seriously considered turning on her

191

beloved Russia. Self-preservation ranked a lot higher than the greater good in her mind.

Bridget sipped her drink. There was nothing to do now but wait for Vladimir to return. She prepared for the eventual attack on the compound. Her eyes traveled to the monitors. So far, the monitors had detected nothing outside the cement building, but that could change at any minute.

Immediately after Bridget heard a ding, Dimitri's face appeared on the screen. "Bridget, John and Mary have not reported back yet. They've activated another team who will strike again tonight—ones who will blend in more if they choose to go to a women's bar tonight. We're running out of agents. He's nervous. He thinks you've betrayed us with so many things going sideways lately. I know you haven't, but I don't think you're safe anymore. Is there anyone you can trust in the bunker?"

"I just sent Vladimir out with the thumb drive. He's the only one I trust. The others are soldiers who will undoubtedly follow whatever orders their superiors give them," Bridget answered.

"Find a weapon and a place to hide. I'll try to get you out of there." Dimitri's head turned to the right as something momentarily distracted him.

"I'll send a message, warning them of the thumb drive. That should buy us more time."

"But I do not have this yet." Dimitri returned his focus to the screen in front of him.

"He doesn't know that," Bridget answered. But Bridget had a bad feeling. When she entered the tunnel, she realized there were no guards around. She began frantically checking every single room and found nothing.

†

"Fuck! Ronda, we have company. Another SUV coming up fast. Looks like he's trying to intercept the first one. I'm taking them both out. Can you handle things until I get there?" Val asked.

"Any chance you know which one has the thumb drive?" Ronda asked.

Val answered before taking a deep breath and squeezing out her first shot. "First vehicle skidding down the road."

Well aimed, her second shot caught the front right tire of the second vehicle. Before a minute had passed, Val had added two more shots. Both cars skidded almost out of control until they stopped on the side of the road. Val scrambled from her vantage point and began running toward the SUVs just as Ronda approached and slammed her car into the driver's side of the first SUV, pinning the driver inside.

Three men scrambled from the second vehicle, guns blazing at both cars. If this was the FBI or some other authorities, why would they shoot at Ronda? Val squatted on the ground and quickly picked off two men, praying they were not from the US Government. Ronda's door flew open, and she rolled on the ground, narrowly avoiding two shots that hit the dirt. Val didn't have a good shot. She hoped Ronda had something on her to take out the third man. The driver in the first SUV had slumped against the steering wheel. Out of the corner of her eye, she noticed the third man crumple to the ground. Carefully approaching the first vehicle, Val arrived beside Ronda's car and leveled her handgun at the shattered window. Ronda swung to the passenger's side, aiming her gun at the man draped over the dash. She pressed her finger against his neck and shook her head.

Almost sensing the impending danger, Val looked up and noticed a dust cloud in the distance. Squinting, she brought her binoculars to her eyes and swore. "Fucking A. What the hell is going on?" A row of at least ten more SUVs traveled along the road. They weren't necessarily in a hurry like the previous two vehicles, but Val didn't want to stick around and find out what new shitstorm was headed their way.

"We need to find the thumb drive and get the fuck out of here. We've got company coming soon."

"Damn, I hate digging into a dead man's pants pockets," Ronda grumbled as she crawled inside and pushed the man back against the seat. Then she began checking his pockets.

Val picked up a padded envelope from the back seat behind the driver and ripped it open. Plucking the thumb drive from inside, she lifted the prize in the air. "Got it. Let's go."

Ronda pushed the man back onto the steering wheel and scrambled out of the car. Val had already slipped into the driver's seat and turned the key. At first, the car wouldn't start, and she slammed her hand against the steering wheel. Ronda slipped into the passenger seat just as Val turned the key again, and the sports car purred to life. They fishtailed away from the wreckage as Val spun the car toward where she'd left her baby. After she reached her own vehicle, she jumped out. Ronda immediately crawled over the middle console and into the driver's seat.

Although Val wanted to pull out her binoculars again and see how close they were to the line of vehicles, she resisted and peeled out, following Ronda down the dusty road. Soon they would reach the highway again, and then she would breathe easy. Hearing a muffled explosion, Val turned her head and watched in shock at the plume of smoke rising in the air. She noted it was still a fair distance away. If not at the Russian bunker, it had to be very close. *What the fuck is going on?*

Tapping her earbud, Val asked, "Toni, shit is hitting the fan here. What just happened?"

"I have no idea. Surveillance just went dark. Describe everything on your end."

"A big line of vehicles was about to intercept, but we got out of there, hopefully in time. Then I heard an explosion that I estimate was five miles away, maybe less. Of course, it's hard to judge distance out here."

"Did you get the thumb drive?" Toni asked.

"Yup. Had to take out three men. The guy with the thumb drive was already dead when we approached the vehicle."

"Shit, okay. Makes sense now. I think the Russians are cleaning up. If I had to make an educated guess, they just took out Bridget and were after the thumb drive. I'm going to backtrack and try to hack into Dimitri's system."

"Who the hell is Dimitri?" Val asked.

"Tell you later. Be careful. If the Russians figure someone else has taken the drive, they won't stop until they find you. Don't make any pit stops on your way back to the house. Speed if you have to. I'm hacking into the highway patrol right now. I'll make sure you have a free pass all the way to San Diego," Toni informed.

"You're paying to get my car fixed," Ronda interjected.

"What happened to your car?" Toni asked. "Never mind. Just get your asses back to the compound. You can tell me all about it then."

CHAPTER FIFTEEN

Wynter watched as two women dressed as paramedics rolled in two gurneys and put the unconscious assassins on them. Her curiosity was getting the best of her, and she blurted, "Those are real medics, aren't they?"

"The less you know, the better. Ignorance sometimes is bliss," Sophie answered.

"What do you plan to do with them?" Sandra asked. "I cannot condone murder, even if they are Russian assassins."

Candy smiled. "Don't worry. While we sometimes play fast and loose with the laws, we aren't planning on killing them. Our trust in our government to keep them detained until they can stand trial is not very high, but we always have a contingency plan."

197

Sophie's phone buzzed, and she answered, "Hey, Toni, I'm a little busy here. What?" She paused as she listened to whoever was on the line. "Well, one problem solved. I'm not crying any tears."

Wynter desperately wanted to know what Toni was telling her. She pretended to focus on something else but remained close enough to hear every word Sophie said.

"Finally, some good news and a certain someone didn't have to go all cowgirl, risking her life. Sounds like we may finally have the ultimate upper hand. Talk to you later." Sophie ended her call and narrowed her eyes at Wynter.

Wynter met her steely gaze. "Aw, come on. You can't leave us in the dark. What if I promise you that everything will remain off the record? We have a right to know what's going on, especially if it impacts our lives."

"No, you don't, Wynter. Toni will continue to feed you information, but everything happens on our timeline, not yours."

"Fucking spies, even if you're the good guys," Wynter mumbled. "Wait. Are you CIA?"

"No," Sophie answered with a tinge of irritation in her voice.

Sandra touched Wynter's arm. "I know following a lead on a big story is important to you, but I'm just happy they were here for us. I'm not sure what to do now. Your association with me is putting your life in danger. Perhaps I should hire extra security for you."

Wynter sighed. "I'd really rather not have someone following me around. It puts a damper on both my personal and professional plans. But you're right about one thing. I should thank these women, not try to get another story out of them. At least for now, we've averted the crisis."

"For now is the operative phrase," Sophie responded. "If you had plans tonight, I suggest you cancel them. Until we learn a little more, there may be others ready to act."

"No, no way. We've already had a miserable two-and-a-half years with this pandemic crap. Now that we're returning to normal, I am not giving up my freedom to enjoy life." Wynter glared at Sophie. "How about if we get you tickets to a Broadway show and you can accompany us? Who doesn't like Broadway in New York?" Wynter turned her attention to Sandra. "Can your contacts get us two more tickets and maybe arrange for the dinner reservations to include two more?"

"Let me see what I can do?" Sandra responded.

Candy smiled. "I do love Broadway. I wish Dani was here. She would be over the moon for a chance to see a Broadway production."

"Who's Dani?" Wynter asked. "Your girlfriend?" She grinned unrepentantly.

Sophie growled, "I don't think this is a very good idea."

"I'll bet Kim drug you to several plays with her background in theater. I've never been to any, myself. I doubt they'll stage another assault so soon. They probably won't even know we blew apart this attempt. Come on, Soph, live a little," Candy pleaded.

"Yeah, Soph, live a little. Who's Kim? Is she your girlfriend?" Wynter teased.

"Fine," Sophie huffed. "But in exchange, no more questions. And don't call me Soph. I don't know you well, and I don't intend to get to know you. Reporters are as bad as politicians."

Wynter shrugged. "Maybe, but Sandra doesn't fit into that neat little good or bad box you've created in your head. Have you always made ethical decisions, Sophie? If my philosophy classes have taught me one thing, it's that there are different perspectives surrounding ethics. Very few individuals can claim purity of motives with every decision they make. Maybe not even one person in this world, because most of us are self-serving, and the rest only believe they are taking the moral high ground."

While Wynter was debating philosophy with Sophie, Sandra had stepped away and made a call. When she returned, she updated the group. "My assistant got two more tickets, but they're a few rows away. It was the best she could do."

"Let me go on record and state I do not like this." Sophie's mouth formed a grim line.

"It's not like they know we're heading to a Broadway musical or know what seats we have. Won't the most dangerous moments occur when we're on our way, not while we're in the theater?" Wynter asked. "Besides, another attempt so soon doesn't seem likely to me."

"Then you haven't been paying attention. You have no idea who you're up against," Sophie grumbled.

"Russian government colluding with alt-right politicians. I think I have a pretty good idea," Wynter replied. "Sometimes, bringing the horror of politics into the light of day is worth the risk."

†

The four women climbed into the roomy limousine CNN had provided to Wynter during her temporary stay in New York. Sandra watched Sophie and Candy's constantly rotating heads. While she certainly wasn't oblivious to the dangers, Sandra's level of attention did not come close to the taciturn woman sent to keep her and Wynter safe. Candy seemed less stringent but equally observant of her surroundings. Sandra wondered if her powerful mother had anything to do with the cloak and dagger security detail assignment.

"Did my mother arrange for you to follow us around?" Sandra asked.

"No," Sophie answered. "No more questions from you, either," she added.

The conversation was stilted at dinner. Candy tried, but the recalcitrant Sophie remained quiet during most of the meal. This was not how Sandra wanted her evening to unfold. She'd been having so much fun getting to know Wynter, relishing every moment with her. She knew that in the not too distant future, that would come to a screeching halt with their jobs taking them miles apart.

After they had taken their seats, Sandra turned around and noticed Sophie touching her ear. A frown appeared on her face. Then, both women abruptly stood and made their way to the aisle, continuing to scan the crowd, causing seated patrons to grumble as the show was about to begin.

Sandra's anxiety skyrocketed when the women exited the theater. She grabbed Wynter's hand, squeezed it, and whispered in her ear, "Something spooked our friends. They just left the theater."

"I sense they are very good at what they do. I trust Sophie and Candy to keep us safe." Wynter moved her other hand on top of their clasped hands. She gently caressed Sandra's hand. "It'll be fine."

†

Sandra tried hard to concentrate on the stage during the first half of the musical, but it was hard to enjoy the production, wondering where their two protectors had gone. Distracted by the impending doom she felt, Sandra didn't notice when the lights in the theater came on, indicating it was intermission. Wynter stood and stretched.

"I need to use the restroom," Wynter announced. "I sure hope the lines aren't too long."

"I'll come with you. I have a bad feeling that I can't seem to shake ever since Candy and Sophie left the theater." Sandra followed Wynter down the aisle.

A long line had already formed outside of the closest restroom. An attendant pointed to a staircase and instructed, "There's another restroom on the second floor. It usually has a shorter line."

Wynter nodded and hurried up the stairs. Sandra followed closely behind. Sandra thought it was strange that the attendant followed them to the alternate bathroom. Wynter grinned and pointed to the door where only one other woman, dressed casually, waited outside. After that, several women exited, but the woman didn't enter.

Sandra looked at the woman expectantly, and she smiled and answered. "It's a smaller restroom than the one downstairs. I prefer to wait outside rather than try to cram myself into a small space with more people than the fire marshals allow."

Sandra nodded. Another woman exited, and the claustrophobic woman pushed the door open, revealing a nearly empty room with four available stalls. Sandra and Wynter followed her inside the space. Wynter rushed to an open stall, and Sandra leaned against the sink, waiting for her.

Sandra could hear a muffled altercation outside the restroom, and goosebumps appeared on her arms. The other woman who had entered the other stall burst out and glanced at Sandra. As the remaining door opened, Sandra noticed the knife in the woman's hand. She met Wynter's startled eyes before the door nearly splintered when Sophie burst inside, dragging an unconscious woman.

Wynter kicked the woman's hand, and the knife clattered to the floor, skidding to the far corner. Unfortunately, Sandra didn't have time to celebrate Wynter's quick reaction before the woman pulled a gun free, and the horrific event unfolded before she had a chance to react.

†

Toni's voice interrupted Sophie and Candy as they took their seats three rows behind Governor Murphy and Wynter. Sophie touched her ear to turn down the volume so nobody around her detected any sound through her earbuds.

"There's going to be a second attempt tonight. My guess is that the Russians are going to send two women. I'm waiting for Ronda and Val to return with a thumb drive that might provide additional information. It's possible we might have pictures to send."

Sophie had made it to the cove outside the orchestra seating and responded, "Copy that." She turned to Candy. "We're flying blind here."

"They've locked the doors. We won't be able to go inside until intermission," Candy noted.

Sophie nodded. "If I were to arrange a hit, I'd probably want to isolate them."

"Bathrooms," Candy stated.

"Yup. Take the first floor, and I'll check out the second-floor facilities."

Candy nodded.

Sophie made a beeline up the curving staircase and noticed a woman exiting the bathroom in a uniform with a small duffel in her hands. The woman tugged on her shirt, which appeared one size too small for the brawny woman. Sophie had a bad feeling. Pushing her way inside, she checked each stall and spied two legs under a locked stall.

"Hello," she called.

When Sophie didn't hear any response, she crouched and peeked under the door, finding a small woman with her head resting against one side of the stall. Her dead eyes stared blankly ahead with a small bullet hole in her forehead. "Son of a bitch," Sophie swore. She'd have to deal with the woman later.

Rushing outside, she searched the empty space, not finding the assassin. After Sophie hurried down the stairs, she pushed the door to the closest bathroom and found Candy checking each stall.

"Dead woman in the upstairs bathroom. A brawny woman with short blond hair is wearing her uniform. I guess they're going to direct Governor Murphy and Wynter into that bathroom."

"Pretty risky. How do the assassins know the governor or Wynter will need to use the restroom at intermission?" Candy asked.

"They don't, but it's their best option to get them isolated in this crowd. It's what I would do. Then I'd have a backup plan. Russian assassins work in teams, so I suspect the other will try something else if their bathroom ruse doesn't work," Sophie answered. "I'm going to find this woman and take her out before she has a chance to activate their plan. If you find her first, go ahead and eliminate the threat."

Candy patted her pocket. "I love these dart pens. So much cleaner than using a gun, plus we get to interrogate them before handing them over to the authorities." Candy continued to move in the open area, heading for the various bars and merchandise booths inside the large theater.

Sophie took the stairs to check out the second floor where additional concession stands were located. She became increasingly frustrated when she didn't find the woman she was looking for. A little over an hour passed, and neither Candy nor Sophie saw the mysterious woman. Sophie glanced at her watch and realized that intermission was, at most, five minutes away.

Speaking into her communication device, she clipped out an order. "Cover the second-floor bathroom. I'll take the doors outside the orchestra seating."

"Copy that," Candy responded.

Attendants rushed to the doors right before they opened, and men and women began pouring out. Trying to go against the flow of the crowd was proving impossible, and Sophie started to panic until she saw Wynter and Governor Murphy exiting through a different entrance.

"Shit," Sophie muttered as she pushed her way back through the crowd, but this time she was going with the flow instead of against it. However, the amoeba of theatergoers still blocked her way. She watched helplessly as the brawny blonde directed Governor Murphy and Wynter to the restroom on the second floor. She hoped Candy was already there and had taken care of whoever was this woman's partner.

Pushing against men and women who blocked her way, Sophie ignored the dirty looks and multiple comments about her rudeness. Instead, she listened intently while the blonde directed patrons to another bathroom stating the one she was standing in front of was out of order. The outside door had a sign that said *Out of Order*.

Sophie didn't have any other option. She would have to take this woman out and potentially expose herself. Rushing up the stairs, she briefly caught the woman's eyes before sending a dart into her neck and catching the woman before she slumped to the ground. Sophie hastily pushed inside the restroom, holding the woman up and carrying her inside.

Where the hell is Candy? Now that Sophie was inside, she quickly surveyed the scene in front of her. Letting go of the unconscious woman, she turned to face a woman with a gun, who had pivoted in her direction when she burst through the door. Her peripheral vision caught Wynter diving for the corner. Fortunately for Sophie, the momentary distraction caused the woman to aim her gun at Wynter, giving Sophie enough time to kick the gun from her hands and follow with a punch to her face.

With the knife in her hand, Wynter scrambled to her feet as Sophie and the blonde exchanged blows.

"Get the gun," Wynter screamed.

Sandra seemed frozen in place before reacting and reaching under one of the stall doors for the gun. Then, screaming, she crawled away but held the gun in her hand.

Sophie finally retrieved her dart pen, and a dart found its mark as the blonde slumped to the ground. Both assassins blocked the exit.

Sandra stood wide-eyed and blurted, "There's a dead woman in that stall."

"Yeah, I know," Sophie answered.

Sandra's eyes widened further.

"No, I didn't kill her," Sophie huffed.

"Hey, there's another person in this stall," Wynter announced.

Sophie lowered herself to the floor and peeked inside the stall. Seeing Candy slumped on the toilet brought Sophie's anger to the surface. She crawled into the tight space under the door and put her finger against Candy's neck. "Oh, thank fuck," she declared.

Detecting a slight ether-like odor, she assumed the assassins had used chloroform. Sophie touched her earbud. "Toni, I need that team to come to the theater for clean-up. We're in the second-floor bathroom with an out-of-order sign on it. The open area should be relatively clear in about another five to ten minutes. It's intermission right now. Candy's down."

"What?" Dani screeched.

"Don't worry, they didn't kill her. She's just going to have a hell of a headache when she wakes. Maybe a little puking, but she'll be okay. Just in case, you might also want to send someone with medical training." Sophie opened the stall door and awkwardly moved inside the small space to carry Candy outside.

"They're on their way. Should be there in about fifteen minutes. Can you hang on for that long?" Toni asked.

"Yeah, sure, we'll just have a little tea party in the bathroom," Sophie grumbled as she gently placed Candy on the floor propped against the wall.

"I'd prefer a stiff drink right about now. Damn, I really wanted to see the rest of the show," Wynter quipped.

Sandra and Sophie turned to Wynter with twin expressions of exasperation.

Wynter nodded. "Too soon again? Sorry, jokes are my defense mechanism."

"Want some good news?" Toni asked. The lilt in her voice suggested it was something big.

"Yes, I could use some right now since this nearly went up in flames," Sophie answered.

"That thumb drive has the names and locations of every Russian agent in the US right now. We even have their photos. I've already sent this to Steve and Hank. We'll let them take credit for it. But it's a major blow. They'll take years to regroup."

"Does that mean no more babysitting duty?" Sophie asked.

"Probably, but I would recommend that Governor Murphy employ regular security. There are still all those domestic terrorists, and while they aren't well-trained, they could be as lethal as the Russians," Toni answered.

"I'll make that recommendation. Okay, we're heading to the main compound tonight. Any estimate on how long you'll be in San Diego?" Sophie asked.

"Char needs to recover. I don't want to chance traveling while she's still on the mend. Dani might want to fly out tonight, though."

"Yes, I'll take the next flight I can get," Dani interjected.

"See you soon. Don't worry. I promise Candy is fine," Sophie assured those listening through the earbuds before moving her gaze back to Governor Murphy and Wynter.

"Anything we can do to help?" Wynter asked.

"Nope. Now we wait," Sophie answered.

"Candy is going to be okay, right?" Governor Murphy asked.

"Yes," Sophie answered as she sat next to Candy, ensuring she didn't fall over and hit her head on the floor.

†

The efficiency of the mysterious Organization removed the two assassins from the restroom, leaving zero evidence behind. Wynter would have no proof of either attempt at Sandra's life. Back at the hotel, Wynter paced nervously, mulling over how she would broach the topic of an exclusive interview with Sandra. Her reporter's sixth sense also told her something significant had happened, and Wynter was dying to know what Sophie had learned from her earlier phone conversation.

Finally, Sandra stood up from where she had settled on the love seat with a stiff drink. Making her way to Wynter, she gently took her hand and stopped her pacing.

"Come, sit." Sandra turned to face Wynter and put her hands against her face. Then, with a gentle caress to her cheek, she said, "I am so sorry, Wynter. You don't deserve to be caught up in any of this. I've placed your life in danger. Twice. I don't know that I can continue to do that."

"What? Please don't tell me you're ending things. And here, all I've been worried about for the past hour is how to approach you." Wynter stared glassy-eyed at Sandra.

"What do you mean, how to approach me?" Sandra asked.

"I want to do an exclusive interview with you," Wynter confessed.

"Okay. Why does that worry you? Of course I would grant you an exclusive interview. Did you promise that to CNN?"

"No." Wynter furrowed her brow. "Although that was in the back of my mind to have you comment on the tapes, the assassination attempts happened after my stint on CNN."

Wynter saw recognition dawn on Sandra's face, and the horror and disappointment made Wynter question what kind of person would take advantage of their situation.

Sandra created distance between them. "I'd like to believe I'm not just another story to you. These women risked their lives to keep us safe. The least we can do is respect their need to stay under the radar. They've gone to great lengths to remain undetected, and we've accepted those decisions."

"I promised them I would not reveal their identities. I've never exposed a confidential informant," Wynter defended herself.

"Wynter, you're a bright woman. These women, except for this Toni person whom you've obviously had contact with before, are not confidential informants," Sandra explained patiently. "Can't you let this go? Arrange an interview with me if you need to bolster your career more, but I won't confirm anything that happened today. I refuse to put these women at risk."

Wynter put her head in her hands. "Shit. I am displaying the worst elements of my profession. I don't even know how to be a human being anymore. And, for the record, you are not just a story to me. So please, don't shut me out. I'm pretty sure I'm falling for you. I doubt they would have left us alone if they thought there was still a risk that others would come after you."

Sandra laid a hand on Wynter's back. "Is this the kind of life you really envisioned for yourself? Goddess forbid I actually become the president of the United States. Secret Service agents will follow us around twenty-four-seven. Privacy is limited. The press will hound *you* instead of the other way around."

Wynter lifted her head and smiled. "Totally worth it. The sex alone makes it worthwhile."

A half smile appeared on Sandra's face. "I doubt I'm the best you've ever had."

Wynter grabbed Sandra's hands and answered with a level of seriousness she didn't know she possessed. "Never,

ever, doubt yourself. I'm up for being followed twenty-four-seven, especially if we can request some hot FBI or attractive Secret Service agents when you become president. I'm in this for the long haul. I apologize for my assholery before. You're right. Those women were impressive, but if they wish to remain ghosts, I need to respect that. Can I still take you up on that exclusive interview?"

"Absolutely."

Wynter smacked her hand against her forehead. "Hey, I just thought of something. Remember when you wanted me to track down Emma Schmidt and Jimena Aguilar's addresses?"

"Um, yes," Sandra answered hesitantly.

"Emma is a slippery devil, but Jimena still lives in her parent's old home. I found her address and phone number. They're both competent women. And easy on the eyes, too. I asked Toni to track Emma's address, but she wouldn't give me that information."

"You don't think they're also part of this mysterious group of women, do you?" Sandra asked.

Wynter shrugged. "I don't think so. Both Emma and Jimena work for the government. While Sophie had that FBI vibe to her, Candy was clearly not a government type. I could do some digging on Sophie, see if I can find out if my gut on her is correct."

Sandra shook her head. "Looks like I am going to have to be your Jiminy Cricket. Separating the reporter from the woman is going to be tough, isn't it?"

"I have an overdeveloped curiosity gene, huh? What if I do that research only to satisfy my need to know? Does that eliminate your concerns, Jiminy?"

"Fine, Curious George. I suppose we can't let your skills go to waste. I'll take that contact information for Jimena."

"See, my skills are useful," Wynter taunted before pulling out her phone and accessing her notes app. Then, grabbing a pad of paper, she scribbled the contact information for Jimena Aguilar and pushed the notepad to Sandra, who smiled back at her.

"Never said they weren't. Thank you."

"So what's my reward for all my hard work getting that information?" Wynter asked.

Sandra took Wynter's hand and pulled her to a standing position, leading her to the bedroom. "Follow me, and you'll find out."

CHAPTER SIXTEEN

Em had called for room service after deciding a leisurely breakfast on the veranda would be a good start to the day. They'd mostly been relaxing on the beach, but today they had an excursion planned for later, and Em wanted to have something in her stomach before the boat captain began mixing drinks. Apparently, it was a thing to start cocktails early. Jimena had a hard and fast rule of never before noon, but they usually had lunch later in the day.

Em had just taken a sip of her coffee when she heard one of their phones go off inside. Shortly after, the other phone started ringing. Jimena shot her a perplexed look but stood to retrieve the phones.

Jimena handed Em her phone, then looked at the screen before her nose wrinkled in confusion. When Em saw who was calling, she quickly pressed the button to answer the call. She noted how Jimena let her call go to voice mail and assumed it was a number she didn't recognize.

"Hank, what's up?"

"It's been an eventful twenty-four hours. Look, I didn't want to disturb you on vacation, but I thought you should know."

"My mother is dead," Em answered.

"Yeah, did Toni already call? How do you know?"

"Toni called to let me know she escaped a few days ago, and they were pursuing a more permanent solution. Given the efficiency of The Organization, I figured they achieved their goal," Em stated without emotion.

"It wasn't The Organization, Em," Hank responded. "Plus, there's a lot more."

"What do you mean it wasn't The Organization?" Em asked.

Jimena's worried look caught Em's attention. "Hey, Hank, can I put you on speaker? Jimena is right here, and I want her to hear everything."

"Sure, that's fine," Hank answered.

Em pulled her phone from her ear and activated the phone speaker.

"As best we can figure, the Russians determined Bridget was too much of a detriment to their plans. She'd been compromised and was no longer valuable to them. Mikhail has a twin brother, and he was the one that arranged for her escape, not the Russians. She tried to get a thumb drive to him, but Val and Ronda managed to steal it from her man. Long story short, the thumb drive had all the names and contact information for every Russian agent stationed in the US. We've rounded up all of them except for Dimitri. He's gone underground."

"Who the hell is Dimitri?" Em asked.

"Mikhail's twin brother."

"Why would Bridget put such sensitive information on a thumb drive?" Jimena asked.

"Insurance. Bridget already suspected that the Russian government would turn on her," Hank answered. "I guess since Dimitri helped Bridget, the Russians assumed he was compromised as well."

"Well, that is all good news. I'm glad you called to let me know. Now don't call again. We're still on vacation," Em teased.

"Sorry, that isn't all. The Russians made two assassination attempts on Governor Murphy and Wynter Holmes, the reporter that broke the story."

"What story?"

"The one that CNN reported on while they still had Bridget in custody. Since your mother was on those tapes, the assumption was that the Russians cleaned up their mess. Mikhail was already dead, so he was no longer a problem to them. Governor Murphy must be a larger threat to their plans than we originally thought."

"You said attempts, right? I presume that means they weren't successful," Em stated.

"Nope, The Organization sent Sophie and Candy to protect the governor and Wynter."

"Candy?" Jimena asked.

"You haven't met her yet," Hank answered.

"Are they still assigned to the governor?" Em asked.

"No, we've determined the threat was reduced after the FBI and Homeland Security rounded up all the other agents except Dimitri. Dimitri isn't much of a threat without resources, especially since he is now on the run. The governor still has the alt-right domestic terrorists to contend with, but most of them are idiots who couldn't find their ass with both hands in broad daylight."

"I wouldn't be too sure of that. Remember, my brother was one of those assholes and was far from stupid."

"True. Listen, Toni has been feeding Wynter information. That's how she broke the story."

"I thought Anderson Cooper broke the story?" Em was confused.

"Wynter worked for TRU, and when they wouldn't run the story, she asked Toni to send the information to CNN with the details that Wynter was the one who uncovered the tapes."

"Okay, that's interesting, but why is that important to me?" Em asked.

"Toni said that Wynter tried to get your contact information. She's a reporter and a damn good one," Hank said.

"Great, now I have to worry about this one hounding me, like I didn't have enough of the vermin following me around," Em groused. "Thanks for the heads up. Anything else I need to know?"

"Nope. Enjoy the rest of your vacation," Hank said.

"Hey, you should send some agents to shadow the governor for a while or convince her to hire a good security team," Em suggested.

"You interested?" Hank asked.

"Not really. I prefer undercover work," Em answered.

"Too bad. The governor seemed impressed with you and Jimena. I wouldn't be surprised if she didn't ask if you were available."

"Well, I'm not because I'M ON VACATION."

"Got it. Bye, Em. Bye, Jimena." Hank clicked off, and Jimena started laughing.

"What are you laughing about?" Em asked.

"A little protective of our time together, aren't you?"

"Damn right I am because we both deserve this. So who called you?" Em asked.

Jimena shrugged. "Don't know. I didn't recognize the number, so I left it to voice mail. Probably a scammer. I rarely answer if I don't recognize the number." Jimena glanced at her phone and wrinkled her nose. "Somebody left a voice mail. I suppose I should listen if it's something important and they blocked the number for a reason. Maybe it's Toni. She would definitely block her number. But why didn't she call you if she wanted to give us an update?"

"No clue. Now you have me curious," Em answered.

"I'll put it on speaker." Jimena picked up her phone and activated the voice mail.

"Hello, Ms. Aguilar. I'm sorry to bother you by calling on your personal phone. This is Governor Murphy.

I've been attempting to contact you and your colleague, Agent Schmidt, for some time now. Unfortunately, you are both nearly impossible to track down. Neither of your agencies was very helpful. Besides thanking you properly, I was hoping we might meet and discuss another matter. You can reach me at 619-235-4011. That is my personal cell number."

"Should I call her back?" Jimena asked.

Em threw her hands in the air. "Sure, why not? Our leisurely breakfast has already been utterly demolished."

Jimena dialed the number and waited a few seconds. The governor answered on the second ring.

"Hello."

"Um, hi. This is Jimena Aguilar returning your call."

"Oh, thank you, Ms. Aguilar. I appreciate your prompt response to my voicemail. Would you know how to contact Agent Schmidt? I'd also like her to be a part of this dinner."

"She's here with me right now. Shall I put you on speaker?" Jimena asked.

"Yes, please," Governor Murphy answered.

"Hello, Governor," Em greeted.

"Agent Schmidt, thank you for joining the call," the governor answered.

"Em, please call me Em."

"And please call me Sandra. The reason for my call is to arrange a dinner to thank you properly. Unfortunately, the efficient agents in the FBI whisked me away before I had a chance to express my sincere appreciation for your heroism.

I'm alive, thanks to you. I also wanted to discuss the possibility of you joining my team. It seems I've attracted the unwanted attention of a few loyalists to the former president. The FBI has offered to provide a security detail. Naturally, I thought of both of you. I recognize that Ms. Aguilar does not work for the FBI yet—"

Jimena interrupted Sandra. "Jimena. Ms. Aguilar just sounds so wrong." Jimena chuckled. "It seems you may have more information than me."

"Oh, they haven't made the offer yet?" Sandra asked.

"No, we're on vacation," Jimena answered.

"I'm so sorry to bother you on vacation. Perhaps you can contact me when you return, and we can make arrangements. That will also give you the chance to think about my idea. I wouldn't necessarily expect you to personally follow me around twenty-four-seven, but perhaps coordinate the security. Hopefully, this won't go on forever. Either I'll succeed in my bid to become president, or I won't. Either way, it would be a temporary assignment. Will that work for you?"

"Um, sure. I can't speak for Em, but I'll give it serious consideration," Jimena answered.

"I'm flattered, Sandra, but I'm not so sure my skill set is what you need. We'll talk this over, though," Em added after glancing at Jimena and noticing her eager expression.

"That's more than I can ask for. Please enjoy your time off. I won't keep you any longer." Sandra Murphy ended the call, and Em stared at Jimena.

"Wow!" Jimena exclaimed. "I have to say, it's kind of tempting. At one point, I considered the Secret Service, but the pull to follow in my father's footsteps was far too great."

"Glorified babysitters," Em grumbled.

"I take it you aren't as enamored with the opportunity. It sounds like the job might be a bit more than just shadowing Governor Murphy. I know you've done mostly solo work while undercover, but it would be nice to shake things up occasionally. And you're an outstanding leader. Coordinating a team utilizes those skills. Plus, we'd be working together."

Em smiled at Jimena. She looked so hopeful that Em didn't have the heart to say no. "Well, there is that. And if I survived twelve years in the military, a couple of years with Governor Murphy should be a walk in the park."

†

Wynter rolled over, and her eyes blinked open. The pout that appeared on her face might have been comical had there been anyone to see it. Not only was Sandra's side of the bed empty, but the coldness of the sheets indicated she'd been gone for some time. After making love well into the night, Wynter had slept hard and woken much later than normal. She could hear the murmur of Sandra's voice in the other room. After grabbing the robe from the closet, she padded her way to the suite's sitting area.

As she ended her call, Sandra looked up, telling the person on the other end to enjoy their time off. Wynter scrunched her face in confusion. Was Sandra talking to her assistant? It seemed like even when Sandra flew to New York and wasn't in the office, she still contacted her assistant for things like last-minute Broadway tickets or reservations to fancy restaurants. Wynter could get used to the perks of dating the governor.

A tray with a carafe of coffee and various pastries sat on the coffee table. Wynter wasn't necessarily a big fan of breakfast, but she reached for a cinnamon roll and took a large bite because she was starved.

"Finally gave Carla some time off?" Wynter asked after she had chewed and swallowed her bite of the roll.

Sandra poured Wynter a cup of coffee, adding a healthy amount of cream and sugar, just like Wynter liked it. That was something Wynter loved about Sandra. She was very observant and had watched when Wynter prepared her coffee the previous morning.

Sandra's brows knitted before she answered, "No, Carla is the only one who keeps the office going when I'm gone, although it has been a while since she took a vacation. I should probably encourage that before things get crazy. I think I rely way too much on my assistant."

"Why would things get crazy?" Wynter asked.

"I'm going to announce my candidacy during that exclusive interview I've agreed to do with you." Sandra grinned.

"Wow! That's awesome. So if it wasn't Carla, who were you talking to? You don't have a secret girlfriend you sent away while wining and dining me in New York, do you?" Wynter teased.

Sandra threw her head back and laughed. "No. That was Jimena Aguilar and Emma Schmidt. No time like the present to get in contact with them."

"So, how did they respond to your proposal?" Wynter asked.

"Well, it wasn't a no. So that's a good sign. I left the ball in their court to contact me after they return from vacation. I was hoping you might come with me when I meet with them, provided you aren't in New York at the time."

"They're on vacation? Together?" Wynter asked.

"Mm-hm. Why does that surprise you? You were the one who mentioned they're a couple," Sandra answered.

"True, but from what I dug up, it's fairly new."

Sandra shook her head. "And you wonder why people have poor opinions of reporters. You dig into people's personal lives. That should be off-limits."

Wynter shrugged. "While it shouldn't be in the public's interest, it is. They want to know more than the façade presented to the cameras. This is true for any public figures, including modern-day superheroes."

"Doesn't make it right." Sandra's clipped tone sounded critical to Wynter, probably harsher than intended, as Wynter detected her attempt to modulate her voice.

"Do you honestly believe I'm a pariah simply because I am thorough with my research for the stories I plan to cover?" Wynter didn't even try to hide the hurt.

"Oh, Wynter, I'm sorry. I know the media has a role to play in our democracy, but sometimes the constant attention gets to me, especially when they dig into my private life. And, of course, I signed up for this gig. This means I have to accept that my choice of vocation comes with a tremendous amount of unwanted scrutiny. Surely you can see things through my perspective."

"No, I'm sorry. I have experienced unwanted attention, but not from the media. And that certainly did not feel great." Sandra began to respond, but Wynter held her hand up. "Don't even go there. I also signed up for this gig. I want to be here with you as long as we have badass women to protect us. It's been exciting."

Sandra shook her head and chuckled. "Only you would dive into danger and call it exciting."

"So, have we concluded our first fight? I want to get to the good part," Wynter said with a twinkle in her eye.

"What's the good part?"

"Make-up sex, of course," Wynter answered.

CHAPTER SEVENTEEN

Sandra made lazy circles over Wynter's stomach. "Any idea what time it is?"

Wynter glanced at her watch. "Wow! It's almost noon. I'm starving, and I need to call the studio. Are you still serious about that exclusive interview?"

Sandra nodded. "Yeah, why?"

"How about if we do it today?"

"So soon?" Sandra asked.

"You're a hot topic lately with the attempts on your life and questions around your possible candidacy. Before I call, can we order more food? I'm starving. And maybe we can catch up on the news. Besides the two assassination attempts, I know something big went down last night. Too bad Candy was out. I might have been able to wiggle it out of her."

Sandra smiled. "Always the reporter. Why do you think something big went down?"

"Logic. No way would Agent Tightass and her colleague leave our side unless they eliminated the major threat. This news story is moving at lightning speed. It wouldn't surprise me if the FBI was forced to provide more details. I'm not saying I regret spending the last few days with you, but I could have been following up on the story," Wynter explained with a tinge of regret in her voice.

Sandra leaned over to grab the remote from her nightstand and clicked on the TV, scrolling through the channels until she landed on CNN. Then, climbing naked from the bed, she announced, "I'll order some lunch for us."

Sandra put on the robe and headed to the other room to make the call so she wouldn't disturb Wynter as she caught up on the news. However, before she had a chance to make the call, she heard Wynter exclaim, "Holy shit."

Sandra ran into the bedroom and flicked her eyes to the television. The Breaking News logo flashed on the screen, and the news anchor reported, "CNN has now confirmed that the Russian spy, Bridget Schmidt, is dead in an apparent explosion. Authorities are not releasing any additional information at this time."

Wynter smacked the bed. "I knew it. I wonder if Bridget was pulling the strings for the latest attempts, and they took her out. Do you think our government or those badass women eliminated Bridget? Didn't the FBI have her in custody?"

Sandra strode to her phone and found the missed texts and voice messages. She hadn't wanted anything to interrupt her time with Wynter, so she had specifically ignored everything. When Carla told her that Adam Carter had called looking for her, Sandra had decided not to let whatever was going on impact what little time she had with Wynter. Now she was kicking herself for ignoring the signs that something significant had occurred.

Selecting the number for Adam Carter, she waited until he answered.

"Carter, Special Agent in Charge."

"Hello, Adam. I'm sorry for not returning your calls earlier. Please tell me what happened. I just flipped on the news and heard about Bridget Schmidt. I thought you turned her over to Homeland Security."

"We aren't exactly sure what happened. It wasn't us. Bridget had some outside help, which we are still trying to track down. Shortly after Bridget's escape, we received top secret information with the names and contact information of every Russian agent in the US. When we tracked the location of a second bunker in the desert, nothing was left but rubble. DNA confirmed Bridget's body. That's all we know at this point. I tried to reach you after I learned Bridget was in the wind," Carter explained.

"Thanks, Adam."

"While there are still serious threats against your life, a great number of them are contained at this time. I know you weren't interested in having Pete or Frank continue providing protection, but I would still recommend you employ a security detail."

"I'm working on that," Sandra answered before ending her call.

Wynter looked at her expectantly. "Anything you care to share with a curious reporter?"

Sandra narrowed her eyes. "On or off the record?"

Wynter sighed. "Fine. Off the record."

"Carter claims it wasn't the US Government who took her out. And somehow, they got their hands on a list of all active Russian agents living in the US. I got the sense that a confidential informant provided the data."

"Shut the front door. Really?"

Sandra nodded. "Yes. Kind of unbelievable."

"My bet is on whatever organization those badass women work for. I'd give my left tit to know more about them. Toni has mad hacking skills. Maybe she's the informant? I doubt Toni will spill anything, but it might be worth a shot. I could ask for an off-the-record statement. Are you still up for the interview?"

"Yes, but tread lightly on this latest development. I know you'll have to ask me about Bridget, but I won't give you much on that front. Is that acceptable?"

"Yeah, I'm used to the duck and cover from politicians," Wynter teased.

†

Wynter was uncharacteristically nervous as she sat in the studio chair facing Sandra. CNN had enthusiastically jumped on the opportunity. Wynter hadn't yet broached the idea of following Sandra on the campaign trail. She wasn't sure if this would be beneficial or an opening that her detractors couldn't wait to exploit. The alt-right had already labeled the media biased or fake news. Their relationship was sure to cause issues for Sandra, and Wynter didn't wish to add to those. It was a conundrum Wynter wasn't sure how to resolve. She would worry about that later. Wynter had a lot of soul-searching to do. Why did she really want to work as an investigative journalist with CNN? Was that really her dream job? Or did she simply enjoy chasing a story to its conclusion?

Straightening her jacket, she went directly to the heart of the story. "Governor Murphy, thank you for agreeing to this interview. You must be relieved to learn that one individual behind the attack against you and your mother is no longer a threat."

"I'm not sure relieved is the correct emotion. There's still a lot we don't know, and I certainly would not have wished for Bridget Schmidt's life to end," Sandra answered smoothly.

"Do you believe the three Congressmen and the Senator caught on tape deserve to be indicted for treason?" Wynter asked.

"That is not for me to judge. I trust in the men and women in law enforcement and in the Justice Department to make the right decisions for our country. Colluding with a foreign government is a grave matter, requiring a measured and thorough response, but I think it's too early to weigh in on the matter until we learn more."

"The tapes were pretty clear. At the very least, don't you believe all should submit their immediate resignations? We've heard crickets or suggestions that this was a setup with fake tapes from their Republican colleagues. Don't you think it's time to hold people accountable?"

"Well, certainly, if the evidence points to a crime or crimes, no one is above the law. I believe that with all my heart," Sandra answered.

"Including a former president?" Wynter probed.

"Yes."

"Speaking of the presidency, any news on that front?"

Sandra smiled. "If you're asking whether I plan to enter the race, the answer is yes."

Wynter chuckled. "Just like that you're confirming that you will run for president?"

"Yes, just like that. I know reporters must remain neutral, but I hope I have your vote." Sandra smiled serenely at Wynter.

Wynter chuckled. "Now that you've formally announced your intentions, do you worry about your safety? I've seen some posts on various social media platforms. You seem to be the number one target of the radical right. The threats are real."

"Yes, they are. And yes, I am aware of those threats. But what kind of leader would I be if I turned tail and ran? I may have my weaknesses, but cowardice is not one of them.

The divisiveness in our nation has gone too far. I am not the only person who has had to deal with the dangerous rhetoric. It's time to mend the rift and bring all parties together for the good of the country. We may not always agree, but decency, respect, and kindness never go out of fashion. There are still many colleagues across the aisle who would agree with that."

"And there is an equal number who gleefully stoke those fires. So what do you propose to do about those individuals?" Wynter asked.

"Find common ground. We may disagree on many things, but there are certainly opportunities for agreement and things we can work on together."

"Ah, an optimist. Some might say you are being entirely unrealistic in your assessment that you will be able to find common ground. At least not in the current political climate. What do you say to those naysayers?"

"Aren't you tired of the divisive politics? I know I am. According to recent polls, the public wants accountability and action. They are just as tired of the excuses and recent shifts as I am. We will never break that logjam if we can't come together. Perhaps someone new can take us in a different direction. I'd like to be that person."

"If you win the presidency, this nation will have two historic firsts. Some don't believe a woman, especially a woman who identifies as a lesbian, can possibly win. Also, while not a first, you will be only the third unmarried president to take the oath. James Buchanan never married, but Grover Cleveland managed to tie the knot during his presidency. Any chance you'll take a wife in the near future?" Wynter grinned unrepentantly.

"I don't believe you're ready for an answer to that question," Sandra teased, "but I will indulge you. I never lose hope of finding the right person to stand with me and endure what will certainly be a rough ride. It can't be easy to marry a politician."

"How about we go onto lighter topics? Do you plan to bring a pet to the oval office? Cat person or dog person?"

†

Sandra wasn't angry or frustrated about the interview. It had primarily gone as planned, but the question about taking a wife had confused her. Did Wynter expect Sandra to reveal their relationship on air?

Both women had remained quiet during their return trip to the hotel. Sandra stayed lost in her own thoughts and wondered briefly what had Wynter so introspective. That was out of character for Wynter. Sandra knew she would need to broach how to handle their relationship with the public, but she didn't plan on doing that in the back of a limousine. They had one more evening together in New York, and Sandra planned to take advantage of that, knowing their schedules would get crazy in the coming weeks and months.

When they reached their room, Sandra broke the silence. "Any particular food you're in the mood for?"

Wynter's eyes blinked. "What, sorry? I wasn't paying attention." A wrinkle formed in the middle of her forehead.

Sandra took Wynter's hand and led her to the love seat in the room. "It wasn't that awful, was it?"

"Was what?" Wynter asked.

"The interview. You've not been yourself since we left the studio. Did your meeting not go well? I know you had your attorney check the contract and suggest a few changes. Were they not amenable to those changes?" Sandra asked.

"No, they didn't even blink an eye at the proposed changes and told me I should have a revised contract by this evening." Wynter stared ahead.

"That's good news, then. So, why do I get the impression that you just lost your best friend?" Sandra caressed Wynter's hand as they remained seated.

"I told them I need one more day to consider their offer."

Sandra wrinkled her brow. "Why? I thought this was your dream job. I take it you didn't float the idea of following me on the campaign trail or reveal that we're dating?"

"No, I didn't. But, honestly, I'm questioning many things right now," Wynter answered.

"Oh," Sandra began to remove her hand from Wynter's, but Wynter held tight.

Wynter smiled. "Not that. The possibility of a serious relationship with you is the only thing I am sure of right now."

"I don't know how to ask this, so I'll just put this out there. Did you want me to expose that we're dating on air tonight? Is that why you asked the question?"

"I suppose that's just one of the many things I don't have an answer for. I know it's prudent to plan every communication with the media carefully, especially a juicy tidbit about your private life. Still, if I were honest, I think I would have been okay with you telling everyone we're dating," Wynter explained.

"I've already told you I won't lie or hide our relationship. I deliberately left that unsaid because the decision of when and where has to be ours, not mine. If I'd known prior to the interview that was your desire, I would have answered that question differently." Sandra looked earnestly at Wynter.

"And, if I'd been transparent about my expectations, which for the record, I don't even have clear in my own mind, I would have followed up with a more pointed question—like whether you're currently seeing anyone."

"Well, that certainly would have shaken things up and made for an interesting conversation with the mucky-mucks at CNN." Sandra laughed.

"I've been thinking a lot about what I really want. Two attempts on our lives in such a scant time have a way of sharpening my viewpoint. Life is way too short for many people. I hope we aren't in that group, but if we are, I don't plan on missing out on the most important things in life. What I enjoy about investigative reporting is the chase."

"The chase?" Sandra asked.

"Yes, chasing down a particularly momentous story. Sure, I like the recognition that accompanies being the one to go on air and report it, but that is not what really gets my motor running. So I'd be just as happy doing opposition research for you. And to satisfy that little part of me that enjoys the spotlight, being the point person for your press conferences will do nicely."

Sandra could feel the smile grow on her face. "Really? Does that mean you'll turn down CNN and take the job I offered after all?"

Wynter nodded. "Yeah, I think so. And, as your new communications director, I recommend keeping our relationship under wraps. At least for now. I don't want anyone questioning my motives for breaking what will probably be one of the year's biggest stories. Timing is everything in this business."

"You're the expert. I bow to your divine wisdom." Sandra bowed in exaggeration.

"Hey, don't make fun of me. This is serious stuff I've been working through, practically on-demand."

"On-demand? You have the most interesting way of framing things," Sandra noted.

"Yes, like in one of those RVs I rented one summer that had on-demand hot water. You pushed my feelings button, and I blurted everything I've been mulling over for the past two hours. You have a way of helping me navigate the weeds."

"I don't care how you came to this conclusion, but I'm over the moon with it. I didn't want to hold you back, but if I'm honest, I look forward to not having to find spare time in either of our schedules just so I can look into those beautiful eyes and do this." Sandra leaned in and captured Wynter's bottom lip, sucking gently before slipping her tongue inside.

The kiss took on a life of its own and would have evolved into another long session of making love, but Wynter pulled back. Sandra realized their discussion wasn't over yet.

"Now that you've formally announced your candidacy, I worry about your safety. You know the fringe will be on the warpath, especially as soon as the unhinged find out I'm your new communications director. They will cry foul soon. Did you know that CNN journalists, especially Anderson Cooper and Don Lemon, receive death threats? Stories that shed a negative light on the former president and his staunch allies, including the ones I just exposed, bring forth defenders who stoke the fires of violence."

Sandra frowned. "I know it is way too soon to move in together, but at least that would mean I only have to hire one security detail versus two. Would you consider moving into my home? I have plenty of space. We've gone from the challenge of rarely seeing one another to conjoined lives that might have you running for the hills after having a front-row seat to all my flaws."

Wynter didn't answer immediately, making Sandra nervous as she jumped in to fill the void. "Never mind. I'll hire a separate security detail for you."

"No, no. Sorry. I was just thinking. I have a confession to make."

"Okay," Sandra answered hesitantly.

"I've never lived with anyone before. Not even a roommate. I've always been somewhat solitary. Not antisocial or anything, more like ultra independent," Wynter explained.

Sandra smiled. "We're not that different. While I've always been surrounded by people, that doesn't necessarily mean I've had many close relationships with others. I've never lived with a lover before, either." Sandra laughed. "But I'm willing to expose myself, warts and all. My house is large enough for both of us to have our own space, should the need arise. Does that make the offer more tempting?"

"Can I think about it?" Wynter asked.

"Of course."

CHAPTER EIGHTEEN

Toni hated scrolling through alt-right social media sites. Still, something told her to pay close attention to the chatter online, especially with the bombshell news that Wynter had reported and the dangerous rhetoric about the tapes being false, once again calling it a witch hunt against the former president and his allies. The vitriol was appalling, calling for the death of the FBI agents who had taken the congressman and senator into custody. Even worse, the TRU Network had thrown their listeners a particularly tasty morsel of red meat by outing their former investigative reporter, Wynter Holmes, and suggesting she was part of the conspiracy against the former president and the alt-right. The recklessness of that reporting was beyond disgusting.

Wynter's interview with Governor Murphy only ratcheted up the calls for violence, crescendoing into calls for the rape and murder of both perverts because they were coming for your children. Fringe politicians jumped on the bandwagon, stating both were "groomers" and dangerous to the country.

Sophie and Candy had already made it back to home base but were still the closest, most experienced agents to send. However, Candy was still experiencing the adverse effects of her chloroform exposure. Toni could send Sophie and ask Wynter and Governor Murphy to lie low until someone else could make the trip to New York. Sometimes Sophie and Val were like oil and water, but Val was the best they had, and the two women were just going to have to deal with their alpha shit and do their jobs.

Toni nodded to herself. With Char still recovering, the weight of the decision to act remained squarely with her. She had access to the most recent intelligence, and Char had repeatedly told Toni she trusted her to take care of things until she was one hundred percent.

Picking up her phone, she dialed the number for Wynter.

"Hey, Wynter, T here."

"Oh, hi, Toni," Wynter cheekily responded.

"Funny. Okay, so you know my first name now. Listen, I have a bad feeling about all the chatter on social media. Your fucking network outed you and just made you and Governor Murphy enemies number one and two in their ridiculous war against the liberal, 'woke' traitors. Oh, and the fringiest politicians added their two cents, calling you groomers and enemies against good Christian values. Any chance you two can lie low for another day or two?"

"Um, I don't know. Sandra has been away from her office for several days now, and with her just announcing her candidacy, she needs to hit the ground running. We had a flight scheduled for later tonight."

"Cancel it," Toni directed.

"What specifically have you picked up?"

"You don't really want to hear the grizzly details. But suffice to say, the death threats are oddly specific and gruesomely detailed," Toni answered.

"All right. You've never led me down the wrong path. I'll talk to Sandra."

"Sandra, huh? You two an item now?" Toni teased.

"None of your damn business, and don't hack into our computers or phones, or I will find a way to track you and your mysterious colleagues down."

Toni laughed. "I'm your top informant. Good luck with that. Just be safe. I would like to see a woman become president in my lifetime. The lesbian part is just a bonus."

"Me too, Toni. Me too. Okay, we'll order room service and hang out in the room. As long as I can convince Sandra to stay another day."

†

Although Sophie grumbled a bit, she agreed to head back to New York to ensure none of the fringe made good on their promises. Over the years, she had learned to trust

241

Toni's gut and her nerd skills to siphon through the enormous amount of data and ferret out the actual threats. Toni seemed spooked, which was enough for Sophie, even if she had to work with the surly fellow agent. Val wasn't her favorite colleague, but Sophie had come to understand the stoic woman much better and recognized why she was the way she was. Most would have crumbled under the enormous weight of her experiences. Besides, since Gina and her daughter had come into the picture, Sophie saw signs of Val softening, which made her easier to deal with.

Not more than ten minutes later, while Sophie had already made her way to her car, Toni called again. Sophie pushed the button to answer the call through her call speakers.

"I'm on my way," Sophie answered.

"Um, Val isn't coming."

"Okay. Not that I really care all that much, but why not?"

"She promised the peanut that she would take her to Disneyland," Toni responded.

"That's fine. From what you said, we aren't dealing with trained professionals or anyone particularly bright. I can handle it on my own. It's fine, Toni," Sophie assured her.

"You sure?"

"Yep. Haven't most of the assaults by these dicknobs been solo attempts?" Sophie asked.

"Um, January sixth? Did you forget that little stain on history?" Toni reminded.

"Good point, but he who shall not be named hasn't called for an all-out assault on the governor or planned a rally in New York, has he?" Sophie countered.

"No, I guess not. But, yeah, you're probably right," Toni agreed. "It will likely be a solo actor if anything happens."

"Since our most experienced agents are still in San Diego, why don't I escort them back to San Diego tonight?" Sophie suggested.

"Good idea. I'll let Wynter know there's been a change in plans and get you a ticket on the same flight. Gotta go because they've probably called the airline already to change their flights. I'll just hack into their system and make the necessary changes."

"Thanks. Can you also get me marshal's credentials so I can carry my firearm?"

"Got it. I'll send the credentials to Wynter and Governor Murphy to give to you. Stay safe," Toni said.

"Always," Sophie answered.

†

Sandra worried more about Wynter's safety than about the delay in her return home, so she hadn't even blinked at the suggestion to stay another couple of days. It had prompted a flurry of calls to her assistant and Adam Carter, hoping to arrange for a security detail for herself and Wynter, as well as new travel arrangements. Carla, her ever-efficient assistant, had emailed the confirmation ten minutes later, and they were set to fly out a day and a half later.

Sandra made the plea once again for Wynter to at least temporarily move into her home until things calmed down. Wynter had acquiesced, mostly because she didn't want Sandra to continue worrying. Adam had assured her he would make the arrangements but couldn't make that happen until her return to San Diego.

Wynter nibbled on a snack leftover from the large gift basket CNN left in the hotel room before Wynter's arrival. There wasn't a lot left to pick through, but being the sugar hound she was, anything would do to satisfy her craving. Her cell phone rang again and Wynter sighed.

"What now?" Wynter grumbled before answering her phone.

"I made new reservations to replace the ones that Carla arranged. Sorry for that."

"Toni?" Wynter scratched her head in confusion.

"Yeah, change of plans. Sophie is going to accompany you tonight. You leave at seven."

"Why?" Wynter motioned for Sandra to come closer and put the phone on speaker.

"We weren't able to get another agent on short notice, and since most of our agents are temporarily in San Diego, it made sense to get you both there as quickly as possible while we identify the threat level. Oh, and I'm working on marshal credentials for Sophie that I'll send to the Four Seasons. Please make sure you give them to Sophie when she arrives."

"All right, and I won't even ask if it's legal. But, geez, I wish you people would make up your minds. Should I stay or should I go…" Wynter sang.

"It's fine," Sandra said. "I'm sure Carla will be happy that I'm returning tonight. The sooner I get with her to plan my schedule, the better. Plus, I really need to deal with my mother. She'll be irate that I didn't consult with her before announcing my candidacy."

"Yeah, I caught your interview," Toni noted. "While personally, I thought it was great news, your detractors don't share my view, and that has ratcheted up the violent rhetoric. I think they're truly rattled about your chances of winning. Good news, bad news," Toni added.

"Thanks. I think," Sandra responded. "If we're going to leave tonight, we better pack up and be ready."

"Sophie should be there soon. Wait for her. She'll accompany you to the airport."

"Got it. Later, Toni."

"Be safe." Toni ended the call.

"Well, Sandra, you've certainly added excitement to my life," Wynter teased.

CHAPTER NINETEEN

When the front desk called to let Sandra know a package had arrived for Wynter, Sandra offered to retrieve the envelope with the credentials inside. While collecting the documents, she bought a Yankees baseball cap on a lark from the gift shop in the lobby. Then, after zipping her suitcase, she'd uncharacteristically placed the ball cap on her head, and Wynter had laughed.

"Are you wearing that to the airport?" Wynter asked.

"Yeah, why not? I'll be incognito," Sandra teased. "Although, I must say that since I've been to New York, you are the only reporter who has mauled me."

"Mauled you? Is that what I've been doing?" Wynter laughed. "I suppose I have devoured you several times since you've arrived."

"Honestly, I think that Sophie escorting us back to California is overkill," Sandra noted.

"Maybe, but better safe than sorry."

Sandra sighed. When a crisp knock on the door interrupted them, Sandra strode to the door to answer it. Without thinking, she pulled the hotel door open.

Sophie scowled. "I hope you looked through the peephole before answering the door."

"I didn't think it was necessary since we were expecting you," Sandra answered sheepishly. She picked the package up from the small desk in the suite and handed it to Sophie. "The credentials from Toni."

"Thanks. You're going to need to be more cautious, Governor. Ready?" Sophie asked.

"Yeah, I'll call for the driver," Wynter stated.

"No need. I have a car. Besides, I would prefer to control all the details related to your trip home." Sophie led the two women to her car without incident.

Sandra's thoughts about the unnecessary cloak and dagger seemed spot-on as no one paid attention to the three women while they made their way through the airport, boarded the plane, and settled into their first-class seats. Sandra reminded herself that she needed to reimburse Toni for the tickets. They couldn't have been cheap. In fact, she needed to compensate Sophie and the other woman for the security services they had already provided. She wondered if either or both of them were available to hire on a more permanent basis. Perhaps she would have time to talk with

Sophie later because, at the moment, the woman seemed too focused on their surroundings to discuss future employment.

†

Sophie remained vigilant, scrutinizing every person who boarded the plane until she was satisfied there weren't any threats on the flight to San Diego. By the time the plane landed, she was grumpy and exhausted. Hopefully, whoever they sent to pick them up from the airport could take over the point position, and she could relax. At least both women packed light, and there wasn't a need to go to baggage claim.

Ronda leaned against the wall, and Sophie saw her push off when the three of them walked toward the exit to ground transportation.

"You look done in," Ronda remarked as she greeted them. She nodded her head at Wynter and Sandra. "Governor. Ms. Holmes. I'll be your driver today." She grinned.

"You're taking the lead to the governor's home," Sophie directed. "I'm afraid I'll miss something."

"Fine by me. Do you want to drive?" Ronda asked.

Sophie nodded. "It'll be easier if we take both of them to Governor Murphy's home. At least she has gate security."

"Not that we have much say in this, it seems, but I will need to go to my place at some point to retrieve a few items," Wynter interjected. "How long were you two planning to shadow us?"

"Until the governor makes arrangements for proper security," Sophie answered.

"What exactly is proper security?" Sandra asked with a bite to her words. "I believe the FBI offered to provide temporary assistance until I hire my own team. I've contacted Agent Schmidt and Agent Aguilar, but they haven't given an answer yet. Plus, they're on vacation right now."

"Emma Schmidt and Jimena Aguilar?" Sophie asked.

"Yes. Do you know them?" Wynter asked.

Sophie and Ronda shared a look, then Sophie answered, "They would be acceptable."

"Well, thank you for your approval," Sandra answered sarcastically. "While I appreciate all you have done for Wynter and myself, and I'll make sure I compensate you appropriately for your services, I'm not sure I like you calling the shots regarding whom I choose to hire."

Ronda chuckled. "Yeah, Sophie can be a little overbearing at times."

"Shut it, Ronda. Come on, let's go." Sophie continued to survey the area but didn't notice anyone who might be out of place or prepared to take action.

†

Sandra had underestimated her interview's impact on the news cycle. Several news vans waited outside of her gate. She had assumed they would have left after not finding her at home over the last several days, but unfortunately, that was not the case.

"Shit, we do not need the press taking photos."
Sophie lowered her head, deftly avoiding the flash of
cameras. "Ronda, any chance Toni can get these yahoos to
leave?"

"How in the actual fuck is she going to do that?"
Ronda asked.

"I don't know. Use some nerd magic or something,"
Sophie answered. "The last thing we need is some reporter
trying to find out who we are."

"Unless there's a bigger story to chase, I'm afraid
they aren't going to leave. Wynter, do you have any
suggestions?"

"Feed them something. I can work on that tonight
with you. Then, we'll do a brief press conference tomorrow
morning. It can be a twofer. First, we'll announce my new
role as the communications director and give them
something new to chew on," Wynter answered.

"Pull up to the keypad, please, and you might want to
turn your heads. I'm going to roll down the window and tell
them about the press conference tomorrow morning," Sandra
announced.

Flashes nearly blinded Sandra's eyes the minute she
rolled down the window. "Good evening. I know you are
eager to ask your questions, and I promise to answer them
tomorrow morning, but it's a bit too late to respond tonight. I
hope you all understand and respect that."

Before pushing the button to roll up the window,
Sandra extended her hand to the keypad to activate opening

the gate as a cacophony of voices yelled, "Governor Murphy!"

"Go ahead and drive through now," Sandra directed.

Sandra hoped her mother wasn't still up. She'd made a quick call to let her know she planned on returning home that evening, but it would be late, and Rose shouldn't wait up. However, making suggestions to her mother didn't guarantee Rose would listen. In fact, more often than not, she ignored Sandra's wishes. Sandra wondered what Rose would think of the two women sent to ensure her safety from an organization she knew very little about. Rose would have questions that Sandra did not have the answer to.

†

Sophie was increasingly uncomfortable with the exposure this mission presented to The Organization. Wynter was like a dog with a bone. The press was all over the governor, likely aiming their long-range cameras at the mansion, increasing the odds they would capture a decent picture of her face. Being an ex-FBI agent, she could not risk anyone tracking her down. Now there was one more person with connections to whom she would be exposed. An older version of Governor Murphy gracefully rose from her chair to greet the governor and her guests.

"I told you not to wait up, Mother." The governor shook her head.

"I didn't realize we were having guests, nor did I expect you to be gone for three days and announce your candidacy in that short time." Governor Murphy's mother shifted her eyes to Wynter, Sophie, and Ronda. "Did I miss the planning for a girl's weekend?" she asked while quirking her eyebrow.

"Can we please talk about this tomorrow? Everyone has had a long day," the governor stated.

"Of course," the stately woman answered while pinning her daughter with a gaze that left no room for misinterpretation. Sophie knew the woman would thoroughly interrogate her daughter. She was known for her tight grip on the governor's career.

"Governor, I assume you have a security system," Sophie said. "May I have a look? Just what is inside because I don't want to provide the reporters an opportunity for a picture."

"Will you please call me Sandra?" She gestured for Sophie to follow her and gave a brief tour of her home along with the location of security cameras and other equipment for the doors and windows. When Sophie and Ronda followed Sandra, Wynter made herself at home in the parlor. Rose made her way to the curving staircase, bidding everyone goodnight.

The setup impressed Sophie, and she deemed it temporarily adequate. She'd arrange for Toni to send over additional tools to make the place a fortress and give The Organization control over the system should they need to access it.

"This will do for now. Tomorrow, we'll add additional insurance," Sophie remarked.

"Let me show you to the guest rooms," Sandra offered.

"We only need one room because we'll be taking shifts," Sophie stated.

"I'll take the first shift since I'm more rested," Ronda offered.

Sophie nodded. She wasn't going to argue. So far, the night had gone smoothly. Sophie had been on the money with her assessment of the threat level. Home-grown domestic terrorists, for the most part, were not much of a challenge to trained professionals. She had to admit that Karl Junior had been the exception. Without Em and Jimena, she wouldn't even be here because the governor would already be dead. Karl had made an elaborate plan to blow up her mother's home during a visit from the governor, and had almost succeeded.

"The guest rooms are on the first floor. Come with me, and you can take your pick," Sandra directed.

"I'll just roam the house if you don't mind," Ronda said.

"Of course. Make yourself at home. I'm not sure what is available to heat up if you get hungry, but I'll be sure to make arrangements for food first thing tomorrow morning."

"Do you have a cook, housekeeper, gardener, or other staff we need to worry about?" Sophie asked.

"No cook or gardener. I have a housekeeper that comes once a week, but she would have come today and won't be back until next week," Sandra answered.

"Good, the fewer people, the better," Sophie remarked.

As Sophie followed Sandra to one of the guest bedrooms, she continued to survey the home, looking for any weaknesses. She wasn't particular and took the first bedroom they came to. Setting her overnight bag on the floor, Sophie thanked Sandra, then shut the door for privacy. She had one more call to make.

Sitting on the bed, she contacted Toni.

"Hey, Soph. What's up?" Toni greeted.

"Two things. I want to beef up the security in the governor's home. Can you send some additional equipment? Cameras, outside sensors, and any prototypes you think might be helpful. Oh, you'll need to hack the system to ensure we have control at all times."

"Got it," Toni answered. "What's the second thing?"

"When are Em and Jimena expected to return?"

"At least another week, I think. Why?"

"Any chance we can talk them into taking over the security detail?" Sophie asked.

"Long-term? I doubt it, but we can always ask. Em's got this over-inflated sense of duty to her country, so it might work. And Jimena will follow Em wherever she goes. That might be a selling point. They'll get to work together for the next couple of years while Governor Murphy is on the campaign trail," Toni answered. "Maybe Hank and Steve will join them. Governor Murphy might not know it, but that'll certainly be a dream team to employ. I'll make the calls tomorrow."

"Thanks. I'd like to get home to Kim. It seems we've been like two ships passing in the night lately." Sophie sighed. "Char and the baby are doing okay now, right?"

"Yeah, she's grumpy because she hasn't been in the thick of things, but they're good. After taking the peanut to Disneyland, Val was in a better mood tonight. She even brought back one of those mouse ear hats but gave us all the warning death stare. Only Gina got away with teasing her about it." Toni chuckled. "Maybe you should ask Kim to fly to San Diego."

"No, there's already too many people in that house. I'd rather go back to home base and work from there."

"Makes sense. I'll send either Hank or Steve with the equipment. Talk to you later, pal."

"Thanks, Toni." Sophie ended the call and flopped on the bed, not bothering to undress. She was out in less than ten minutes.

Chapter Twenty

Em lounged on the beach, glancing at her watch and waiting until the noon hour approached when she would allow herself a refreshing mojito. She wasn't sure why she continued to carry her cell phone. She was supposed to be on vacation, not tethered to the damn thing. Jimena teased her about being far too responsible for her own good.

Glancing over at her fiancé, a smile blossomed on her face. She was the luckiest woman in the world to have reconnected with her first love, her only love if she were honest. And now, Jimena had agreed to marry her. Life was good.

When her phone rang, she looked at the number and groaned. "I'm beginning to think you have a crush on me,

Toni. You keep calling while I'm on vacation with my fiancé. You're just lucky Jimena isn't the jealous type."

"Who says I'm not the jealous type? Hot, fiery, Latina. Remember?" Jimena joked.

Em looked around and found the beach was nearly empty. Jimena scooted closer, and she placed the call on speaker.

"Sorry to bother you lovebirds on vacation, but Governor Murphy just announced that she was running for president."

"Okay. What does that have to do with us?"

"Well, I'm sure you realize she now has a huge target on her back. Every backwater white nationalist and fringe alt-right fanatic will gun for her. I had a bad feeling, so Soph and Ronda are on security detail for the interim, but we need a more permanent solution. Actually, not completely permanent. Only for the next couple of years until after the 2024 election," Toni explained.

"And you think Jimena and myself are the perfect solution."

"Uh-huh. Don't you want to ensure that we protect the next president of the United States? It's like your patriotic duty to care deeply about that."

"Stop buttering me up," Em groused.

"I told the governor we would consider it." Em looked at Jimena, who nodded. "Fine, not my favorite thing to do, but two years is not forever."

"If it helps, I convinced Hank and Steve to join the team. They're talking with Carter later today," Toni added.

"I'm not cutting our vacation short. We earned this time off. If we agree, will you stop calling and interrupting us?" Em teased.

"Yup. Unless there is something big that goes down," Toni amended. "One more thing. Remember that matter you asked me to look into? It's been resolved. Hank personally delivered the evidence to the local PD. They're toast."

"Thanks, Toni, I guess I owe you on this," Em answered.

"Consider the debt paid with your willingness to join the protection detail for Governor Murphy."

Jimena furrowed her brow and Em, mouthed, *later*.

"Are y'all still at your house in San Diego?" Jimena asked.

"Yeah, we'll be here for a while. Well, most of us. Soph is itching to return to our main compound because she misses her partner."

"Sophie has a partner?" Em asked.

"Oh, yeah. Kim is Soph's one great love. Kim, Soph, and I went to college together. Before joining The Organization, we were like the Three Musketeers. Kim is a master of disguise with her theater background."

"Maybe we'll meet her someday," Jimena said.

"Maybe. Okay, I'll let you two get back to whatever you were doing before I called. Enjoy the rest of your vacation." Toni ended the call.

Em looked at Jimena. "Okay, what was that all about with Toni?"

"I asked her to help out with uncovering who killed your papa."

"Oh. She already found them?" Jimena asked with a quiver in her voice.

"Sounds like found and arrested. I hope you can rest easy that justice will be served." Em caressed Jimena's face.

"Thank you. You're amazing. I love you."

"I love you, too. If it's important to you. It will always be a top priority to me. That will never change," Em answered.

"I don't want you to take this protection detail because you think you owe Toni or because I'm interested. Are you sure it's what *you* want? Two years is a long time."

Jimena nodded. "Yeah. I'd feel terrible if something happened to Governor Murphy. I like her and her politics. She's just what this country needs right now. Should I call her back and let her know?"

"Nope. We are not letting that drama impact the rest of our vacation. No more work. For the remainder of our time in Mexico, I want my focus on you and only you."

Jimena grinned. "Sweet talker."

†

Sophie rubbed her face as she woke to whatever kerfuffle was happening in the kitchen. She could hear voices, and knowing Ronda as well as she did, she sensed her deep frustration. Besides needing an enormous cup of coffee, Sophie wanted to take a nice, long shower. Instead, she stalked toward the voices.

"What the hell is going on?" Sophie grumbled.

"The governor wants to go outside right now and answer questions," Ronda responded.

Sophie glanced at Sandra, who looked like the ultimate Commander-in-Chief, dressed in her stylish power suit. Wynter had chosen more casual attire, with cream-colored pants and a light-blue silk blouse.

"Not before Toni checks out every single person and van outside the gate," Sophie responded.

"That's what I told her. Unfortunately, neither of us can take the chance that they'll capture us on camera. I was hoping we would have something in place soon to allow them to have a press briefing, but Toni said that Hank and Steve aren't available until after they clear things with Carter," Ronda answered.

"Is she running everyone through her face recognition software?" Sophie asked.

"Yup. She just got off the phone with Em and Jimena, and they've agreed to join the team. We've been busy while you were snoring away. I'm so ready for a bed right now." Ronda yawned.

"How well do you know Emma Schmidt and Jimena Aguilar? How are you connected to them?" Governor Murphy asked.

Sophie turned her steely gaze to Sandra. "Not important right now. What has you so hellfire bent on giving a press conference right this second?" Sophie noted the coffee pot resting on a hot pad in her periphery and asked, "Is that coffee up for grabs?"

Sandra retrieved a cup from the cupboard and filled it almost to the brim, pushing it along with the cream and sugar in Sophie's direction. "Here. I made a promise that I would answer their questions this morning. I was merely going to keep my promise. In my line of business, that's a rarity. I'd prefer not to start my campaign with empty promises that I have no intention of keeping."

Sophie sighed. "Toni is very good at what she does. She'll have an answer for us within the hour. So, I suggest you exercise some patience because there is no way we are allowing you to hold a press conference in the open until we've cleared everyone. I'll hogtie you myself if I have to."

Wynter held her hand over her mouth while she snickered. "I think you just met your match, Sandra."

Sophie heard Ronda's phone buzz before Ronda swiped to answer the call.

"Hey, Toni." Ronda listened intently. "Okay, that's great news, but the other piece will not go over too well. I'll let Soph know." Ronda ended the call and turned to Sophie. "Toni says Hank and Steve will be here in another hour or so, but there is an interloper in the crowd of journalists. Bald guy wearing a camo vest. I didn't see him earlier. So he must have shown up when I came into the kitchen for food."

Sophie grabbed her coffee and directed, "We better check it out." Heading to the room with the monitors, Sophie grimaced when not only Ronda but Wynter and Sandra also followed.

When the group reached the room, Sophie watched in horror as a group of angry white men wearing MAGA hats gathered around the bald man. Sophie heard Sandra gasp and leaned closer to the monitor, noting that several men wore T-shirts that said, "Kill Your Local Pedophile." Others had donned T-shirts with a large red X over "Dyke President."

"Well, that's not good," Ronda noted.

Sandra adjusted her posture and seemed to gather some internal strength as she stated, "California does not allow protests on private property. I'll simply invite the cameras and reporters just inside the gate."

"You are not getting anywhere near that crowd," Sophie stated while pinching the bridge of her nose. "Let me think."

"Hank and Steve should arrive within the next hour. We can have them call in additional agents to use as a backup to clear the illegal protesters," Ronda suggested. "Toni can communicate directly with them as she surveys the crowd. Besides checking their press credentials, Hank and Steve will have the advantage of Toni letting them know who is legit and who is not. Although, it looks pretty obvious from here who are the asswipes and who is the press."

"All right. That makes sense. I wish we could just take out every one of those homophobic pigs," Sophie growled.

"I don't know." Wynter frowned. "The optics will not be in our favor if the FBI uses strong-arm tactics to disburse this small group of protesters. Bashing the FBI seems to be the latest craze with the MAGA base. The media will have a field day with that because I'm sure this group will play to the cameras and shouting their first amendment rights."

"Unfortunately, Wynter is correct. A simple show of force without the FBI physically removing them might work better," Sandra suggested. "Let me know when they arrive, and I'll greet them at the gate at the same time I invite the reporters inside. I plan on acknowledging the protesters. It's important to show everyone grace, including those that oppose you. Those are the optics worth catching on camera."

Wynter nodded. "Impressive."

Sophie ran her hand through her hair. "I don't like it, but I suppose if we can have Toni link us all to the same channel, we'll be able to provide information to Hank and Steve while we watch the cameras for any sign that either of you is in imminent danger."

Ronda clapped her hands together. "Perfect. We have a plan. Now can I get some breakfast? I'm starved. If I'm up for a few hours more, I better have a cup of coffee."

"No, I can handle things here. Just get some sleep," Sophie directed.

Rose strolled into the kitchen, every hair in place, fully made-up, wearing an equally impressive power suit. "Did I miss the pre-party?" she drolly asked.

†

Rarely had Wynter seen a politician with as much grace and class as Sandra Murphy. As soon as the agents arrived, Sandra went into action. First, she pulled a case of water from her spare refrigerator and brought it out to the crowd that had gathered outside her gate. Then, while Hank and Steve checked press credentials to usher only the reporters inside the entrance, Sandra handed out water to the angry mob of men.

"It's going to be a scorcher today, gentlemen," Sandra announced. "I wouldn't want any of you to pass out from heat exhaustion."

One camera swiveled toward Sandra, capturing the scene, and Wynter smiled as she watched Sandra handle the angry crowd with ease. Most of the men were too shocked to react quickly. A few batted the bottle from Sandra's hand, but she kept going as if nothing had happened. When an angry man approached and began screaming slurs in Sandra's face, she didn't flinch, but the two male agents quickly intervened and guided Sandra back onto her estate, closing the gate to the angry crowd.

The reporters barely waited for the gate to close before hollering their questions. Some were related to her recent announcement, but others tried to explore why she would hand out water to the unruly crowd.

"I hope you don't mind a short walk. If you would follow me, I'd like to hold the press conference in my garden. I believe it'll be more comfortable for everyone," Sandra directed.

Earlier, Sophie had grumbled about not only being a glorified babysitter but also suddenly relegated to stagehand while helping Sandra, Wynter, and Rose set up chairs in the garden. As the reporters settled into chairs and the camera crew remained on the periphery with their cameras pointed at Sandra, Wynter noticed the two male agents touch their ears and subtly acknowledge whatever information was being fed to their earbuds. Wynter would have given her right arm to have one of those devices so she could hear everything going on. The whole cloak-and-dagger routine with the mysterious women who'd come to their rescue was beyond fascinating to Wynter.

Wynter received multiple questioning looks from reporters who often covered the same beat as herself as she took the seat next to Sandra.

Sandra held up her hand to quiet the crowd. "Before answering your questions, I'd like to introduce my new communications director, Wynter Holmes. While I'm still happy to answer questions and agree to on-camera interviews, Wynter will organize all future communications. You may also have questions for Wynter since she is the reporter who broke the earlier story. I am sure you're curious about that."

Wynter wasn't shocked by Sandra offering her the spotlight because they'd talked about it the previous evening. Unfortunately, one weasel from TRU was the first to ask Wynter a question.

"When did you accept your new role, Wynter? Did you begin your opposition research while you still worked for TRU?" He shouted his question.

"Hello, Harold," Wynter answered. "It's good to see that TRU has given you my old spot. After considering a contract from CNN, I accepted an offer from Governor Murphy, which happened several days after my appearance on CNN. The story was good old-fashioned journalism, not opposition research. TRU might not have recognized the tremendous importance of the story, but CNN certainly did. I had planned on giving TRU four weeks' notice, but when TRU decided to kill this historical reporting, I figured it was more prudent to depart immediately. That left room to consider other opportunities."

"Governor Murphy, you didn't seem too bothered by the protesters outside your gate. With the recent attack on your life and deep unpopularity with a subset of the nation, aren't you afraid of another attempt on your life? I doubt they have a permit to protest outside of your home. Why not send them packing?"

"I believe strongly in the First Amendment. While I may disagree with their perspective, especially regarding my qualifications for president," Sandra joked, "I will defend their right to free speech. Everyone deserves respect, kindness, and courtesy. I'd like to think that has not yet gone out of fashion. Besides, if you haven't noticed, those two immensely qualified agents were quite capable of ensuring that nothing got out of hand. Violence is never the answer."

"Governor Murphy, did you decide to run for president before or after the story broke? Why did you make the announcement so soon after the alleged collusion? The timing seems convenient," Harold asked.

"It seemed like the right moment to announce what I'd already contemplated before the recent allegations against sitting members of Congress. I've been considering this for quite some time," Sandra answered carefully. "Understanding politics as I do, the announcement is anything but convenient. In fact, it's probably a distraction to a press digging more into the story that is far more important than my announcement," Sandra added, then continued her explanation. "Ms. Holmes inquired about the possibility of an interview, and I agreed. After I learned about the dangerous connections between Russia and members of Congress, I felt it was my duty to enter the race. We need a strong leader to navigate these treacherous waters. I don't know who leaked those tapes, and I would never pressure the free press into revealing their source. However, I believe we must put more resources into the intelligence community. The strength of our nation depends on it. Rooting out any threat to our democracy will be one of my first priorities. No one is above the law."

Wynter was glad the reporters left her alone after Harold's questions. The experience was utterly foreign to Wynter. Suddenly, she appreciated what Sandra and other politicians had to go through on a nearly daily basis. Considering Wynter would be front and center, she might have to elicit a few pointers from Sandra or Rose on handling the media. No wonder some people thought the media were just a bunch of pariahs. Walking in someone else's shoes was downright uncomfortable.

Sandra handled all the rest of the questions like a pro, keeping the reporters entertained for nearly two hours. Sandra and Rose had prepared a small spread of food and drink before Sandra led the reporters to the garden. It was the most unusual press event Wynter had ever attended. Some looked at the spread cautiously while others dug in, waiting their turn to ask questions.

Finally, Sandra made a point of looking at her watch and announced that she needed to bring the press briefing to a close. Hank and Steve led the group to the closed gate as Sandra and Wynter retreated inside the large home.

Rose greeted the two women and started to comment on the press conference when Sophie came running out of the security room hub. Hank and Steve had just entered the house when Sophie yelled, "Security breach on the south side. One of those assholes actually scaled the fence. I don't know if others followed."

Hank grabbed Sophie's arm. "Wait. Let Steve and I handle this. You take care of Wynter and Governor Murphy. The press is probably filming Mr. Commando and his abysmal decision to enter private property."

"I'll call for backup," Steve announced. "We probably should have asked them to stay until the crowd disbursed."

Sophie touched her earbud. "Shit. Got it, Toni. There are now twenty of them climbing the fence," Sophie announced as she pointed to Sandra. "Go wake Ronda. We need her. Now," she ordered.

"Fuck. We have ourselves a mini January 6th," Hank groused.

"I don't suppose you'll let me pick them off, will you?" Sophie asked.

"Don't even joke about that. Look, I didn't see any weapons, but that doesn't mean they aren't carrying. A few could have concealed weapon permits. We'll lock the doors until support arrives. Do we have a way of remotely letting in backup?" Hank asked as he checked the front door to ensure someone had locked it.

"Yeah. Almost everything is remote. Toni also has control of the entire security hub. She's been monitoring the situation. Val is on her way, too," Sophie answered.

"Good, good, but Toni needs to tell Val not to go wild on the trespassers," Hank added.

"Can you use those little dart thingies?" Wynter asked.

"Only as a last resort. I'd rather not have to answer questions about tech the FBI does not possess," Hank answered.

The banging on the door startled Wynter but didn't seem to phase Sophie, Hank, or Steve. Finally, Ronda and Sandra entered the chaos, and Ronda rubbed her eyes, asking, "What the fuck is going on?"

"Overzealous MAGA party guests weren't satisfied with water. They'd like to have afternoon tea now. They heard about the spread in the garden and felt discriminated against," Wynter deadpanned.

Sophie glared at Wynter. "Not helping."

Sandra whispered in Wynter's ear, "I don't think this crew appreciates your jokes."

"Do you?" Wynter grinned.

"I might after this is over," Sandra answered.

"Maybe this will help your campaign," Wynter suggested.

Sandra shook her head. "Either you're joking again, or your inner cynic decided against taking a vacation."

"No, really. We can use this to our advantage. Aren't Republicans supposed to be the party of law and order? This can't look good for their brand, just like January 6th leveled a significant blow to the former president."

Sandra shrugged. "Maybe, maybe not. Facts no longer matter to their base."

"At some point, the overwhelming evidence will make a difference. I have to believe that, and I know you do. You're more optimistic about most things. Don't be a cynic like me."

"Okay, my wise communications director. I'll leave the spin to you." Sandra smiled.

"You three, get your asses into that secure room until we've eliminated the threat. This is no time for idle chit-chat," Sophie directed.

As Rose, Wynter, and Sandra made their way to Sandra's panic room, Wynter leaned in again and whispered, "Never a dull moment with you, is there? Oh, and by the way, did you at least get a permit for building this panic room?" Wynter laughed.

"Smartass," Sandra answered.

Before they entered the panic room, Wynter heard a loud noise that sounded like breaking glass. "Uh-oh, time to lock ourselves inside. I don't think that was a very comforting noise."

CHAPTER TWENTY-ONE

If Sophie had questions regarding the governor's need for a complete security team, they went out the window the minute the large rock came barreling into the room. She had just enough time to pivot to the noise before engaging with a large man huffing while he attempted to crawl through the window. Ronda took the next person who used a rock to break the glass on the edges. Sophie and Ronda had quickly bound the men's arms and legs with zip ties while they screamed profanities. Hank and Steve had both ventured outside, presumably hoping to calm the angry group of men. While Sophie could hear the sounds of fighting, she trusted Hank and Steve to hold their own until Val arrived.

None of the men seemed very bright as Ronda and Sophie immobilized several more with little effort. Sophie decided it was worth the chance that cameras might capture the scuffle because she wasn't about to let Hank and Steve handle the rest of the small mob on their own. She listened to the string of profanities and slurs littering the air and turning it foul.

Crawling through the window the men had broken, Sophie looked around and smiled. Val was a veritable one-woman wrecking crew. Neatly lined up on the lawn were fifteen men, struggling against their bindings and screaming at Val.

"Shut the fuck up, or I'll gag every one of you," Val threatened. "You're lucky I'm not putting a bullet in your head."

Hank approached Val cautiously. "Why don't you go on inside? I've got this now." He turned to Sophie. "I presume everything in the house is copacetic."

"Yeah, six more are next to the broken window. The assholes are ready for you to take into custody," Sophie answered.

Sophie lifted her head as she heard sirens in the distance.

"I'm not quite sure how I'll explain all this, but you three should go inside now," Hank said. "Thanks for the assist, Val."

Val nodded and followed Sophie. Ronda stood tall and glared at the six men sitting on the floor. Sophie gestured with her head for Ronda and Val to follow her.

"The police will be here any second. Hank and Steve will handle things now. We need to make ourselves scarce," Sophie whispered.

They made their way to the panic room, and Sophie announced in front of the camera installed above the door, "All clear."

Wynter looked wide-eyed at Val. "Holy shit. Who are you? I only saw part of the fight outside through the security cameras, and you took ten men by yourself."

Val grunted, "I don't give information to reporters."

Wynter laughed. "Fair enough, but I'm not a reporter anymore."

"We don't have time for this. Hank and Steve are going to work with the local authorities. In the meantime, we need to stay out of the fray. We can either remain inside this room for the next couple of hours or find somewhere else to lie low while the police gather up the unwanted guests," Sophie said.

"It might be a little crowded in here. How about we all retire to the library?" Sandra suggested. "It's in a remote corner of the house and has plenty of seating and creature comforts for everyone."

Val glanced at the blood on her hands and asked, "Is there somewhere I can clean up?"

Before anyone could ask if Val was hurt, she clarified, "It's not mine. Bunch of amateurs that couldn't fight their way out of a paper bag."

The governor nodded. "Follow me. There's a bathroom next to the library. You can use that and then join us after you're done."

†

Wynter and Sandra sat in a corner away from the others, murmuring between themselves. However, Wynter was far too curious about what might be happening outside the library, so she decided to access the live streaming app on her phone, hoping to catch a news report about the attempted assault on Sandra. And, she supposed, herself as well.

The screen on her phone wasn't very large, but Wynter could clearly see the line of cars entering Sandra's estate. Fortunately for the three women who had come to their rescue, it didn't appear as though any of the networks caught the women on camera since the bulk of the fighting occurred close to the house. Wynter watched as the local police directed the reporters away from the gate, blocking even more of their view inside.

For a brief moment, Wynter lamented she wasn't out there with the other reporters attempting to get the story. She had to admit, she would miss the excitement of the chase. Sandra shot a concerned look in her direction.

"You okay?" Sandra asked.

"Yeah." Wynter sighed.

"Already missing your life as a reporter?" Sandra asked.

"Yes and no. Who would have thought I'd be in the center of a major news story?" Wynter attempted a smile.

"It's not going to get any better, Wynter. Are you sure you're up for this? I would understand if you want to go back to the life you had before we, uh, you know...." Sandra let the sentence dangle.

"Fell in love?" Wynter quirked an eyebrow.

"Is that what we've been doing?" Sandra asked.

"Pretty sure that's what I've been doing. So, no, I don't want to return to my old life. That's not to say that there aren't parts of it I'll miss. But I wouldn't change a single thing about the past couple of weeks. In case you haven't noticed, I'm an adrenaline junkie and you've more than fed my need for excitement. I'm all in. Are you?"

"One hundred percent, yes. How can I lose with you by my side? I've grown accustomed to your face."

"*My Fair Lady*? Really? You're quoting that old classic?" Wynter chuckled. "I suppose it fits. You're this high-class woman who is part of the political elite, and I'm a work in progress. So, what else will you teach me besides better manners?" Wynter waggled her brows.

"I think we have many things to teach one another," Sandra answered before stealing a kiss.

"Why, Governor Murphy, not in front of the children," Wynter teased.

All eyes turned to the doorway into the library when Hank entered. "Well, the local authorities were more than a little skeptical about how we neutralized twenty-one men on our own. Four against twenty-one seemed like impossible odds, especially without a single shot fired."

"That's because the FBI and local police are a bunch of pussies." The tall woman who had neglected to give Wynter her name smirked.

"I wouldn't be so glib or arrogant, Val. At least one camera caught your ninja act on tape." Hank held his hand up as Sophie opened her mouth to speak. "I'm not sure if they have the equipment to enhance the video, but it was too blurry to get a good look at your face. At least you had your black hoodie on. I'm not even sure if they could identify your hair color."

"Do you know which station got the video?" Sophie asked.

"The local TRU station has the best video to work with, but I don't believe that's our biggest concern. That group of yahoos got a tip about your press conference this morning. And I'm willing to bet my house that one reporter in the crowd is their source of information. So expect this clusterfuck whenever you have a gathering of reporters."

Sophie nodded and touched her earbud. "Hey, Toni, any chance you can hack into the local news station?" She paused as she listened. "Yeah, okay. The local TRU news station has a video of Val. They might try to enhance it. Can you make it worse instead of better?" Sophie directed her attention to Sandra. "Governor, can you get me a list of the reporters at the press conference this morning?"

"Sure. I recognized everyone but the new reporter from TRU," Sandra answered. "Wynter seems to know him, though."

"Yeah, it was Harold Smith. He's a real piece of work. My money is on him as the person to call forth the angry crowd. He probably thought he could ratchet up the story by adding more conflict, or he's a white nationalist," Wynter added.

"Why do you need their names?" Sandra asked.

Sophie waved her hand as if she were swatting away the pesky question. "You're on a need-to-know basis, and you don't need to know why. Trust me, you don't want to know all the ins and outs of our business. Plausible deniability. Isn't that what politicians need?"

Wynter leaned in and whispered, "Toni's probably going to tap their phones and find the culprit."

"She can do that?" Sandra whispered back.

Sophie pointed at the whispering women. "No secret conferences over there. We're still responsible for protecting you. At least until Em and Jimena take over when they return from vacation."

"I sure hope Emma and Jimena are more fun than Ms. Personality one and two," Wynter mumbled just loud enough for Sandra to hear. Or so she thought.

Ronda grinned. "I hope you aren't lumping me in with Val and Soph," she teased.

Sophie and the new woman both turned their humorless glares to Ronda, who only laughed in response. Wynter was far too curious about these women and vowed to do a little digging. Ronda and Val might not be ex-FBI, but Wynter was convinced that Sophie had spent some of her career in law enforcement, probably FBI. She had that air about her.

CHAPTER TWENTY-TWO

Ten days had gone by, and in that time, Wynter had moved some of her clothes to Sandra's home after reluctantly agreeing it made sense for her to move into Sandra's mansion. After that, everyone settled into a relatively normal routine. Sandra was happy that Wynter seemed to know when she needed a little time and space from the almost dorm-like atmosphere at the house and would retreat to the library during those times. It reminded Sandra of her boarding school days. Finding quiet time was nearly impossible, but the library was often a place to hide.

Val had chosen not to remain at the house. Wynter had learned that Val had a wife and child and relayed that surprising information to Sandra. Although Sophie hadn't exactly opened up to Sandra and Wynter, she had softened her edges, especially when the small group gathered each morning for coffee and to plan out the day. Bits and pieces of their personal life would sneak out, which seemed to pique Wynter's interest more than Sandra's. Sandra had wanted to respect their privacy, but Wynter's natural instincts and curious nature meant she couldn't stop digging. Although, the only thing she found was an old news story about an undercover operation that ended in tragedy. Sophie had left the FBI after her former partner had died when the mission went sideways. Wynter had been excited to share this with Sandra, confirming her earlier assessment that Sophie was ex-FBI. Sandra had already developed considerable respect for Sophie, but now she better understood the seriousness with which Sophie approached her job.

The group had just conferred on the schedule for the day when the doorbell rang. Sophie swiveled her body to face Sandra. "Are you expecting someone this morning? You need to let us know everything," she griped.

Sandra frowned. "No, I am not expecting anyone."

"Okay, hang on while I check the cameras," Sophie directed as she made her way to the security hub.

A minute later, she headed for the front door, opening it and letting in whoever had rung the doorbell. "About time you two showed up. I've almost forgotten what my girlfriend looks like," Sophie teased.

Sandra slipped from the chair, surprised by Sophie's jovial tone. Emma Schmidt and Jimena Aguilar stood in the foyer, each with an overnight bag slung across their shoulder. Both had a healthy glow from their tans as they smiled at

Sophie. Wynter quietly joined Sandra, smiling as she watched the interaction between Sophie, Emma, and Jimena.

"You better put a ring on that lest you lose Kim to some hot thespian," Emma teased.

"I don't think she wants to get married," Sophie defended.

Jimena shook her head. "Typical butch. Have you ever talked about it with her? Jeez, Soph, even Val is married. You and Ronda are the only two holdouts."

"Hank and Steve aren't married," Sophie answered.

"Hey, don't bring us into this," Hank interjected. "We have our reasons to stay under the wire." Then Hank and Steve approached Emma and Jimena, giving each a hug.

Ronda saluted the newcomers. "Leave me out of this, too. Everyone knows Cindy rules the roost. If she wants to marry, she'll ask." Ronda ran her hands over her body. "Don't let this fine butch specimen fool you. Cindy is the real boss."

Sophie startled Sandra when she threw her head back and laughed. She'd seen Sophie smile once or twice but never laugh before, especially not a deep, hearty laugh like she was witnessing in this rare moment.

†

It was their last day at Sandra's house. With the arrival of Em and Jimena, Sophie planned on returning home, and Ronda would stay in San Diego along with Val, Char, and Toni. Rose had arranged for a nice meal before the literal changing of the guard. They all settled in the formal dining area for one last communal gathering. Sophie and Ronda's small bags waited by the door, and Sophie had to admit that she would almost miss the two women she'd been tasked to protect.

She had grown to admire both Wynter and Sandra. Despite the number of attempts on their lives, neither seemed rattled. Instead, both committed themselves to not letting the threats impact their goals. Wynter had been the first to approach Sophie and ask her to teach her self-defense. When Sandra had learned about their early morning lessons, she'd wanted in. Sophie admitted the job wasn't as bad as she thought it would be. She would have offered to stay on if Kim hadn't been so far away. With most of the original agents temporarily residing in San Diego, Sophie and Kim practically had the main compound to themselves.

Sophie didn't think that Wynter or Sandra had noticed the occasion when Val had discreetly disarmed the odd solo attacker during the small test rally Rose had arranged to kick off their campaign. Her respect ratcheted up when at dinner that evening, Sandra casually asked, "Are you and Ronda planning on hanging around like Val?"

"What? Val is not on your security detail. Besides, Em and Jimena are equally qualified to take our spot," Sophie answered.

"Did anyone tell Val that? She removed someone from the crowd the other day. I hope she wasn't just being overzealous. I still maintain every person has a right to protest," Sandra answered. "Even if they are disruptive."

"He was not merely disruptive but carrying a homemade knife made of plastic," Sophie patiently explained.

"Oh." Sandra's face lost its color. "How in the world did she figure that out? I can't imagine he was waving it in the air for all to see."

"Um, the drone that Toni flew over the crowd that day has special tech that can identify weapons not picked up through the metal detectors," Sophie reluctantly answered.

"Any chance Toni would like to sell her inventions to the government?" Sandra asked.

"Nope, they're strictly for our use. We prefer to remain outside of government control. I know you, and especially Wynter, have a lot of questions, but I strongly recommend not asking. Remember plausible deniability." Sophie turned her penetrating gaze to Wynter. "I know you checked into my background and learned I used to be with the FBI. Trust me when I say you'll only learn information we choose to allow you to dig up. Understand?"

Wynter hung her head. "Sorry, Sophie. It's not like I'm going to run to the networks and do a story on any of you. I was simply curious."

"It's good that you didn't try to learn more about Val. She's not as nice and forgiving as I am." Sophie hoped her warning would cool Wynter's reporter instincts.

"I wouldn't exactly classify you as nice and forgiving," Wynter mumbled. "Efficient, observant, a surprisingly patient teacher, yes, but gentle and kind are not necessarily adjectives I would use to describe you."

Ronda chuckled. "She pegged you, except when you're around Kim, and then you turn all soft and gooey."

"Shut it, Ronda," Sophie said with a tiny bite as Ronda grinned unrepentantly at her.

"Too bad you're planning to return to the main compound. I was starting to get used to your curmudgeonly ways," Ronda teased.

"And where is this main compound?" Wynter asked. "Can I take a tour?"

"No," both Ronda and Sophie shouted.

Sandra shook her head. "Didn't Sophie just give you a warning about sticking your nose into their affairs? I'm going to have to give Wynter more work to keep her busy," Sandra teased before her face turned serious. "I don't know how to thank both of you. The least I can do is write a large check for your services. I'll miss our self-defense training."

"Unnecessary. We have all the funding we need. Keep your money. In fact, I believe a sizable chunk is coming your way for your upcoming presidential bid," Sophie answered.

"Self-defense training, huh?" Em inquired. "Good idea. I could take over the training if you want to continue. It might keep me from becoming too bored. Did you conduct the classes in that large workout room I saw?"

Sandra nodded. "We've been meeting every morning at around six. At first, Wynter balked at the time, but now I think she enjoys getting it out of the way before we start our day. It's been fun and rejuvenating."

"Six? I was going to say I'll join the class, too, but count me out at that ungodly hour," Jimena added.

The doorbell rang, and all eyes pivoted toward the sound. Then, as if a switch had turned on, the six agents transformed into tightly woven balls of pure energy, ready to pounce on anyone threatening their charges.

Rose smiled. "Relax, Super Six. It's probably the food. I don't think a domestic terrorist cell would ring the doorbell to come in and execute us all."

Hank stood. "I'll get it."

†

Wynter lay on her back with her hands behind her head, looking up at the ceiling fan in what she now considered her bedroom and Sandra's. It hadn't taken her long to settle into the large home. She hadn't even minded the constant parade of people through the house. Em and Jimena had dumped their bags into Sophie's old room. Wynter decided that living in what she had affectionately labeled the *glammune*, the upscale version of communal living, with other lesbians and gay men was something she never thought she'd enjoy, but she did. Wynter had always loved the slang term *glamping*, and now she had her own new word.

Sophie had softened as the days progressed and even shared a few personal tidbits about herself. Wynter was dying to meet her girlfriend, Kim, because she seemed the opposite of Sophie, whom Wynter had named Sophie Sourpuss. Wynter paid attention to the little clues, hoping to learn more about the mysterious group of women. She'd learned that recently Emma, Jimena, Hank, and Steve had joined The Organization, and she wondered how that worked since they were all still employed with the FBI or Border Patrol. Of course, they all had fighting skills, which Wynter lacked but was working on.

"I think I'm going to miss Sophie Sourpuss," Wynter blurted.

Chuckling, Sandra turned to her side and propped her head in her hand. "You better never let her hear you call her that."

"You heard Ronda. Sophie is like a roasted marshmallow, all crusty on the outside but warm and gooey on the inside. I might have seen glimpses of the Sophie that melts under her girlfriend's glow."

"Do you think Sophie handles the training for everyone?" Sandra asked.

Wynter turned to mirror Sandra's pose. "Maybe. She certainly is an excellent teacher. Although I doubt Val let Sophie train her. She doesn't seem like the type to take instructions well. And from the looks of it, Val doesn't need any pointers. She's like a one-woman wrecking crew. I'd love to interview Val. She's such a fascinating dichotomy of strength and compassion."

"And you know this how?"

"Ronda told me why Val wasn't assigned to security detail, temporary or permanent. Apparently, Val's daughter has Val wrapped tight around her pinkie. She's also very protective of Candy's fiancé, Dani. She's another tech expert like Toni and got caught up in the same undercover mission that went wrong for Sophie and caused her to leave the FBI. Dani was seriously injured. Took a bullet to her back and still struggles with crutches." Wynter pulled herself into a sitting position and let the sheet drop against her waist, showing her naked breasts.

"You got all of that out of Ronda? How did you manage that feat?" Sandra asked before also sitting up in bed.

Wynter shrugged. "I have an honest face. People tell me stuff. Sophie even let a few tidbits slip. Mostly about Kim, but she has a lot of respect for her fellow agents. She'd die for any of them. Almost has on a few occasions. But, apparently, when she first met some of the other agents in their mysterious Organization, she wasn't too keen on joining."

"Not that I'm not grateful for their expertise, but there is a part of me that wonders what they might want in return, especially if I manage to do the impossible and become the next president. Unfortunately, politics can be a very transactional business. That's why I wanted to pay them for their services. I don't like owing favors, especially ones I'm not sure I would want to pay. I get the sense they make their money through less than reputable means."

"Maybe," Wynter answered. "But don't you also suspect that whatever bending of the rules is for the greater good?"

"I've never favored the idiom *the ends justify the means*." Sandra wrinkled her forehead.

"Maybe they're like some modern-day Robin Hoods, stealing from the rich and redistributing the wealth to those that need it. If the politicians would get off their asses and tax the one percent fairly, we wouldn't need anyone to break the laws. A few years ago, I looked into this story about missing funds from places known to shelter money, like Cayman Islands bank accounts. Coincidently, several charities received windfalls from an anonymous donor at about the same time those funds went missing," Wynter shared.

"You aren't suggesting that these women were behind that, are you?" Sandra asked.

Wynter shrugged again. "Possibly. Would it be so far-fetched? Toni is a genius who seems to be able to hack into any security system. They have tech I've never heard of."

"So, what did you find out?" Sandra asked. "Now you have me curious."

"I hit a massive wall. Dead end. That was right about the time Toni started contacting me and feeding me information on other stories that were too tempting not to follow. So I let go of the threads to the Robin Hood story and began chasing other more interesting leads to different stories. Since I don't believe in coincidences, I assume Toni and this group did not want me digging into the Robin Hood rumors."

Sandra smiled. "Still conjecture on your part."

"Yeah, but wouldn't it be cool if it was true? Although, I won't pursue the story because, as Sophie has warned on several occasions, plausible deniability is important. I wouldn't be able to contain my enthusiasm if I learned it was true. I'd have to at least tell you." Wynter glanced at the clock. "Do you think Em was serious about continuing our training? It's after six."

Sandra threw off the covers and rummaged in her drawers, grabbing her workout gear. "Em seems like a person who doesn't make offers she doesn't intend to follow through with."

CHAPTER TWENTY-THREE

Despite all the travel and busyness of a presidential campaign, Sandra still felt the need to listen to the news in the evenings. Wynter would often receive a heads up to a major story, relying on her sources to keep her ear to the ground, especially related to recent polls or anything that might affect the campaign.

Sandra had hoped to get a little work done while Wynter was looking over the draft of a speech she was about to give. Two quick knocks on Sandra's office door preceded Wynter bursting inside.

"The FBI just finished searching the former president's home. They took away eleven boxes of what some are presuming are more classified documents he isn't supposed to have. The far right is going crazy. Just when we thought his influence was fading." Wynter sighed. "Damn, I wish I was still a reporter right about now. I can't believe I didn't even hear a whisper about this."

"Well, that's how it's supposed to work," Sandra answered.

"Do you think Hank, Steve, or Em knew about this?" Wynter asked.

"I doubt it." Sandra frowned. "I sure hope this does not change our plans to travel to Michigan for the rally there."

"Why would it?"

"When we stir up the right, bad things happen," Sandra answered.

"I think for right now, they've focused their ire on the FBI. We're merely an afterthought at this point. It would certainly be a stretch to blame you for this latest bombshell. You have no sway over the Department of Justice. However, we must be prepared to respond to questions about this. So let me think about it." Wynter ran her hand through her hair.

"You know, you really are very good at this. I wouldn't want anyone else by my side for this adventure. Win or lose; I've already won because you came into my life." It was now or never. Sandra decided the time to hold back on expressing her feelings had long passed. "I love you."

"Enough to make me press secretary when you win?" Wynter teased, then her expression turned deadly serious. "I love you, too."

Sandra smiled. "Well, that's a given that you would become press secretary. If the former president can hire his daughter and son-in-law as senior advisors to the president, surely I can hire you as my press secretary."

"We have to get through the election first. But, I have a very good feeling. You're going to make history, and I feel privileged to travel this historical road with you. I'll stay by your side for as long as you'll have me."

"Well, that's good because with you there with me, there's no mountain too high to climb. I hoped that since the living arrangements have worked so well, you might decide to sell your condo and make this a permanent arrangement." Sandra crossed her fingers that Wynter would agree to move in officially with her.

"I think that's a splendid idea. Although, I'd like to hang onto my condo as an investment and turn it into an Air B&B. That seems to be the rage now. I just can't see myself making you my sugar momma. Having my own money is very important to me. Maintaining a certain amount of independence will always be a given."

"Of course. It's one of the things I love most about you—that fiercely independent streak. It's sexy as hell to me."

"Sexy as hell, huh? Well, what's sexy as hell to me is you naked, writhing in pleasure underneath me while I take my time teasing an earth-shattering orgasm from you. And no time like the present. I think you need a quick break. Right now." Wynter held out her hand, and Sandra eagerly took it. She could make the time for Wynter.

They still had a lot to work out, including when they would make an announcement about their relationship, but Sandra knew they had plenty of time for that. Serious consideration about marriage would need to wait until after the election. She only hoped the craziest surprises of the following year and a half would not derail the plans she was already starting to make in her mind about their future together.

EPILOGUE

It was late, and everyone was tired and running on pure fumes, but the good news that kept coming injected fresh energy into Sandra's inner circle. Wynter anxiously waited as the results rolled in. She kept her eyes glued to the massive monitors in the large hall Sandra had rented for election night. Wynter knew it was a silly superstition, but she crossed her fingers when she saw the Breaking News logo flash across the screen, and Anderson Cooper called Florida. Sandra had done the impossible and captured the sunshine state. It guaranteed her path to the presidency unless she lost every other state that still had not been called.

Like glorious dominos, it only took another hour for CNN to call the race. Sandra Murphy would be the forty-seventh president of the United States. Wynter leaped into Sandra's arms and hugged her.

"You ready for this?" Sandra whispered in her ear.

"I can't wait," Wynter answered.

Sandra took the three steps to the stage, and Wynter could see her take a big breath before starting her speech. They had decided weeks ago that she would not wait to make a speech if she won. A concession would never come Sandra's way from that vile man. He hadn't conceded before, and they knew hell would freeze over before he ever conceded to a woman.

As Sandra adjusted the microphone, Wynter looked to her right, noticing a disturbance in the crowd. Somehow, a relatively large group of the MAGA base held unoriginal signs stating, "Stop The Steal." They began chanting, "Illegal president," along with multiple slurs. She couldn't believe they also stole the slogan, "Not my president," from nearly eight years ago when men and women on the left came out in droves to protest the MAGA leader. Then the violent shouts began, including a reprise of, "Hang Sandra Murphy."

Here we go again. Wynter wasn't sure how the assholes saw the writing on the wall and made their way into the ballroom where Sandra's supporters were already celebrating the victory. After a year and a half of training, Wynter wanted to walk over and join Em, Jimena, Val, Ronda, Sophie, Steve, and Hank, who didn't really need her assistance. But she stopped in her tracks when she heard Sandra say her name. In her distraction, Wynter had missed a major part of the speech. However, she wasn't too concerned since Sandra had practiced both versions in front of Wynter. Plus, Wynter had written a good portion of the speech and could recite it herself, word for word.

Wynter reluctantly turned her focus back to the stage and the love of her life. Sandra beckoned Wynter to join her on stage.

"Finally, I wish to thank my communications director, for none of this would be possible without her steady guidance and unwavering support for me both personally and professionally."

Wynter finally reached Sandra and kissed her cheek. "Hello, President-Elect Murphy." Sandra's smile lit up the stage.

Not too long after their major campaigning push began, the two women had contacted a trusted reporter that Wynter knew to announce they were in a relationship well before election night. Wynter had argued for getting that bombshell out of the way. They didn't need a perception that Sandra was hiding something major to avoid providing political fodder for her critics. Sandra had agreed, and the interview had gone better than expected. They were the new power couple. And although they had their fair share of genuinely horrific criticism, there were more Americans that supported the budding romance.

Confetti continued to rain down on the crowd of supporters as Sandra finished her speech and moved gracefully through the packed room. Offering hugs to some and accepting handshakes from others, Wynter saw Em and Jimena rapidly making their way toward Sandra. The scowls on their faces told the story of their displeasure. It was a running argument in the house. Each time Sandra finished a speech, she would jump from the stage and spend hours with her supporters. Em, Jimena, Hank, and Steve often had very vocal hissy fits about this practice, warning it was nearly impossible to screen every person in the sizable crowds that Sandra attracted as she traversed the country. Sandra had insisted that she could fend off any risk until they could neutralize a potentially violent person.

Wynter had learned to read micro-expressions, and when she noticed a woman making her way to Sandra with a fake smile, alarm bells started ringing in her head. Something in the woman's hand caught one of the fluorescent lights, and Wynter had barely enough time to react. She kicked the piece of jagged glass from the woman's hand. Two seconds later, Em had reached Wynter and Sandra and quickly bound the woman's hands, leading her to the exit doors.

Wynter wasn't sure whatever happened to the individuals that Sandra's very efficient security team would handle, although she suspected that there was always a police presence at the events. Tonight Wynter assumed that Hank and Steve had also called in a few favors because several FBI agents roamed the ballroom, ready and able to arrest anyone who had crossed a line.

One thing about Sandra was that she was unflappable. Leaning in, she whispered to Wynter. "Nice roundhouse kick, Wynter. It's a good thing we practiced those last week. I might have to take back my offer to make you my press secretary and instead hire you as my personal bodyguard."

Wynter chuckled and whispered in Sandra's ear, "I've been dying to get in the muck of things. It's why I almost missed you calling me to the stage. Something was happening in the back of the room while you were making your speech, and I wanted in on the fun. Do you think they'll consider letting me join their club? I can fight almost as good as Em now."

"Don't even joke about that. I want you by my side for a very long time."

Jimena deftly led Wynter and Sandra away from the dense crowd. "Are you two done here? Em is going to read you the riot act later. You know that, right?"

Sandra nodded. "I suppose it is late, and you all are exhausted. I'm sorry you had to do triple duty tonight. I'm really going to miss you two. Any chance you would consider joining the Secret Service?"

"Anything is possible. Em didn't think she would like this gig as much as she has. It wasn't as boring as she expected," Jimena answered.

"Unfortunately, I have a knack for attracting MAGA zealots who don't exactly share my view of how the world should work," Sandra quipped.

"That's one way of looking at it," Jimena responded. "Hank and Steve are bringing around the car. Shall we?" Jimena gestured for Sandra and Wynter to walk to the right and take the side exit they had presumably cleared.

†

For once, Sandra wasn't eager to jump from their bed and start the day. It had been a long night waiting for the results to come in. Wynter was curled up on her side with her hand against her cheek, snoring softly. When Sandra shifted in the bed, Wynter stirred, turned, and opened her eyes.

"Good morning, Madam President."

"Not quite yet," Sandra answered. "Are you ready for breakfast, or probably brunch? It's late. I have something to ask you. I briefly considered asking last night but didn't want it to come across as some cheap political trick." Sandra pushed aside the covers and walked to the master bath to retrieve her robe.

Wynter's face scrunched in confusion as she crawled from the bed and then rummaged through the drawers to retrieve a pair of shorts and a tank top. "What kind of question would you perceive as a cheap political trick?"

"I know we made a formal announcement over a year ago about our relationship because we wanted to be as transparent as possible. However, I didn't want to share this moment with anyone else. Perhaps this isn't the most romantic way of doing things…"

Wynter's eyes went wide. "Holy shit. Really?"

"My knees aren't what they used to be, so I hope this still works." Sandra opened the top drawer of her dresser and pulled out a small ring box. "When we started this amazing adventure, I said to you, win or lose, I felt like I'd already won when you came into my life. However, I'll consider this a bigger win than the one last night if you say yes. Wynter, will you agree to become my first lady? I am stronger with you by my side, and I'm sure everyone wants the strongest leader possible to navigate these challenging times."

"Does that mean I get to live in the White House with you? Probably wouldn't look good if the president of the United States was living in sin with their girlfriend. I suppose for the sake of propriety, we should get married, but only if we get a cat. I can't wait to create an official Twitter account for him or her," Wynter deadpanned.

Sandra threw her head back and laughed. "If a cat is the price I need to pay to get an affirmative response, then let's head to the shelter today. Are you ready for the next leg of our adventure?" Sandra slipped the ring onto Wynter's finger.

"Absolutely. We also need to find a jewelry store. I'm not letting you go too long without putting a ring on your finger. Gotta lock that shit down before another beauty comes along, angling for a shot at being the first lady. Speaking of putting a ring on it, Em told me that Sophie finally asked Kim to marry her. Ronda is still waiting for Cindy to pop the question."

"How do you know all this?" Sandra asked.

"Hank is the worst gossip I've ever met. I think he was jealous. Both of them are still in the closet. Honestly, I don't know which agency would be more accepting, the FBI or Secret Service. Maybe they can also apply to the Secret Service, and we can keep our security team intact."

"That would be ideal, huh? You know that there will be a lot more agents assigned to both of us," Sandra said.

"You can request specific agents, though, right?" Wynter asked.

"I believe I can name whomever I want as the head of the Secret Service and then let that person know if we have preferences for specific agents," Sandra answered. "Plenty of time to make those decisions. Besides, I'm not worried. I have you, my personal bodyguard, and you're a force, as evidenced by that martial arts move you made last night."

"I certainly can't have anyone assassinating my future bride. I love her too much."

"I love you too and can't wait to build a life with you and our new kitty. I think we should look for an older cat. They need love, too. We old folks need to stick together."

Wynter shook her head. "I hardly think one of the youngest presidents in our history would be considered old. You're the perfect age for me."

Sandra laughed. "A spin doctor to the bitter end."

"Only for you, darling. Only for you."

AUTHOR NOTE

Thank you for your support of my books. You are the reason I continue to write and am inspired to spin these tales. If you enjoyed this book, I hope you will consider leaving a review or rating the book on Amazon, Goodreads, or wherever you are comfortable. Look for the third book in the series, Love Bonds, due out in August, 2023. A sneak peek follows this note. Additionally, as a thank you to all of my subscribers on my mailing list I offer links to free short stories. Here is the link to subscribe: http://eepurl.com/cS7nr9 I promise not to bombard you with messages, but will only send an email when I have a new book release or a new offering of a free short story.

Peace,

Annette

SNEAK PEAK LOVE BONDS
AUGUST 2023

CHAPTER ONE

The dank interior of the rotted-out shelter barely shed light on a man huddled in the corner, sipping a cold cup of coffee laced with vodka. Although it was the middle of the day, very little sunlight leaked inside since the previous owner had boarded up every window. The man ran his hand over the stubble on his face, contemplating his options.

Dimitri didn't enjoy the position he was in. His superiors had assumed he double-crossed them merely because he'd helped Bridget escape. But that wasn't accurate. William was the one who had arranged everything.

Dimitri was merely the lackey William used to secure her transfer to the safe house. Unfortunately, facts did not matter to the Russians. Even a hint of disloyalty would get you killed.

He knew of only one way out of this mess. Somehow, he would need to convince the Russians they had eliminated the wrong target, and that Bridget was still alive. He'd been hiding in this literal rathole for two weeks while the US government had rounded up his comrades, except that snake, William.

"I'm going to make that *mudak* pay for what he's done," Dimitri screamed at the rat who casually strolled by. Dimitri paced the dark interior, kicking up dust and God knows what else. When another rat crossed his path, he brought down his heavy boot, crushing the annoying rodent beneath. A satisfied smirk grew on his gaunt face.

William's name was not on the list because Bridget hadn't known about him, but William didn't know that. William was always careful to keep his fingerprints clear of any mission. He had men to do his dirty work.

It was a desperate plan, but these were the only cards he had to play. If Dimitri's plans worked the way he envisioned, all he needed to do was ensure anonymous intel reached William, proving Bridget had survived. Then he'd have the body double eliminated once he was in the clear. Maybe he could ensure the mysterious women received the same intel, and perhaps they would do the job for him. He'd leave bread crumbs, just enough for an assassin to be conveniently sent to take care of the imposter. Or he'd let

William think he'd found Bridget and let him take care of that loose end. Of course, by then, Dimitri would be long gone.

He had a few allies he could turn to that owed him a favor or two, but he didn't have a lot of time. It was a miracle the US government had not swept those allies up in a clean-up mission after obtaining that fucking thumb drive.

Dimitri had thought it divine intervention when he'd crossed paths with the woman he and William assumed dead. He couldn't believe she was now living in San Diego instead of DC. Bridget hadn't shown any interest when he'd shared the information with her—a blood relative. Damn, she was a cold fish. But that worked to his advantage. It was also fortunate Bridget hadn't known about William and his role in assisting with her escape, but the Russians didn't know that either. William would assume that Bridget knew all along about his double-cross.

It was stupid of Bridget to make that thumb drive, even though the list had excluded William's name and his own. "I know there are more high-level Russians still in strategic positions. It won't matter that I don't know who they are because William will assume Bridget has a lot more intel beyond his name and position in the government," Dimitri mumbled to himself and the rodents occupying his temporary lodging.

Even if William didn't make that presumption, Dimitri would drag him in that direction until he understood the risks. He would want to ensure that Bridget did not survive the blast.

Lifting the burner phone to his ear, he contacted his friends. "I have a package for you to pick up. *Da*, yes, I'll send the location and details on the car. In the parking lot, before her shift."

A quick grab was necessary, and then he'd need to attract William's attention. Dimitri suspected the women were very good at what they did. They'd somehow managed to capture Bridget. He'd just have to attract their attention and William's. Let those women and William duke it out. The more William occupied himself with continued threats from that mysterious Organization, the less time he would devote to tracking Dimitri down. William had a reason to hate them, and it would not bode well for him if they knew who he truly was. But then, why should he care? So be it if they got to William after he was free and clear.

William had kept his true identity hidden for the past thirty years, rising to a place of prominence and influence in the United States government. He was even more cunning than Bridget. At this point, Dimitri didn't particularly care about the competent women in the illicit Organization. Poking that bear was merely a means to an end. William, on the other hand, hated them with a passion. Dimitri heard how William had tried to convince everyone that the women were responsible for the death of his younger brothers, Leonid and Alexei. But the Russians weren't buying his tale, not believing a group of *biyads* had prevailed over his brothers.

William was his only chance to escape his predicament. He had the resources to buy him off. Dimitri would find his own fake documents to leave the country, but he needed money to do that. That didn't mean he wouldn't ask for ten sets of false identities. Knowing William would follow every lead, he'd have fun making the Russians run after their own tail while he was escaping right under their noses. At this point, retirement was his only option.

†

An impeccably dressed man in an expensive Armani suit slammed the secure phone on his desk. His richly decorated office, with paintings of American heroes, enclosed William in a cocoon of luxury. Unfortunately, the mahogany desk gave the room an oppressive feel, along with the muted color on the walls and other antique furniture. But William didn't mind the ambiance of the office; it suited him.

"I'm working with fucking amateurs," he shouted in the empty chamber. Thick walls separated him from his assistant on the other side of the closed door.

Not only had the US government retrieved the thumb drive with names of nearly every Russian operative placed in the US, but now that bitch was running free, with God knows what damaging information. And she'd likely developed additional insurance regarding her survival from the authorized hit he'd personally ordered.

William had no choice but to round up most of his comrades because too many individuals had access to the sensitive data on the drive. He'd wondered at the time why his name was not on the list. Perhaps this was their plan all along. Did Dimitri expect they were about to double-cross Bridget?

At the time, his men had assured him they had resolved the problem. Then again, they had also convinced him that the thumb drive was in safe hands until it wasn't. Now, his intel had informed him the damn cockroach was still alive. And how the fuck did they blast the wrong woman? The intel came through the secure Homeland Security channel, and the CIA was many things, but inaccurate wasn't one of them. He wasn't all that concerned about his superior in the US government. That man was an idiot. William would take his lumps, but there was no real threat to his position. On the other hand, Bridget and Dimitri had him by the balls.

Somehow, they'd switched Bridget with what the government thought was her doppelgänger. If they only knew what the actual story was. The truth was stranger than fiction, but only a few people knew she was alive.

So many years ago. That had also been a botched killing, but it didn't seem crucial to complete the job. Then they'd lost track of the blasted woman. Fucking Dimitri, he was the one that was supposed to take care of Sasha. How in the world had he found her? William should have tracked her down all those years ago and ensured she wasn't an issue.

Of course, this had Dimitri's fingerprints all over it. He was the only other person who could have possibly known to make the switch with this other woman. He must have tracked her down for Bridget and sent her to the safe house in Bridget's place. That's why you never combined business with pleasure. Bridget had outmaneuvered him. Again.

Sweat dripped down his handsome forehead. It was only a matter of time before the cunning bitch contacted him. William would have to wait until they made their play. Blackmail for sure, but for what? Freedom? A new identity? This time, he might have to give her exactly what she wanted. That would most certainly include enough money for Dimitri's freedom, but maybe not. Bridget seemed to use men as pawns. Her self-interests always prevailed. It was too bad, really. She was an excellent agent. She'd managed to further their cause. Although they'd not achieved their goal with the governor, Bridget had set the more pressing outcome in motion—increased extremism and divisiveness in the country. They might not even have to take out the governor because the American extremists would do it for them.

That didn't make Bridget any less dangerous and someone they needed to eliminate. Permanently. Although William feared that even without the information she undoubtedly kept in a secure location, the US government wasn't a bunch of imbeciles. At some point, they would ascertain that someone in the upper ranks of Homeland Security was a double agent.

Drumming his fingers on the massive imported desk, he walked to the safe behind the fake wall and plucked his secure phone from inside, the one with a direct line to the Kremlin. Punching in the number to his superior, he began reporting, "Bridget Schmidt is alive. Permission to exercise clean-up protocol."

After listening to the man on the other end of the phone, William responded, "Yes, I am aware of that. I suspect the same group of women are working with Bridget and Dimitri, but I haven't located their complex. Nor have I determined exactly who these women are. All I have is the intel obtained based on previous interference, including the scant evidence of their involvement in Leonid and Alexei's deaths." William tried again to convince his superior these mysterious women existed, but he wasn't biting.

"We still have not determined how they were able to track Bridget Schmidt or obtain the thumb drive. If only you would listen," William pleaded again. "I believe these women command cutting-edge tech that even the US government does not possess. Therefore, we must presume Bridget controls additional information that would embarrass the Kremlin and place all of our operations at tremendous risk."

Leaning back in his comfortable leather chair, he assured his handler. "No, I'm quite positive I am not compromised." That was a lie, but he wasn't about to reveal his suspicions. "I don't believe Schmidt was privy to that level of confidential information. Although, she is certainly intelligent enough to make some suppositions. Yes, but that just reinforces my position that we eliminate the threat by activating our clean-up protocol. I don't believe we can take that chance. Very well. I'll take care of it."

William needed air. The walls were closing in, and he couldn't breathe anymore. Two fucking weeks. It had been two weeks since this mess had blown up in his face. He'd survived, but barely.

He knew it was only a matter of time before they discovered his real identity. While his brothers had taken a different path, one that did not directly help the motherland and that he personally found distasteful, he couldn't really blame them. They hadn't grown up with the same privileges as he had. He'd been fortunate to attend private schools and secure a master's degree from a first-rate university in the United States. His placement in a prominent family in the US to groom him for greater glory was far different from growing up in the slums of Russia. Leonid and Alexei's only choice to rise above the filth was to become ruthless mobsters. It wasn't their fault. At least they'd contributed a portion of their earnings to the Russian government. That was something.

As he exited his office, squinting into the sunshine and taking in large breaths of air, his burner phone rang. "Hello. Ah, Dimitri. That didn't take long. I was expecting to hear from Bridget. Yes, I've been authorized to do whatever it takes to ensure it does not compromise our mission. Name your requirements."

The insignificant cockroach had the audacity to inform William he'd be in touch with further instructions, or all hell would break loose. At least he'd sent the asshole scrambling by insisting he provide proof of Bridget's survival. No video corroboration. No exit package. That would give him two opportunities to catch the bastard. The video proof would need verification, and that meant two meetings or two drops.

"Could Dimitri and Bridget really be so stupid to think they can get away so easily? I'll track every fake ID included in the package," he mumbled to the empty room. The self-assurance was a desperate attempt to ease his doubts about having everything under control.

CHAPTER TWO

Mila ran her hand through her sandy blonde hair. Her caramel-colored eyes stared blankly inside her patrol vehicle. She was sure something was wrong; her cop instincts told her so. Simply because she'd only just completed her police academy training, and was a lowly patrol officer, didn't mean that her routine-driven mother wasn't missing. Her mother hadn't shown up for her shift at the local hospital which was not like her. At all.

The first thing Mila did was check the *Find My Phone* link she'd placed on her smartphone. Her mother hadn't understood the new tech, but Mila had, and she made sure she linked their whole family. Unfortunately, her mom was always misplacing her phone. As a police officer, Mila knew every phone was trackable, even burner phones unless someone used a special burner app and was sophisticated enough to alter the phone. But that was not her mother. Besides, utilizing the *Find My Phone* tool made it quicker and easier to locate a lost phone immediately. When she saw the phone was in the general vicinity of the hospital, that told her she'd made it to her place of employment.

She knew she might get in trouble for taking a quick detour to the hospital during her watch, considering Mila had only just begun, but that was where she had located her mother's phone. What if something happened to her before she entered the hospital, and no one thought to look for her? Her mother was healthy, but that didn't mean she hadn't suffered a heart attack or aneurysm.

The hospital had first called her father, but he hadn't picked up. She loved her father, but he often left his personal cell phone in his office and forgot to check his messages. His work phone was always with him because, as chief of police, it was almost a requirement to stay connected twenty-four-seven to the politicians.

Mila resented how all the other officers presumed she'd gotten her position because of her connection to the chief. Gritting her teeth, she reminded everyone she'd graduated at the top of her class and received the highest score on her physical agility test. Misogynous assholes. Every. Single. One.

Mila wasn't very tall, but she was a force to be reckoned with. Compact and muscular, she often appeared more imposing than someone taller. Marching up to the first detective she could find at the station, fire in her amber eyes, she pleaded her case.

"Frank, I'm telling you something is wrong. Mom never misses a shift. Ever. Not that I would pull the chief card, but when it comes to my mom, I'm not above doing whatever it takes for you to get off your lazy ass and pursue this." Mila's jaw tightened as she made the impassioned plea. Or was it a threat?

Frank, a slovenly detective with a noticeable pot belly pushing against the buttons of his too-tight shirt, answered, "Aw, come on, Mila, quit busting my balls. She hasn't even been missing twenty-four hours."

"You know as well as I do there is no set amount of time for a person to be missing before the police can begin investigating. That's a bullshit myth you can feel free to peddle to someone not in the know."

Frank sighed and pushed his fingers through his unkempt graying hair. "Okay, tell me everything you know, and I'll do some follow-up."

"I want Bernie on the case. Where is she?" Mila looked around the office.

"You've got to be fucking kidding me. Bernie's been through six partners. She's a bigger ball buster than you." Frank grimaced before bringing the coffee to his pale, bulbous lips.

"Fine, tell me where she is right now, and I'll approach her. I'll even give you a pass and work with her myself as long as you cover for me." Mila smirked, knowing this was what she had hoped for all along. Frank might be a halfway decent detective, and that was being generous, but he didn't go the extra mile like Bernie.

"I'm a detective, not a patrol officer. I will do no such thing," Frank huffed, hiking up his pants.

"Then call in a marker and get my shifts covered for the next few days." Mila batted her amber eyes. "Come on, Frank, you owe me for not telling your wife about that bachelor's party where the stripper gave you instead of the groom-to-be that lap dance."

"Fuck," Frank hissed. "Why were you even there? It was supposed to be a guy's thing."

Mila shrugged. "Can I help it if the groom is a good friend, and he knows I like the ladies? You might have gotten the lap dance by mistake, but I got her number."

"All right. I'll find your replacement. Pete owes me." Frank chuckled. "But, good luck with Bernie. She was in a particularly foul mood this morning. I think she's talking with the captain in his office. Getting her butt chewed, if I'm not mistaken." His eyes shifted to the closed door with the blinds shut tight.

"Thanks, Frank. Consider the slate clean. My lips are sealed forever." Mila pantomimed zipping her lips shut.

"Yeah, yeah. It's a good thing I like you, kid."

"Don't call me kid." She scowled at him.

†

Mila waited outside the captain's office with one foot propped against the wall and her arms crossed over her chest. When Bernie stomped out, she immediately tossed a coffee cup into the trash can several yards away. Dark liquid erupted from inside the can, and several drops spilled over the side. Mila rushed to catch up with the recalcitrant detective.

315

Bernie was an imposing woman, standing nearly six feet tall with short, perpetually disheveled hair that fell to just the top of her shoulders. The color reminded Mila of the coffee that dripped down the sides of the trash can where Bernie had tossed her cup. When she'd first seen Bernie, she thought she'd lost one of her colored contacts because one eye was a vibrant blue and the other a muted hazel. But Bernie had gruffly explained that she had a rare condition called heterochromia, and those were her natural eye colors. Bernie had held up her hand and warned Mila about not making a joke about huskies. Mila wasn't about to do that. Instead, she'd wanted to tell her how cool that was. Sexy, actually, but she wouldn't say that out loud.

"Bernie, wait up. I need to talk to you." Mila hurried to catch up with Bernie's long legs as they strode away.

Bernie turned and narrowed her gaze at Mila. The harshness of her eyes seemed to soften a tiny bit before looking Mila directly in the eye, as if evaluating something only she could assess.

"Mila, what's got you all worked up?"

"I'm not worked up." Mila shook her head. "Okay, I am worked up. Mom is missing." Mila rushed to finish her plea. "Frank got my shifts covered for the next two days, so I can work with you to find her." Now that Mila was close enough to touch her major crush, she tried hard to avoid staring at her, lest Bernie get the wrong idea. This wasn't about her attraction, it was about Bernie's exceptional abilities as a detective.

"Whoa. First, I work in homicide, not missing persons. And second, even if I were to take the case, you know I can't bring you along. Your father will have my ass. I haven't exactly given him many reasons to cut me slack lately." Bernie glanced back at the office she'd just exited.

"Sure you have. You've closed all of your last ten cases. Dad respects you, and so do I. I know I'm only a lowly patrol officer, but I won't be one for long. I'm going to be the youngest person to ever make detective, and what better way to get my feet wet than working with you? Besides, it's my mom. So I have a vested interest."

"So does your father. Why isn't he all over this?" Bernie narrowed her eyes.

"He doesn't know yet." Mila looked away.

Bernie's face screwed in disgust. "Yeah, that's right, he's in meetings with some big political mucky mucks. Part of the reason I just got my ass chewed by the captain. But that's all beside the point. Because you have a vested interest, that's exactly why you need to stay far away from this. Look, Mila, I'll do my best to find out what happened, but I work alone. Okay?"

"Not okay. I figured I could get a jump on this and maybe find Mom before Dad even has to get involved," Mila pleaded, adding, "because this will destroy him."

Bernie shook her head. "I can't have some wet behind the ears, rookie, tagging along like a lost puppy while I work."

"I might have just graduated," Mila grunted, "but I grew up listening to my father, hanging on his every word when he talked about his cases. I know a lot more about how to follow up. The average rookie doesn't know how or what questions to ask. Please, Bernie, I have to help. It's my mother. The first twenty-four hours are crucial. Our family can't be this unlucky to have it happen again."

Bernie held her gaze with an appraising eye. "What do you mean, happen again?"

Mila slapped a hand over her mouth. She'd gotten into police work because she was bound and determined to find out what had happened to her half-sister, but she wasn't supposed to know anything about it.

"Shit, forget I just said that." Mila lifted her booted foot and pressed her toe into the floor.

Bernie grabbed Mila's arm and pulled her into an interrogation room.

†

Mila sat in the hard-backed chair, waiting for Bernie to sit as well. Before resigning herself to her fate, Mila tried a diversion tactic to give her a bit more time.

"So, why was the captain reaming you?"

"Fucking politics. The captain wanted me to join the FBI, Homeland Security, and whomever else they invited to the party to escort that Russian spy. I can't even imagine what shitty hole where they planned to store her until they got every possible bit of intel out of her." Bernie squinted her eyes and shook her head, taking a seat across from Mila. "Fucking A, most obvious trick in the book. Clearly, I'm not at my best this morning. So...no more stalling. Spill it."

318

Mila recounted the story of how she'd overheard her mother and father one evening after waking to the soft sobs of her mother. Peeking from the top of the stairs, she listened to their murmuring voices.

Her father was rubbing small circles over her mother's back. "No, honey, I'm sure it wasn't her. I studied the picture you gave me, and even with age, this young woman was definitely not your daughter. Besides, I had them run a DNA test, and it wasn't a match. I promise I'll keep looking. If she's out there, we'll find her."

"It's been ten years. They could have sold her off or even taken her back to Russia by now. We'll never find her." Her mother swiped the tissue against her eyes and continued to sob.

Mila had slipped quietly back into her room and vowed that when she got older, she would be like the great female detective, Miss Marple. It didn't matter that Miss Marple wasn't a real person. Mila also enjoyed reading the *Harriet the Spy* books, but Harriet didn't solve grown-up mysteries like Miss Marple.

"Wow! I never knew that. You know your dad keeps his cards very close to his vest. I know I only started here five years ago, but I would have helped him track down your sister if only he'd asked," Bernie noted.

Mila shrugged. "I think he'd given up hope by the time you'd joined this precinct. I'm not sure my mother ever has. There's always this residual sadness in her eyes. I know she loves me and was thrilled when she got pregnant after marrying my dad, but does a mother ever get over losing their child? Especially when you don't know whatever became of them."

"I guess not." Bernie sucked in a mouthful of air and shook her head. "I'm probably going to regret this, but I have a soft spot for you, kid."

"Don't call me kid," Mila spit back. "For fuck's sake, you're what, ten years older than me? I am not, nor will I be, young enough to be your child. That's just gross to think about."

"Why in the world would that be gross to think about?" Bernie's perplexed expression had Mila rushing to change the subject.

"Can I tell you what I've learned so far?"

Mila couldn't very well admit that she had a massive crush on Bernie. She'd pleasured herself enough to the fantasy of Bernie and her making mad passionate love in the back of her cruiser. The beach. On her kitchen table. In front of a roaring fire. At a five-star hotel. Hell, there weren't many places she hadn't imagined the sexy detective fucking her.

Finally, Bernie motioned with her hand for Mila to continue.

"Okay, so I went to the hospital, and her car was in the parking lot…"

Release Date: August 2023

ABOUT THE AUTHOR

Annette is an award-winning author, published by Affinity Rainbow Publications, who lives in the beautiful Pacific Northwest with her wife and their five furry kids. With twenty-nine published novels, three Lesfic Bard Awards, and one Goldie Award for her fourth novel, *Locked Inside*, she finally feels like a real author. Annette is as much a reader as a writer and is always looking for the next sapphic novel to queue up. She came up with the One Fan at a Time tagline, because it rolled off the tongue much better than One Reader at a Time. After pondering who she was at her core, she feels it was all about connecting to each reader on a personal level. Annette would be the first to admit she doesn't do well with the masses. If someone picks up her book and it touches them, she believes she has achieved what she wants with her writing by reaching each reader. It is who she is at her core. Drop her a line. She loves to hear from readers.

Email: annettemori0859@gmail.com.
Sign up for her mailing list: http://eepurl.com/cS7nr9
Check out her blog: Everyday Occurrences:
https://annettemori0859.wordpress.com/
Visit the Affinity Rainbow Publications website for her books and many other outstanding authors:www.affinityebooks.com

OTHER AFFINITY BOOKS

Remember Me by Del Robertson
Sarah Lindley followed her brother into the untamed Wild West in search of adventure. She found it – in the form of a woman unlike any she'd ever met before.

Buckshot Bailey Bowen thought she had settled down as a ranch hand. That was until a chance encounter with a feisty, Irish redhead turned her world upside down.

Sarah and Bailey meet again in San Antonio in an old, crumbling mission. As the infamous thirteen-day siege rages about them, they fall hopelessly in love. Surrounded by enemy forces, their future looks uncertain. Will they – and their love – survive against such insurmountable odds?

The cry "Remember The Alamo" has long echoed throughout history. Now, the women that were at the Battle of The Alamo ask you to *Remember Me*.

Out and Loud by Ali Spooner
The Bentleys have begun celebrating their success by performing live in small venues and outdoor concerts. Their

music and love for one another continue to grow as their number drops to four. Stone is needed at home to run the business during his father's rehabilitation, but the Bentleys drive forward. Cedra's challenge to her bandmates to create original songs for their next album turns into brilliant love songs, rockabilly, and a Pride Festival anthem. Ride along with the Bentleys as they capture the hearts of country music lovers across the nation.

Undercover Love by Annette Mori

When the domestic terrorist cell Emma Schmidt has infiltrated summons her to an abandoned warehouse for a loyalty test, Emma immediately recognizes the battered woman. Emma must act fast to protect her cover and save the woman, Jimena Aguilar, she's never forgotten.

Emma and Jimena team up on a dangerous mission to take down the terrorist cell and save the life of the popular California governor.

Will this lead them back to the closeness they once shared or have the years in between hardened their hearts to love.

Changing Times by Jen Silver

Thirty years on from when we first met Dani Barker and Camila Callaghan in *Changing Perspectives*, they're enjoying marriage and semi-retirement in a luxury flat near London.

Dani's niece, Holly, runs their mixed media business, now gaining a foothold in the highly competitive online games market. Holly's older sibling, Luc, influences people to take action on climate issues with their website, Gaia One: One Earth, One Chance.

Romance has been in short supply for both Holly and Luc. Immersed in her work, Holly's dating life is non-existent. For Luc, family prejudices stand in the way of a relationship with the love of their life.

Can Holly and Luc succeed in making the changes necessary to achieve their own happy ever afters?

Midnight in Nashville by Ali Spooner

The Bentleys have successfully finished cutting their first album, *Six Strings, and a Dream*. When the Covid-19 epidemic hits, tours and live performances are cancelled as the world goes into lockdown. With the closing of the restaurant, employment for the band members has been severely impacted. The group comes together to make life work at Ma Bentley's Boarding House. They take advantage of their down time and use of the studio to record more songs. Cedra has challenged each of her bandmates to create a song for their next album. Juliet's song, "Midnight in Nashville," is chosen as the title track. Join the group as they venture into new marketing avenues and create their first music video for the title track.

Compound Interest by Annette Mori

The kick-ass women in The Organization are back and they have their sights set on a few new recruits. Not everyone is jumping for joy at the choices, considering subterfuge is front and center in the games the new recruits have been playing.

Dani is supposed to get her happily ever after, but she's not sure what's real anymore including Candy's feelings for her. When a new enemy takes Candy captive, Dani vows to uncover the truth by insisting on going on the mission to save her. Candy is not what she seems, and that presents a new set of complications for Dani and her feelings.

The Organization continues to have challenges when those damn book magicians and book witches keep popping back in to warn them of new catastrophes on the horizon. She doesn't have time for their warnings, until their enemies intersect once again to keep them working together.

From award-winning author, Annette Mori, find out what happens in this final chapter of the combined Asset Management/Book Addict series.

Affinity
Rainbow Publications

eBooks, Print, Free eBooks

Visit our website for more publications available online.

https://affinityebooks.com/

Published by Affinity Rainbow Publications
A Division of Affinity eBook Press NZ LTD
Canterbury, New Zealand

Registered Company 2517228

Made in the USA
Monee, IL
17 May 2023